THE GOLDEN CHRYSALIS

Pressman
House

By

Stan McMurtry

ISBN: 978-1-915657-12-1

(Also available as an eBook ISBN 978-1-915657-07-7)

A CIP catalogue record for this book
is available from the British Library

MMXXIII

Published by
Pressman House Publishing Ltd.
Boston, Lincs, PE20 3BT
England +44 (0)1296 695 588
www.pressman-house.co.uk

For Stephie

CONTENTS

Chapter

CHAPTER 1

The Butterfly Effect

A *butterfly flaps its wings in Tokyo and a tornado occurs in Tennessee.*

It probably doesn't happen often, maybe only once in a lifetime, when out of the blue some tiny insignificant action escalates dramatically and unexpectedly into something large. A massive tsunami of change, a whole world turned upside down. I know this because it happened to me... yes, me... meek and mild Eddie Wheatley.

If I hadn't taken the dog for a walk that fateful night just over two years ago, eight people would still be alive. They died and my humdrum existence was transformed completely and forever. It seems strange now but at the time I wasn't aware that anything needed to change. I had accepted the status quo. I assumed everyone was like me, plodding along, going with the flow, every day being much like the one preceding it. Uneventful, dull and monotonous, until without warning and when I was least expecting it. *WHAP!* That big red bus my mother had constantly warned me was lurking around the corner if I didn't wear clean underwear each day, hit me and set in motion events which I couldn't have conjured up in my worst nightmare. Eight people dead! One of them I grieve for, the other seven I hope are rotting in hell. I don't feel sorry for them. Maybe I should but I don't, not one bit. The bastards deserved everything they got. The only remorse I feel is what led up to their deaths, coupled with sympathy for their families. But hey, maybe, just maybe, those newly widowed wives or girlfriends are still partying now, grateful that someone had removed the heartless, greedy

1

parasites they'd been stupid enough to get linked up with from their lives. Who knows? I just hope so.

Like I said earlier, my name is Eddie Wheatley. I'm thirty-nine years old, on the small size—five feet seven inches in my socks, have my own teeth, a thick mop of reddish hair and I've worn glasses since I was a kid.

Looking back to the time before all this stuff happened, I suppose a reasonable description of me then would be shy, unassuming and extremely timid. Happy to let things happen, to let others take the lead. I'd accepted that this was my lot in life. Small with glasses, red hair and a stammer was like holding up a placard reading 'Come and get me, bullies!' and so they did, almost forming a queue. My nickname at school was 'Weakly Wheatley' or sometimes 'Never Ready Eddie'. I hated it but fighting back never worked. It always ended up with me being bruised and humiliated so I just crawled back into my shell. It was safer in there.

This then was the groundwork for the adult I turned out to be. A first-class nonentity. A complete no-no, who had achieved nothing, absolutely zilch. And had taken thirty-nine years to get there. Unless, of course, living in my mother's ancient cottage in a scruffy cul-de-sac in East London, earning a pittance as a shop assistant can be considered successful. I suppose I had always lacked the vital ingredient for climbing ladders: ambition. Oh my, how things have changed. It's hard now to recognise that person was me. I seemed to have become the modern equivalent of Jekyll and Hyde.

But let me scroll back to when all this happened. It was two o'clock in the morning, raining, and I was walking the dog. An hour when most people were probably tucked up in their beds. But it was my favourite time. In the wee small hours problems could be thought through, decisions made without being overruled, together with that delicious feeling of being totally alone. For me it was as soothing as slipping into a warm bath. It swallowed and relaxed me as soon as I closed the front door and stepped out on to the pavement. Out there in the narrow street, cut deep between the high grimy buildings of London, was a place where I could be myself. Indoors was tension, being at the beck and call of relatives and never having the time or space to think one's own thoughts. Indoors was Miriam the puppeteer who controlled my every string, while out here the drunks and the muggers who only wanted my wallet and not my soul had mostly gone home—freedom!

I picked my way across the debris in the front garden. It resembled a building site. Years ago my father, a man of great taste and sensibility who preferred to spend his leisure time in the pub rather than the garden, had bought himself a second-hand car and not wanting to stagger too far after parking it had demolished the old wooden picket fence, torn up the grass and shrubs and replaced them with two or three tons of concrete.

I had decided to pretty the place up a bit and turn it back into a proper garden. God knows this area needed cheering up with a bit of colour. Piles of bricks and mounds of sand covered with plastic sheeting lay between the front door and the pavement and two planks of wood acted as a walkway across the muddy churned-up ground.

The dog, Rufus – a mutt that looked like the result of a one-night stand between an old carpet and a roadkill hedgehog – started to bark excitedly, tugging at the lead, feet scraping uselessly back and forth dragging me along the pavement seemingly intent on strangling itself so I leant down and unclipped the leash. He trotted happily into the darkness. I pulled my collar up and cursed that I hadn't brought an umbrella. The drizzle seemed to be getting heavier and the pavement was wet and shiny reflecting a line of skips, builders' lorries and mechanical diggers stretched along the street from one end to the other, blind and inanimate like fairground machinery waiting for summer.

Apart from me and the dog, the place was deserted. This was how I liked it, what I looked forward to most each day. No

Miriam talking non-stop and making decisions on which direction we should take. All was well with the world. My time. Bliss!

The ancient cottage we shared lay at the end of a cul-de-sac. Until about six months ago it had stood out like a bad tooth at the end of a row of Victorian semi-detached houses. Back then there had been a couple of shops, a community centre and a small Methodist church. All gone now to make way for a vast Ikea store, a carpet emporium and various other retail units selling everything from building materials to industrial paper shredders. The street resembled a bomb site. Half demolished dwellings lay below a vigorous new growth of scaffolding, bricks and spindly one-legged cranes. Our once friendly community had reluctantly accepted the council's compulsory purchase of their homes and now there were only two semis left. Mine and my elderly neighbour's. Our two dwellings had at one time been farm workers' cottages sitting in about sixty acres of pastureland. Possibly three hundred years old and listed so the council had been unable to knock them down, which, given the condition they were in, wouldn't have been difficult. Before I met Miriam, the semi I shared with my mother was about to fall down anyway. Now these two ancient dwellings were separated from any other houses by an ugly retail park like lepers excluded from society.

I had reached the end of the street and turned towards the Market Square. An ambulance swished by sending out a fine mist from the wet road, the graffiti messages on the drab black walls to one side suddenly illuminated by its blue flashing light. Here the ground was still littered with cauliflower leaves, squashed fruit and sodden navy coloured tissue paper from the Friday afternoon market stalls. The square was almost completely dark but on the top floor above one of the shops, a solitary window was lit up and I could hear the muffled angry words of a couple having a blazing row. A man wearing pyjamas appeared briefly at the window. The thin wailing cry of a woman came from somewhere in the room. I heard the man swear loudly then he slammed the window down with a crash and pulled the curtain across. *Poor bugger*, I thought. *He'll be walking the streets soon.* Rufus, alarmed by the noise, scuttled away mid-sniff from an interesting bouquet he'd been savouring at the foot of a lamppost and decided to stay close.

We walked on until we came to a row of shops where quite suddenly the light drizzle changed abruptly into a steady downpour of rain. I cursed myself again for not bringing a brolly, and the weather for spoiling my walk. The water was starting to seep through the shoulders of my coat and my trousers were soaked and clinging to my legs.

I looked about for a place to shelter. The wind was sweeping the rain into the shop doorways but on the other side of the road I could see a covered alleyway between two terraced houses. I splashed across and stood in the darkness dabbing at my face with a wet handkerchief. Rufus followed, his tail drooping and his expression asking the question, 'what the hell are we doing out here when we could be back a home having a nice warm kip?'.

Far off a low rumble of thunder broke the silence then a few seconds later the sky flickered briefly and soon a river of water was pouring along the alleyway bringing with it a regatta of old cans, bits of paper and fag ends.

I groaned. It looked like it had set in for quite some time. I walked further into the alley wondering if I could find a dustbin lid or something to use as an umbrella. It was so dark I had to feel my way along the wall but after a few yards it got lighter and I found that the alley was clear right through to the end of the building. It led out onto a narrow back street. In the dim light I could see piles of orange boxes and plastic rubbish bags stacked against a wall and an old car without any wheels standing in the middle of an assortment of oil drums and planks of wood. On the other side of the lane was a line of dilapidated garages, most of them with corrugated iron roofs onto which the rain was hammering down noisily.

A longish sheet of grey plastic held down by four bricks lay across the bonnet of the old car. Just what I needed. I was already soaked but this would help until I got home. I waited hoping that the storm would ease a little but ten minutes later it showed no sign of stopping so I made a dash for it, splashing through the puddles and between the oil drums. I threw the bricks to one side and grabbed the plastic sheet. It wouldn't budge. Then I saw that one end was still jammed tight under some planks at the front of the car. Swearing loudly I yanked harder but my hands kept slipping from the wet plastic.

Suddenly Rufus who was still standing in the alleyway started to bark furiously. I rushed over and picked him up, clamping my hand across his muzzle. The barking became a low growl.

"Shush," I hissed. The last thing I needed was for anybody to find me lurking like a would-be burglar on their property. How would I convince them I was only sheltering and not there to steal anything at two o'clock in the morning?

Just then I heard the reason for the dog's barking. The sound of an approaching vehicle. I backed quickly into the darkness of the alley, Rufus squirming in my arms, desperate to wake the whole neighbourhood. I squeezed his jaws tightly until he got the message and shut up.

The low whine of the engine got closer. The vehicle was moving very slowly. I could hear the creak of springs and the soft splash of water as it negotiated the potholes in the road. Flattening myself against the wall, I peered out into the lane. From the grey black shadows, an even darker shape emerged and moved slowly nearer. It was a truck, a builder's truck. I could see the silhouette of a ladder and what looked like a pile of rubble at the back. There was something odd about the vehicle's slow approach then I realised it didn't have any lights showing. How strange. It was understandable someone keeping the engine noise as low as possible at this hour for the neighbours' sake but to dispense with lights down a pitch-black lane littered with obstacles? Very odd.

A new sound came from the direction of one of the garages at the other side of the lane. The soft click of a bolt being drawn back. Rufus struggled in my arms and tried to bark again and I had to clamp his mouth shut once more. I glanced over. A thin shaft of light suddenly appeared in the slit between the doors of the garage and one of them was pushed open from the inside.

The figure of a man stood silhouetted against the bright light from behind. He stooped and picked something up from the ground and propped it against the open door then stood with his hands on his hips until the truck drew up alongside. The engine was switched off and a voice growled, "For Christ's sake, turn off that light!"

The man in the doorway said, "Aw, stop worrying, Smalley. We've got to be able to see haven't we?"

"Do it," the other voice hissed.

The man in the doorway shrugged, turned round and disappeared into the garage. A second later the light went off.

The doors of the truck opened and two men climbed out. The first voice said, "Don't slam the truck doors, leave 'em open."

"Jesus!" another voice said. "What about this fucking rain?"

As if in answer the whole lane was suddenly lit up by a brilliant flash of lightning followed immediately by a gigantic clap of thunder.

"Shit, Smalley," the first man said, "and you worrying about leaving a forty watt bulb on."

"Come on!" Smalley grunted. "Get this stuff off!"

The rain continued to fall in torrents. I watched mesmerised by the scene, aware that the gutter in my alleyway had overflowed and the water was already covering my shoes. Rufus was shivering with cold and I felt frozen too, but frozen to the spot. I couldn't take my eyes off what was going on. Occasionally lightning would flicker overhead and I could see the wet faces of the men straining with the effort as they went back and forth from the truck to the interior of the garage unloading their mysterious cargo.

One of the men was very small but squat and muscular with heavy black eyebrows and a square jaw. He wore a pair of grubby dungarees and on his head was a woollen hat with a pom-pom. This would be Smalley I guessed.

The second man was a barrel-chested West Indian. He carried with ease twice the load that the other two could manage on each trip and he did it with a big smile on his face. A great grin flashing a mouthful of incredibly white teeth seemed to be permanently in position as if he had just won the lottery.

The third man was the one I'd seen in the garage doorway. He was the eldest of the three with long white hair poking out from the edges of a black baseball cap. He had a fat flabby face and a paunch of generous proportions. He tired quickly and would stop frequently to lean against the tailboard of the truck breathing heavily and muttering curses to himself. Unlike the West Indian giant, he wore a dour, sullen expression on his face as he worked and looked as though he was only doing what he was doing under sufferance.

At last they were finished. The West Indian scooped up the last of the load in his great, thick arms and took it into the garage. Smalley put the tailboard of the truck back up and slipped its chain silently into place then all three stood in a huddle at the rear having a whispered conversation.

Eventually the older man climbed into the driver's seat and again without lights drove off very quietly down the lane. The other two walked into the garage and the doors were closed.

I put Rufus down on the wet ground and made my way back up the alley to the street. What the hell were those three up to? There was no doubt in my mind that it was something illegal. Normal law-abiding citizens don't drive down dark lanes without lights, unload mysterious loads, talk in whispers and act so furtively at two thirty in the morning. I looked at my watch. *My God*, I thought, *it's twenty to four*. I'd been standing watching that mysterious threesome for over an hour. Out on the street I leant against a wall and emptied the water from my shoes. Rufus stayed close to my legs, his tail down, a forlorn expression on his face. Poor little bugger. I should've left him at home. I broke into a trot in an effort to warm up. My mind kept going over the scene I'd just witnessed. Maybe I should tell the police. The station was only a couple of streets away. But how was I to explain? 'Oh yes, Officer, I always walk the dog at two thirty in the morning then lurk about in somebody's private passageway…' I decided I'd sleep on it. After all, there was the possibility that whatever those three men were up to was perfectly innocent. Improbable maybe, but possible. I thought about the huge bull-like body of the West Indian and the hard faces of the other two and decided that after all, ignorance was best and that if I wanted to stay in one piece it was probably wise to just forget it. The important thing right at that moment was to get home and get warm. The trot became a run worthy of the Olympics and in twenty minutes we were back, wet, cold and completely exhausted in the haven of the house.

CHAPTER 2

The Wall

I knew immediately I woke up that there was going to be an inquisition. Miriam was clattering crockery and banging saucepans in the kitchen. Doors slammed and drawers were angrily crashed shut. I looked at my watch and groaned. It was ten thirty in the morning and I was lying half on and half off the sofa in the living room under a spare duvet. I'd wisely decided last night not to put my freezing cold body in the same bed as my sleeping wife. I felt dreadful. My head was pounding and I ached all over. Maybe this was the beginning of a bout of flu. *Serves me right*, I thought as I staggered up the stairs to the bathroom. I had a pee, a couple of Paracetamol, climbed into a dressing gown then went downstairs again to face the music.

Miriam was standing at the sink when I went into the kitchen. She didn't turn but spoke at my reflection she could see on the window pane.

"I want you to see a doctor."

I didn't answer. I leaned across her and filled the kettle. She turned to face me.

"Or a psychiatrist!" she added.

"I'm all right," I muttered.

"You're not bloody all right!" she said. "Where the hell did you go last night? I've just picked up your wet clothes. They were soaking. It's a wonder you haven't got pneumonia."

"I was walking the dog."

"Bullshit!" she spat. "Nobody walks their bloody dog at that time in the morning... and in a thunderstorm."

I shrugged and busied myself getting tea bags from a cupboard.

She grabbed my shoulders and turned me to face her.

"Are you having an affair?"

"Don't be silly."

"Be honest."

"I'm not having an affair."

She stared into my eyes for a long time then sat down at the table.

"Well, what're you up to?"

"Nothing. I walk the dog. Is that a crime?"

She gave me that penetrating gaze again then said, "Is it me? Am I doing something wrong?" I did not know how to answer that so she continued. "Eddie, you're looking dreadfully tired. Being out half the night is wearing you out. Why don't you walk Rufus when you get home from work then sit and relax while watching TV?"

I smiled to myself, remembering the many times we had tried relaxing together to watch TV. Miriam clutching the remote control like Annie with her gun, zapping through the channels, never stopping for long on any of them, but managing to criticise each one for the terrible action, the music or the foul language. The thought that I might like to choose something to watch never entering her head.

"We hardly see each other nowadays," she continued. "You come back home, gobble your meal down then run off to find some do-it-yourself job around the house. It's almost as though… as though you were trying to escape. It… It's not good to be always wanting to be on your own. I don't understand it. When most couples are going off to bed together, you disappear with the bloody dog." She got up and poured herself some tea. "I'm tired too Eddie. I don't sleep when you're out."

I glanced across at her, remembering the loud snores coming from the bedroom when I'd returned home. But she did look tired, her eyes had lost a little of their usual lustre and her face was pale and fatigued. I felt a rare twinge of compassion and mumbled, "I'm sorry. I don't know what it is. Maybe I will see a doctor. He'll probably give me something for insomnia."

She brightened a little and said, "Yes, some pills. Anything that'll help you sleep. Daddy says you wander around the shop like a zombie sometimes."

I winced and closed my eyes. Daddy, the UK's answer to Attila the Hun was my boss at the small hardware shop in town. We shared a mutual hatred of each other.

"I'll give the doctor a call," I said.

"This morning?"

I looked at my watch. "It's a bit late," I said. "Perhaps this afternoon's surgery."

She stood up and grabbed my arm. "Please go this morning. Even better, I'll come with you. I can explain it more clearly than you. You'll just mumble a few words and come back with a few aspirins."

I pushed her back gently into the chair and gave her what I hoped was a breezy smile.

"I'm okay. Honestly, I'll go and see the quack this afternoon if I have time. I've taken this Saturday off especially to finish that wall outside. I don't want to waste it."

She looked crestfallen so I said reluctantly, "Look, I promise you. I won't go out tonight. I'll stay in." I looked down at the dog curled up in his basket fast asleep and mercifully not yapping. "Rufus can have an afternoon walk for a change."

Miriam brightened up immediately. She put her arms around my neck and kissed my cheek. "Oh, that's music to my ears," she said. "Oh Eddie, let's get back to how we used to be." She landed another kiss on my forehead. "I'm going to make this a really special evening. You'll wonder why you ever bothered to go out."

I wanted to scream at her, 'For God's sake, stop putting pressure on me!' She had her arms clamped around my neck like the tentacles of a giant squid and I felt smothered.

"Right," I said gaily, extricating myself from her embrace. "I must get on, y'know." I backed towards the door. "That wall won't get built on its own." She was sitting down again and staring at me with that hurt look on her face.

I waved my mobile phone at her. "I will call the doctor," I said. "I promise," then pulled the door closed between us… rather like a shield.

*****

One good thing about living in an old house as far as I'm concerned is that there's always plenty to do. If you have a new house all you can do is to potter. There's no fun pacing up and down an already immaculate garden waiting for a weed to pop up or hoping that the paint work of the building might start to peel so you'll have something to do. With my old mum's ramshackle semi, thank God, there was always plenty to do, providing you didn't breach the listed building rules.

I like working with my hands. I pride myself that there are not many jobs around the house that I can't turn my hand to. I'm not as quick as some professional craftsmen but I'm a damn sight better and much more meticulous. I suppose in a rather sad way I have Miriam to thank for my interest in making and mending. I can't remember doing any work around the place when I lived here with my mother. Apart from maybe mowing the lawn or occasionally fixing a fuse. Most of my leisure hours seemed to have been spent sitting on my backside watching rubbish on TV. It was when I married Miriam that I became totally absorbed with maintaining and improving the house. Perhaps it was the new-found responsibility of being a husband or maybe, if I'm honest, it was my way of escaping.

My latest project was to transform the scruffy patch of grey concrete which had been a parking space into a thing of beauty like my next-door neighbour's garden, which was a delight, neatly tended with a tiny lawn surrounded by sweet-smelling shrubs and bushes. So far it had been hard work.

The concrete was at least six inches thick and had had to be pounded with a heavy sledgehammer until piece by piece it could be loaded into a skip which stood by the pavement in the road. I left a small strip of concrete to act as a footing for a low back wall that I was building between the garden and the footpath. I set to work eagerly, piling sand into a neat mound then pouring the exact amount of concrete on top before mixing the two together. I added water with a little squeeze of washing up liquid to make a creamy consistency, turning the mix, smoothing, stirring—complete absorption. Then I spread a thick line of cement on the concrete footing and laid my first brick on top, tapping it down with the handle of a trowel and checking its trueness with a spirit level. Within an hour the wall was beginning to take shape.

I'd just started preparing a new mix when I became aware of someone standing on the pavement watching me work.

"You're doin' a fine job there, Eddie," he said. It was my next-door neighbour. He stood with a big grin on his face, pointing at my handiwork with the stem of a huge briar pipe.

"Oh hi, Mr Paterson," I said. "Yes. It's coming along isn't it?"

He banged out the ashes from his pipe on the heel of his shoe.

"You've worked wonders. This place was a shambles before your poor mother passed away, then suddenly boom! You're out there digging, painting, hammering. I don't know where you get the energy. You put me to shame."

I pointed at his garden. "I'm trying to compete with you."

"Well it's a good job all the other houses have gone. All the wives would've been nagging their husbands to keep up. You'd probably would have been lynched by now."

I laughed. I liked old Mike Paterson. He'd been a neighbour for the last sixteen years moving from a larger house on the other side of town when his wife died to this smaller more compact and easier to run house. It must have been a bit difficult downsizing to this run-down part of town but I guessed it was for financial reasons. I knew that he was renting. There had been a board outside the property announcing it was to rent for several months before he moved in. He was probably in his early seventies but had the bearing of a man half his age. Ramrod back, florid complexion, well over six feet tall with long silver-grey hair under his tweed cap and short silver-grey hair under his large, hooked nose. He carried a walking stick, not as an aid for walking but tucked under his arm in the style of an ex-sergeant major. He looked like an upper-class gent visiting these parts from his mansion in the country and spoke with a soft Scottish accent.

"I always hated it when your mother parked her car on that bit of concrete," he said. "Don't take this the wrong way but she was getting on a wee bit and her eyesight wasn't all that good. Sometimes she'd bump into the wall and I could feel the vibrations come right through my floor boards. There were times when I thought she was goin' to drive right into my living room."

I nodded. "You're right. She shouldn't have been driving at all. She was a danger to everyone. It's a wonder she didn't kill somebody."

Paterson smiled and waved his pipe at the pile of bricks. "What's the plan?" he asked.

I picked up another brick. "It's going back to how it must have been once. A little patch of lawn, some shrubs and flowers… and here," I pointed to my beginnings of a wall, "will be two lines of bricks filled with earth and I'll plant aubrietia and petunias and maybe some begonias…"

Paterson started to move off. "Daffodils," he said. "Daffodils that's what you need. Beats me how you can afford doin' all the DIY that you do. You didn't nick the bullion by any chance?"

Paterson had opened the gate into his garden and was walking towards his front door.

"Bullion?" I asked.

The old man stopped and fished his keys from his pocket. "Yes. Vicious bastards weren't they?"

I shook my head.

"Sorry Mike. I don't know what you're talking about. What bullion, what vicious bastards?"

Paterson left his keys dangling from the door lock and pulled a newspaper from his jacket pocket. "Haven't you read?" he said. "Somebody's been and stolen thirty million quids' worth of gold bullion from the Fletton Stewart security firm." He passed the paper over the hedge. "Here, have a look." I took it, a vague feeling of unease crawling up my spine and although I'd worked up quite a sweat mixing cement I suddenly started to shiver.

GUARD MURDERED IN MASSIVE BULLION RAID! was the headline.

At 8 o'clock last night, a gang of masked men blasted their way into the Fletton Stewart Security firm headquarters near Heathrow Airport and got away with thirty million pounds' worth of gold bullion and precious stones. One man died instantly. The other is critically ill in hospital. A policeman who was patrolling the area at the time was also badly injured when the…

The words started to blur. I could see a builder's truck driving along a dark alleyway with no lights. Three men with grim, hard faces, furtively unloading the contents into a dilapidated garage… could it be? Oh God. Surely not. The burden of perhaps knowing the whereabouts of such a vast amount of stolen money suddenly settled on my shoulders like a lead blanket. I tried desperately to focus my eyes on the small print of the newspaper to find whether there was any description of the gang but the small print of the paper had somehow become a jumble of unreadable hieroglyphics which were shaking about in time with my trembling hands. I dropped the paper and sat slowly down on a bag of cement. Paterson peered anxiously over the hedge.

"You all right, laddie?" he said.

I looked up. "Eh? … Oh yeah, yeah, I'm fine."

He continued to stare.

"I was just shocked by the violence of it. That poor security bloke."

"Nasty business. Horrible world we live in." He stood for a while still staring at me curiously. "You sure you're okay?"

I smiled at him and nodded.

"Oi," he said, "my paper!"

My mind was in a daze. I needed to be on my own to get my head straight. I handed him the paper. "Sorry," I mumbled. "Er… I've got to get on." I gave him a thumbs-up sign and climbed over the wall. I had to read more so I fairly sprinted down the street. I turned after a few yards and looked back. Paterson was staring after me with a perplexed look on his face, then he walked towards his door and left himself into his house.

The corner shop was a few hundred yards away. I arrived there red-faced and out of breath a couple of minutes later, bought two different national newspapers then hurried outside ignoring the good mornings and polite remarks about the weather from the shopkeeper.

Both papers had the robbery as the main headline on their front pages. *The Daily Mail* said that thirty million pounds' worth of gold bullion had been stolen from the Fletton Stewart Security firm by three masked men. *The Daily Express* said that twenty-five million pounds' worth had been stolen by five men in balaclavas. There were no descriptions of the thieves and apart from the one dead security man and a policeman who was still alive but dangerously ill in hospital, there were no witnesses. The police were appealing for anyone who had seen a black Mercedes car parked outside Fletton Stewart's gates an hour before the robbery to come forward.

I threw the papers into the rubbish bin outside the shop and walked slowly home. I wondered how journalists could ever hazard a guess about how many men there were involved. Maybe the wounded policeman had told them. They had to fill their columns with something I supposed, but all they really knew was that there had been a robbery on a grand scale and that there were no clues. The robbers had vanished into thin air and no one knew who they were or where they were. No one apart from me, I thought. But did I know? Surely it was too much of a coincidence for me to be sheltering from the rain at the exact moment a gang of crooks just happened to unload their loot right under my nose. Things like that just don't happen to ordinary blokes like me.

I got back to the house, stepped over the new wall and sat down on a pile of bricks. What to do now? Should I phone the police? All sorts of questions were going through my head. I pictured myself at the police station telling my story, explaining that I had insomnia so took the dog for a walk. In my mind I saw the police hit squad raiding the house, arresting the three men and recovering the gold. The grateful bullion company handing me a substantial reward. My photograph splashed across the front pages of the newspapers. The very thought of a day or two of notoriety brought with it a warm flush of excitement. This is what I needed. A boost to my self-esteem. My spirits lifted substantially. I picked up my spade, gave the pile of still wet cement a few turns and got down to the serious business of laying bricks. After an hour or so my wall was starting to take shape but I couldn't get the robbery out of my mind. The more I thought about it the more worried I became and slowly as I worked all my earlier enthusiasm started to seep away as though some inner tap had been left on. What proof did I have? All that I'd seen were three men unloading a truck in the early hours of the morning. What might happen if the three were found guilty and were banged up in jail? My face would be on the front pages of every paper. They'd soon find out where I live and in no time at all some of their mates would be banging on my door to rearrange my face in revenge.

I sat back on my heels and put the trowel down. Maybe it would be better to forget the whole thing. Yes, that's the best course, I thought. Why turn my life upside down? Why risk getting hurt, having bricks thrown through the windows, always having to look over my shoulder? Then I shook my head. Forgetting the whole thing was impossible and I knew it. I had to know for sure. How could I possibly go about my everyday business from now on and never know if I'd witnessed a part of one of the biggest robberies ever to have been committed in Britain?

I got up from my kneeling position and sat back down on the pile of bricks. There was only one thing to do and deep down inside I knew it was something I'd been longing to do since I waded soaked to the skin from that dark alleyway in the early hours of the morning …… go back and have another look.

Now that I'd made my decision, I turned my attention once again to the job in hand and worked without interruption right through the morning. At midday, a lorry arrived at the house with a load of topsoil which was tipped half into the garden and half onto the pavement. I paid the man and then spent another hour shovelling the earth off the pavement into a neat pile on the other side of the wall. I would have carried on for the rest of the day but Miriam called me in for lunch, which was welcome. My mind had been so preoccupied by plans to revisit the alleyway, I'd not noticed that I was absolutely starving.

It was a salad. Thick, pink slices of ham with lettuce, chopped eggs, celery, cucumber and radish, accompanied by two cans of light ale and doorstep-sized chunks of Miriam's homemade brown bread. I washed my hands and arms in the kitchen sink and looked admiringly at the spread my wife had prepared. "I'll tell you what, Miriam," I said, "you know how to look after the inner man."

She smiled. "This is just a snack. Wait till you see what you're getting tonight."

I pulled back a chair and sat down. "Eh? What's special about tonight? Don't tell me I've forgotten an anniversary. It's not your birthday is it?"

She laughed. "No, but it is a special occasion." Miriam opened one of the cans of beer and poured it into a glass. "Tonight," she said dramatically, following up with an imitation roll of drums, "tonight, Ladies and Gentlemen, we are happy to announce a unique and important event in the history of Daleham Road, E3." She reached over and raised my hand. "Tonight, Edward Wheatley is not out walking his dog Rufus Wheatley, but is staying at home with his wife, Mrs M.W. Wheatley, who is going to prepare him a wondrous candlelit meal, after which they will both retire at the same time and to the same bed followed by which this speech is censored in deference to those of a sensitive disposition…" She walked round the table laughing and stood behind me with her arms around my neck. "It's going to be lovely having you pinned down for the evening, you old insomniac."

I turned my head and stared at her. I'd completely forgotten my rash promised to stay in that evening. All morning I'd worked with enthusiasm and a growing excitement at the prospect of retracing my steps of the evening before. I tried my hardest to smile. "Oh, come on Miriam," I said. "It's no earth-shattering event y'know. You make it sound like I was never in."

"Oh, you're in during the evenings, I know, love. But usually, you're putting up shelves or painting. Then when I'm all cosy and tucked up in bed waiting for you to come up, I hear the front door open and shut and you've gone off on one of your walks." She gave me a squeeze then walked round to her own chair and sat down. "Well," she said, "not tonight. I've got my man to myself."

I forced another smile. "Yes," I said weakly. "Sounds wonderful." My heart sank. Ahead, with depressing predictability, lay an evening involving a sequence that rarely changed. Dinner, dishes and bathroom, followed by bedroom and the ritual removal of the make-up. Bathed and naked in bed, I would wait with less than eager anticipation as the night creams were applied, teeth flossed and brushed and a yellow spiked plastic tube inserted into the curl above her forehead. Here there would probably be a pause as she dimmed the lights and quite likely she would stare down at me deep in thought, a small smile upon her lips. Then having made her decision, she's climb in to her side of the bed, kneel with her face pressed into the pillow, lift her nightdress over her buttocks and whisper seductively, "Let's do it doggy fashion, shall we?" No kisses, no foreplay. Just perform, little man.

Surely piggy fashion was a more apt description of the act. For afterwards I always felt, as I lay in a litter of tissues, like Miriam's prize boar.

Suddenly the ham salad didn't seem quite so appetising. I plodded through it, searching hard for an excuse so that I could go out that night.

But there was no reason I could contrive which wouldn't involve hurting her feelings badly. She was chirruping away happily on the other side of the table about her plans to go down to the shops to buy something for that special meal and I knew there was nothing I could do about it. Frustrating though it was, I would just have to postpone my visit to the alleyway until the next night.

I finished the salad and went back to the garden again. By three o'clock in the afternoon, the wall was complete. Two single brick walls eight inches apart and two feet high. When the cement was dry I would fill the space between the two lines of brickwork with earth, which would then be ready for planting. I started spreading the load of topsoil over the garden leaving enough for the wall infill. Miriam bustled out of the house with her shopping basket and by the time she returned an hour later, I'd cleared away the remaining sand and bags of cement and was standing proudly surveying my handiwork. The bare parking space at the front of the house had been transformed into a garden. The old, drab concrete had disappeared.

Miriam didn't return alone, she had company. Walking alongside and carrying her shopping was a thin-faced elderly man wearing a green trilby hat and a sour expression. I cursed silently. The last person I wanted to see at a weekend was my boss, Geoffrey Hislop. I had to endure that miserable scowling face every other day of the week. Geoffrey Hislop, Britain's own Attila the Hun, was not only my boss but Miriam's father. "Look who I bumped into at the shops," she said brightly.

"Afternoon, Wheatley," grunted Geoffrey Hislop of Hislop's Hardware Store, Wellington Road, E3, not bothering to look at me.

"Hello, Mr Hislop," said his chief assistant, hating himself for almost standing to attention as his employer/father-in-law walked past him. Miriam paused as she opened the door. "Just when my arm was breaking carrying the shopping, Daddy turned up. Isn't that lucky? He's going to have a cup of tea with us. You'll join us won't you Ed?"

It wasn't a question, it was an order. She opened the door and Rufus bounded out barking furiously.

Hislop paused in the doorway and glanced around the new garden. I could see him mentally checking the tools which were scattered around to make sure they hadn't been stolen from his shop. He nodded at me then followed his daughter and dog indoors. Neither of them, I noticed, had bothered to pass any comments about my efforts in the garden.

I stood for a few moments taking deep breaths and doing some more cursing. Eventually I tore off my work gloves and threw them down disgustedly and following them into the house.

Man and dog were already in the lounge when I entered. The old man was seated in his armchair and Rufus was on his knee. Miriam, I supposed, was in the kitchen making the tea.

"Ah, Edward," said Hislop. "Come and sit down."

How very kind, I thought. *To offer me a seat so magnanimously in my own home.* It was noticeable also how the tag 'Wheatley' had been dropped now that we were within the confines of the house. Outside or in the shop it was 'Wheatley' do this, 'Wheatley' do that. But here suddenly I had become the son-in-law and could be referred to affectionately as 'Edward'.

I sat.

The old man fingered the dog's ear, leaned back comfortably in the chair and addressed me as though I was a stranger applying for a job.

"I'm afraid I won't be able to stay long," he said. "We're short staffed today."

"Oh, busy are you, Mr Hislop?" I said.

I was intrigued by his head. How could one's head be so wrinkled from the front to the back? When he raised his eyebrows the furrows on his brow started a chain reaction sending more furrows swirling across his bald dome like ripples on a pool to lap against the collar at the back of his neck.

"Yes," he said. "Damned inconvenient."

These two words seemed to hang uncomfortably in the air for quite some time as we both stared at the empty fireplace,

"I am owed several days," I ventured.

The old man frowned. The tide on his head went into reverse while he wiped something from the corner of the dog's eye with his thumb. He was sitting with his back to the windows and the strong sunlight streaming through the glass made his ears appear pink and translucent like those of a white mouse. His whiskers twitched.

"Well, I hope you won't take any more of them on a Saturday," he grunted.

It was a lie about the shop being busy. Hislop's hardware hadn't been busy on a Saturday or any other day since the new Tesco superstore had opened half a mile away. Business had plummeted and even the customers who'd been with him for years had opted for the convenience of being able to buy everything they needed under the same roof.

I wanted to say, 'Look, if you're so damned busy what are you doing sitting on your scrawny backside in my house waiting to be served?' Instead, I answered, "I'll try to arrange them during the week in future, Mr Hislop."

"A little thought, that's all that's needed," he said.

Miriam broke the strained atmosphere in the room by coming in with the tea.

"Sorry to take so long," she said. "I thought I'd give you two men a little time on your own."

Thank God, I thought. *You've just stopped me from strangling your father.*

She put the tray down on a small coffee table in front of the fireplace. As well as the tea there was a large plate full of chocolate digestive biscuits. Hislop, without being asked, immediately leaned over and took two biscuits, one of which he bit into leaving half a biscuit in his hand a pile of crumbs all over the arm of the chair. Rufus woke up and the old man fed him the other biscuit scattering more crumbs and allowing the dog to lick the wet chocolate from his fingers. Then, with the same hand, he shoved the remaining half of biscuit into his own mouth, licked the fingers and reached out for another one. I winced.

"Well, Dad," said Miriam, "how's Mum feeling now?" She handed out cups of tea and sat herself next to me.

"She's feeling a bit sorry for herself just at the moment," Hislop said, through a mouthful of biscuit. "But I daresay she'll mend."

Miriam's mother had just undergone an appendix operation. In an effort to reassure her before entering the hospital the doctor had said, "Don't worry Mrs Hislop. Nowadays an appendix operation is as easy as having a tooth out. You'll be up and about in no time." Her husband, overhearing the remark, had taken it as a medical fact. Consequently, his wife had received little or no sympathy and was even now behind the counter at the hardware shop, several days sooner than she should have been.

"You'll both make Sunday lunch as usual though?" asked Miriam. Her father slurped his tea loudly. "Wouldn't miss it for the world," he said.

"Sundays wouldn't be the same without you both," said Miriam. "Would they Ed?"

That's true, I thought. *They'd be bloody wonderful.*

"No, they wouldn't," I said.

Watching my father-in-law wolfing down the biscuits was only mildly revolting compared with the usual Sunday lunch ordeal. From the moment of her parent's arrival, Miriam's mouth would open and a torrent of meaningless chatter would pour out, during which Hislop's mouth would also open and he would cram in as much food as he possibly could.

There was no point asking whether he would like another potato or a few more sprouts. Anything left on the serving dishes after everyone had had their first helping he'd shovel on to his plate as though it was his automatic right.

My feelings of revulsion were mixed with those of astonishment that such a thin, little man could put away such vast quantities of food and still stay thin. A long time ago I had decided that within that scrawny frame there lurked a gigantic tape-worm devouring everything that came down. Occasionally, I found myself watching intently that ever open mouth, expecting at any moment the worm to pop out from its dark recess, little evil eyes darting from side to side before lunging forward to snatch the last remaining morsel of food from the serving dishes or from somebody's plate then, with a whip-like snap, disappear back down the old man's throat.

Mrs Hislop would probably utter no more than two words during the whole lunch. A timid little creature, she would eat very little and still retain her homely, round little figure. Like me, she left most of the talking and decision-making to other people and outwardly seemed content to just go with the flow. Doubtless inwardly she had her private torments. Maybe, I thought, I would meet her one day in the early hours of the morning, walking her dog. Why on earth did she, seemingly a nice, quiet and unassuming little lady, marry such a charmless glutton of a man? I glanced across at Hislop who had exhausted the supply of biscuits and was noisily working his way through his third cup of tea. He was nodding his head enthusiastically as Miriam expounded her theories on what the government should be doing about foreigners and how the blame for urban decay could be laid fairly and squarely on the doorstep of Britain's immigrant community.

Come to think of it, Miriam and I were an incongruous couple. I tried to remember if we'd always been so.

We first met in the library were Miriam worked. I was thirty at the time and a sales rep in the confectionary trade. My father had died many years earlier and I lived in this neglected old house with my mother.

I was a hopeless salesman, so although I worked hard my earnings were meagre by any standards. But I was fairly content. My mother received a pension from the government as my father had been killed accidentally during military service so between us we managed to live fairly comfortably.

Looking back, my courtship with Miriam had been an unusual one. A kind of role-reversal one might say. One minute I was plodding through life as a bachelor... The next I was plodding through life as a married man, having been chased, wooed and won by a very determined lady. Not against my wishes, of course. No, not a bit of it. In fact at thirty years of age, when women had played very little part in my life, it was extremely flattering – okay, ego-boosting – to be the focal point of the attentions of an attractive woman like Miriam. I had resigned myself to permanent bachelorhood. Not that I minded. I was really quite happy living with my mother. I detested the usual haunts of the young and single such as bars, clubs and sports complexes, preferring instead to spend my leisure hours reading, playing cards with my mother or just watching television. What a nerd I must have been.

Miriam was a fully qualified librarian and worked at the old red sandstone library in Wickerstreet Road, near the shopping arcade. She was four years older than me. A tall, heavily built girl with auburn hair scraped back in a ponytail, she had a square angular face with large attractive brown eyes and a full, rather sensuous mouth. Most often she dressed in a smart grey suit and a white blouse, which somehow accentuated an extremely ample bosom, and because of her height she wore flat shoes.

She had always been very pleasant to me on my regular weekly visits to the library to pick up books for my mother, but usually confined her conversation to matters about the state of the weather, novels or our mutual good health. So it was quite a surprise when, after the usual small talk as she was checking my books one day, she asked me if I was interested in classical music. Anxious not to appear ignorant, I answered untruthfully, yes. She told me that she had managed to obtain two tickets for a piano recital by a famous pianist at the Royal Festival Hall, but the friend she had been going to go with had fallen sick. Would I like to come instead?

I had been astounded and had tried feverishly to think of all the reasons why I couldn't go.

"It's Tchaikovsky's Piano Concerto No 1 in B flat minor," she said by way of encouragement. "Oh please say you'll come. I'd hate to miss it and I wouldn't like to go on my own."

In a daze I had agreed, thinking to myself that I could always invent an excuse not to go later. But she had turned up, in her little car and so there was no way that I could wriggle out of our date.

I remember being surprised by how much I enjoyed it, although Miriam did have a tendency to make rather loud comments during the performance about the beauty of the music or our surroundings, making people sitting around us turn their heads with frowns of annoyance and me cringe with embarrassment.

A month after our meeting, my mother had died suddenly of a stroke. I remembered Miriam turning up at the funeral and afterwards being very comforting, driving me home and offering me kind words of sympathy.

A week later she arrived again unexpectedly at my house, asking if she could be of any help with the washing or ironing. I felt obliged to invite her in and can still recall my nervousness and embarrassment at having a woman in my home without the reassuring presence of my mother for the first time in my life. (Oh God! Even more nerd-like behaviours. We spent the evening playing Scrabble, for God's sake!) and she had insisted on taking away a pile of dirty sheets and a couple of my shirts for washing.

Two nights later she turned up again with the clean linen, but this time with a large bottle of wine 'to cheer me up' she said, after my tragic bereavement. Immediately she set about cleaning the house. Without being asked, she opened cupboards and drawers looking for cleaning materials and then spent the whole evening vacuuming and dusting and wiping down. I felt a curious mixture of gratitude that she should bother and irritation that my privacy was being invaded. But, as usual, I said nothing.

We drank some of the wine while she talked about her work in the library and asked me questions about the confectionary trade, then she went home. Half an hour later I had to get out of bed to answer the doorbell. It was Miriam. Her father and mother must have thought she was already indoors, she explained, and had locked up and gone to bed themselves. Unfortunately, she had mislaid her key and didn't like to disturb her parents. Could I put her up for the night in my spare room? Reluctantly, but curiously excited, I had agreed. She suggested that perhaps we could have a nightcap before retiring and finish the bottle of wine.

In the middle of the night I woke up to find Miriam standing beside my bed, totally naked. Looking back it all seemed like a dream. I remembered sitting bolt upright in bed with panic rising in my throat. I tried to speak to protest, but nothing escaped my lips apart from a high-pitched whimper. Miriam climbed into bed beside me and stifled my protests with her lips, tugging at my pyjama jacket and uttering little moans and endearing words. Despite myself I felt aroused and, as though in a trance, passively allowed her to take off the rest of my pyjamas. She kissed and stroked the private parts of my body and dug her fingers into my stomach. I watched her move about me as though it was happening to someone else and I was a mere spectator. I looked up and her large white body was astride me and I was inside her. She was now making the little whimpering noises and moving up and down, the huge mountains of her breasts swinging like weather beacons in a gale. And then, way deep within myself, I felt a soft feather brush lightly against an exposed nerve end. The friction became more intense and suddenly I felt my whole insides erupting and spilling out like lava from a volcano. Above me, Miriam shuddered and let out an agonised gasp then fell forward, her hair dangling on my face, a hand on either side of my head. When she was lying beside me, I realised that I hadn't said one word to her, nor had I reached out to touch her. She fell asleep and I lay transfixed, staring at the ceiling until morning came and she slipped out of bed to make some tea.

Later, when she had gone, I felt a great surging sense of elation. Up until that moment I had felt that sex was something which would pass me by. Unattainable emotions reserved only for the confident and strong. Yet here I was being chased and seduced by a very attractive female. I saw myself in a new light, convinced that some new aspect of my nature that I had hidden from myself had all of a sudden emerged.

Shortly afterwards had come the revelation that she was pregnant and so it seemed the decent thing to do to get married.

After that though there had been the intensive investigations by her father to ensure that I was able to provide adequately for his daughter and child. Then the sudden vacancy that had occurred at her father's firm which paid a lot more than I was earning as a representative. Then surprise, surprise: a week after the wedding she discovered that she wasn't pregnant after all. False alarm,

"What's the matter with him?"

I came to a jolt and dragged my mind back to the present. Hislop and Miriam were staring at me, frowning. I sat up straight and tried to look attentive.

"Eddie!" said Miriam through clenched teeth. "Daddy was talking to you!"

"Sorry," I said. "I was far away for a moment."

Hislop grunted and leaned back in his chair. "What's the matter with you Wheatley?" he said. "What kind of bloody host are you? When you have visitors you're supposed to entertain them, y'know, not leave everything to your poor wife. I've been sitting here ages and not heard a peep from you." I opened my mouth to speak but Hislop carried on. "It's the same in the shop. For heaven's sake man, you're supposed to be my chief assistant but you act like it's your first day, every bloody day! People want a smile and a bit of conversation when they come in but they don't get it from you! You can't even force yourself to say thank you when they hand you the money. It's damned bad for business!"

I felt the colour rush to my cheeks. "I… I don't understand, what did I—" I stammered.

"Daddy is right, Ed," Miriam interrupted. "Why can't you try to be a bit more sociable? You sit there with that stupid expression on your face… you may as well not be here. I was just saying that as Mummy's a bit tired I've invited Daddy to eat with us tonight."

I stared at her in astonishment.

So much for the romantic evening she had planned for her nasty, unsociable spouse. So much for the candlelit dinner.

Now she wanted her bloody father along. It was all too much. Something inside my head clicked. Miriam had unwittingly opened the door of my cell. I didn't have to endure an evening with her after all. I had my excuse.

I stood up and walked to the door. Miriam looked startled. "Eddie," she said. "Where do you think you're going?"

I turned. "Like you just said, Miriam dear," I answered. "I may as well not be here. Well, now I'm not! Have a romantic evening with Daddy." I closed the door behind me and walked into the hallway, picking up my overcoat from the hook beside the front door. Behind me I heard Miriam's astonished cry of "Edward!" and Attila the Hun muttering about me being off my head.

CHAPTER 3

The Shadow

I hurried down the street chortling to myself. A wild elation had taken hold of me. I'd done something totally and utterly out of character. I'd actually rebelled, walked out. I'd surprised myself. Those few seconds before standing up and leaving the room had been for me like climbing out of a wartime trench to face the enemy's machine guns. I felt like a small boy who'd done something wrong and was both pleased and slightly fearful about the possible repercussions.

I glanced at my watch. A quarter to six. Too early yet. It would have to be dark before I could go snooping around in that alleyway again. But it was hard to contain the excitement I felt now that I didn't have to wait until tomorrow. My cheeks felt hot and I kept giggling to myself as I recalled Miriam's squawk of astonishment when I walked out. I felt a good deal braver now that I was a safe distance from the house, although even then I kept looking from left to right, as though expecting her at any second to leap out from a doorway or from behind someone's hedge. On the other side of the road was a greasy-spoon type café. I crossed over and opened the door. Inside was a long, narrow, rectangular room with half a dozen plastic-topped tables arranged in a line down one side and three brightly lit fruit machines on the other. I'd passed this place many times before but hadn't come in thinking that the place would be dirty and full of yobs. But the only other occupants were three young lads in overalls who were playing one of the fruit machines. They barely looked up as I entered, and the café was spotless. I bought a cup of tea and took it to a seat nearest the window overlooking the street. Almost immediately I felt my mobile phone vibrate in my pocket. It was Miriam. I pressed decline, put the phone on mute and slipped it back into my pocket. She could stew for a while.

Ten minutes later, I saw Attila walk past on the other side of the street. He had the usual frown on his face and he seemed to be muttering to himself. This was the man who couldn't stop long because they were so busy in the shop. I watched him with loathing until he was nearly out of sight and then gave the retreating figure a two-fingered salute.

There was a sudden clatter of noise and a great roar of delight as the right sequence lined up on the fruit machine and loud, but good humoured voices proclaimed that the manager of the café could stuff his gnat's pee tea because they could now afford a few pints at the pub. The manager replied with a smile. "Bloody good riddance too, and you can buy me a pint when I've locked up."

"See you down the Rose then," they said and left.

The man closed the door behind them and then stared pointedly at his watch.

"Oops, sorry," I said. "I didn't realise you were waiting to close." I gulped down what was left of my tea.

"That's all right, pal. There's no hurry," said the man, opening the door to show that there was.

I stumbled out on to the pavement and the door was slammed behind me. I stood for a while staring at the ground and wondering what I could do to kill more time. It would be best to arrive at the dark alleyway in the small hours of the morning when everybody was asleep and there was less chance of being disturbed. Going back home was out of the question. Miriam would almost certainly do all she could to stop me going out again and, having walked out on her earlier, I didn't want to put myself through one of her screaming rages. Definitely something to be avoided.

The café door opened again and the manager came out dressed in a bulky black overcoat and tweed cap. He locked the door and looked at me suspiciously. "Lost your way, pal?" he asked.

I must've looked a bit odd loitering outside his café so I said, "No. I was trying to think of… of… where the, er… Rose is. That's right. I've lost my bearings a little. Could you tell me where I could find the Rose?"

The man flicked his head sideways. "Turn left at the lights… can't miss it." He turned and walked off in the direction that he had indicated. "I'm going there myself." He didn't offer to show me the way but set off at a brisk pace towards the traffic lights. I followed. I hadn't really wanted directions to the Rose, it was the first thing that had come into my head. But now that I came to think about it, it seemed a good idea. It would be well past eleven o'clock before I would have to leave. I turned left at the lights and a little further down the road followed the man from the café across the car park of a huge Victorian red brick pub, the Rose and Crown. I had driven down this road many times and never noticed that the pub was there.

I pushed open the door and walked into a large room that smelt faintly of furniture polish. There were six other people in the room—the three lads that I had seen earlier were feeding their winnings from the café's fruit machine into a far larger machine in the corner and had been joined by the man who owned the café. An old man sat hunched at a table by an imitation log fire nursing an empty glass and the landlord leaned on the far side of the bar doing *The Daily Telegraph* crossword. Nobody looked up as I entered.

I walked up to the bar. The landlord indicated that he was willing to forsake the crossword for a while to serve me by raising one eyebrow and grunting. I ordered half a pint of bitter and asked if it was possible to have something to eat.

"You're a bit early, old son," the landlord said, pushing my money into the till then talking down at his crossword. "Try again at seven o'clock."

On the far side of the room I sat down, took a sip of my beer, and glanced at my watch. Six-thirty. Closing time was eleven o'clock. I wanted to be at the alleyway about one o'clock in the morning—it was going to be a long night.

At seven thirty, I went to the bar for a refill and ordered a shepherd's pie from the menu on the counter. Nine o'clock came and I'd eaten the pie and was wondering whether or not to have another half pint. The place was starting to fill up now and the landlord had switched on something remotely resembling music. A loud thump, thump, thump beat that was on a loop and was very loud.

Men and women were standing in groups, shouting above the incessant noise and a small crowd was standing below a television showing a game of football in progress.

I wished I had a newspaper. Anything to pass the time. Somehow I felt uncomfortable sitting sipping beer all on my own and staring round the room. I fished around and pulled an old letter from one of my pockets and started rereading it. It was only a document confirming that my building materials would be delivered last week, but it made me feel less conspicuous.

Someone put a full glass of beer down on the other side of the table then pulled a chair out so roughly that the table rocked and beer slopped on to the table surface and over my letter. I looked up indignantly and found myself staring at the sullen face of the man in the baseball cap. My heart lurched and felt as if it had jumped up into my throat. His eyes rested on mine for a moment or two daring me to complain about the spilt beer then he ignored me and stared slowly around the room. I did the same looking to see if the man called Smalley or the grinning West Indian were there too. For a panic-filled moment I thought maybe they'd spotted me, in the alley, and had come to get me but he was on his own, thank God, and seemed unaware of the trembling he'd caused to the wreck sitting on the other side of the table.

Close up the man's face was extremely pale but the cheeks and nose were crisscrossed by tiny red veins. He wore an earring from which dangled a three-pronged fishhook of the type that anglers use when spinning for river pike. He turned round suddenly and picked up his beer and those wet, spaniel-like eyes glanced briefly at my face. Realising that I had been staring open-mouthed, I quickly looked back at my wet letter. Surely the man could hear the loud hammering sound coming from my heart?

He tapped me on the arm. I looked up at him in alarm, prepared to do a runner.

"Where's the bog?" he said.

"Eh?" I managed to croak.

"The bog, where is it?"

Ah. The gents. I'd been there earlier in the evening. I pointed across to the stairs on the other side of the room. "Up the stairs," I said.

Baseball Cap grunted, stood up, drained his glass and walked through the crowd in the direction I'd given him.

A few minutes later he reappeared again and pushed his way through the crowd at the bar. For a while I couldn't see him then he re-emerged clutching a bottle of whisky. He walked across to the door, stopped to light a cigarette, then disappeared into the night.

I stared at the closed door. I had to make a decision. Should I wait until after midnight to visit the alleyway as I'd planned, which meant I would probably see nothing, or should I follow him at a safe distance and maybe find out what was going on? A no-brainer. I stuffed the wet letter into my pocket and made for the exit.

Outside it was quite dark but rows of electric bulbs had been strung all around the pub's car park and I could see the silhouette of Baseball Cap just about to step on to the pavement on the far side. He quickened his pace, crossed the car park and walked into the dark street.

The road on this side of the pub had only limited street lighting and I thought at first that I'd lost my man, but a car passed by from the opposite direction and in its headlights I could see the hurrying figure in the familiar hat about a hundred yards away on the other side of the road. I crossed over, feeling slightly sick with nerves and wondering why I hadn't stayed in the pub until closing time and stuck to my original plan. It was just seeing the man leave the pub and suddenly feeling that he might disappear and that it would be a wasted few hours just staring into an empty alleyway.

Although nervous I was quite enjoying the adventure. My life was humdrum enough. This was exciting. At that moment I felt like a detective in a novel. I turned up my collar and dug my hands deep into my pockets. Eddie Wheatley was on the case!

Up ahead was a solitary streetlamp. I waited for Baseball Cap to show up in the small lighted circle on the pavement but no one appeared. Keeping my back to the wall on the opposite side of the street, I edged forward straining my eyes for movement beyond the lamp. There was none. I cursed softly. Where the hell had he gone?

Puzzled I crossed over the road and retraced my steps on the other side. Then when I was well past the light, I crossed the road again to where I'd been a minute before. I stood perfectly still for a whole minute until my eyes had grown accustomed to the dark, then, very slowly, I started to walk back towards the pub. After ten yards I saw where I'd gone wrong. The pavement dipped down on my right side. I could see that I was standing at the entrance to a small side street I hadn't noticed before. Taking a deep breath and walking as quietly as I could, I turned and walked from the darkness of the main street into the total blackness of the side street.

Almost immediately the paving slabs beneath my feet ended and the ground became muddy and uneven. Then I knew where I was. This was the little lane with the garage where I had seen the men unloading the truck. So somewhere further up on the left-hand side would be the alleyway where I'd sheltered last night.

I moved slowly forward, peering into the almost impenetrable darkness, moving each foot carefully, feeling with my toes over the uneven ground and trying to avoid the deep puddles. But after about ten yards my foot hit something metallic and light: a tin can. It clattered noisily away to my right. I froze, rooted to the spot, my heart threatening to pound its way out of my chest and my brain screaming at me to turn round and get the hell out of there. I stood for a long time listening for the slightest sound. From far off came the whine of a motorcycle and a few seconds later the clack-clack of the rails under a distant train. Then complete and utter silence returned. I edged slowly forwards again, my arms outstretched hoping to find a wall which would guide me along. Then something made me come to an abrupt stop. There was something. It wasn't a sound. It was more of an awareness. A primeval sense of imminent danger. I listened again, my every sense quivering with alarm signals. Then I heard it: a sound... soft but unmistakeable... the sound of breathing. A strange tingling sensation crept up my neck and I felt fear, real paralysing fear. I could feel his presence. Within an arm's length of my body was another human being.

I turned to run. There was a scraping noise in the gravel as though someone had taken a step nearer, then a swishing noise—something heavy and solid crashed into my shoulder with an impact that took the breath from my body and sent me sprawling on the ground with a cry of agony. I scrambled forward again on my hands and knees but the heavy object descended again, this time exploding against the side of my head. The darkness abruptly disappeared and was replaced by a blinding flash of white lights which gradually changed into a deep blood-red colour. Then that too changed slowly back to darkness. A different kind of darkness this time... no shape... no sound... nothing!

CHAPTER 4

Carrie Donaghue

"I warned you didn't I? I told you it would be a big mistake. Hislop helped himself to some more apple crumble, took a mouthful then waved the spoon at his daughter. "But you were determined to go ahead with it."

He looked across the table at Miriam who sat with her chin cupped in her hands, pushing her uneaten dessert disconsolately around the bowl. She nodded.

"Well you can't carry on like this," he said.

She nodded again. "I've tried to make it work," she said.

"I know you have but you married a lunatic. He doesn't deserve you."

Hislop had been away for only a short time to lock up the shop and to pop into his house to check that his wife was still in the land of the living. Now he was back, the meal was nearly over and it was still only seven thirty in the evening. Meals disappeared quickly when Hislop was present. The main topic of conversation was about the empty chair at the table.

"I was thirty-four, dad. Time was running out."

"Nonsense. It would've been better to play single than end up with the idiot you've lumbered yourself with." Hislop poured himself another glass of wine.

"He was different then. Quiet and shy. I thought he needed looking after," Miriam sighed.

"Quiet, shy and stupid," her father said, "and you've lumbered me with him too. He wanders around the shop in a trance."

"It was kind of you to give him a job," she said.

Hislop wiped custard from his chin. "You are my daughter. What else could I do?"

They sat for a while then he leaned forward and laid his hand on her arm. "Why don't you move back in to your old bedroom at home with your mother and me? She'd love having you back again."

Miriam smiled and shook her head knowing full well that if she did move back, within days she'd be full-time cook, cleaner and slave.

"Thanks, Dad," she said. "I'll plod on for a bit. I just can't pin him down to talk over our problems and he won't see a doctor."

"Hmph!" Hislop snorted. "A bit late for that." He pulled her arm. "Leave it with me. I'll give him a good talking to, man to man as soon as I can."

Another hour went by during which the topic didn't change and Hislop wolfed down what was left of the crumble, half a pack of biscuits, a large slab of cheese and three cups of coffee.

She led him to the door.

"Thanks, Daddy," she said. "Give my love to Mum."

He rammed his trilby hat on to his head.

"Will do," he said.

"How is she feeling now?"

"She's fine. Just keeps fussing about her operation. It never ends. She'll mend."

He kissed his daughter on the cheek and disappeared into the night.

Miriam went back into the kitchen and started stacking the dirty dishes in the washer. She knew that she'd done the wrong thing inviting her father to dinner when she'd promised Eddie a romantic evening. It was thoughtless of her. She'd apologise maybe in the morning and explain that she felt that she had had no option. Her father had carried her heavy shopping bag home for her; she had told him what she was going to cook.

He had said that it sounded very nice, that his wife was very tired, didn't want to eat much and that he'd probably have to cook a simple supper for himself. What could she do after such loaded hints? She had to invite him. But then she thought that at least she had had a conversation tonight. Meals with Eddie were always a bit one-sided. She found herself at times wracking her brains to think of a new topic they could discuss instead of the usual mumblings about the jobs he intended to do about the house, the dog, the weather and how he hated his job. She sat back down at the table and poured herself another glass of red wine. There was no doubt about it. She was bored. Numbingly bored. Daddy was right. She should've waited. Getting married had been a mistake. Her fault, she admitted to herself. She'd done all the running, put on all the pressure, but there had never been what she had been hoping for: romance or even a modicum of passion. They had been married for five years yet it seemed longer, much longer. They were like a long-wedded couple who'd run out of steam and were just enduring life together.

She looked at her watch. Eight thirty. Normally at this time she and Eddie would have finished their meal and he would be up a ladder painting a damp patch on the ceiling or hammering a shelf to the wall. Very rarely would he sit with her to watch television. Always fidgeting, for ever on the go until it was time for one of his late-night walks. What a life! She picked up a magazine and scanned the TV pages to see what was on. Nothing grabbed her interest. She sighed and drummed her fingers on the table. She needed someone to talk to. After another glance at her watch, she topped up her glass, picked up her mobile phone and keyed in to a contact.

"Hi," a voice said. "Leave a number and I'll call you back."

Miriam sighed and put the phone down. Almost immediately it rang. She picked it up.

"Hi, Miriam," the voice said. "Sorry about that. I was waiting to check who was calling and you hung up before I could answer."

"Hello, Carrie," Miriam said. "I'm so glad you're in."

"Yeah. Nice to hear from you. To what do I owe this pleasure?"

Miriam hesitated. "Well, nothing really. I just called for a chat."

Carrie Donaghue had been a friend for a long time. They'd worked together at the library. Since then she'd had lots of jobs but was now working quite successfully writing as a freelancer for women's magazines. They had kept in regular contact, often meeting at a small coffee house in the nearby market square when Miriam was shopping or after Carrie had finished one of her regular sessions at the gym. She was a fitness fanatic. Tall and thin with short almost mannish black hair, she'd completed the London Marathon twice and another in New York. Miriam liked her because she was different. She envied her exuberant lifestyle, her quirkiness, her energy and her quick wit. Carrie was an American and had lived in the UK for the last ten years since the break-up of her marriage to an alcoholic actor in Los Angeles.

"You sound a bit fed up, honey," she said.

"No, I'm fine."

"Aw, C'mon. I know that voice. Did somebody die?"

Miriam laughed. "Well, okay. But if I was, you've cheered me up already."

"Okay. Talk to Mommy. What's the problem?"

Miriam hesitated then said, "Hey, I didn't call to burden you with my problems."

"Come on. Out with it!"

"Oh. It's nothing really. Another argument with Eddie, that's all."

"Put him on," Carrie said. "I'll sort the bastard out!"

"He's out. God knows where."

"Aw, shit!"

Miriam tried to change the subject. "What've you been up to?" she asked.

"Never mind about me. What time will he be home?"

"Probably not until the early hours of tomorrow."

"What? Are you kidding me? Where the hell does he go?"

Miriam sighed again. "Who knows?"

There was a long pause then Carrie said, "He's having an affair."

Miriam laughed again.

"I don't think so. He's more interested in DIY than sex."

"Maybe he's into DIY sex."

"I wouldn't know about that."

There was yet another long pause, then Carrie said, "I'm coming over."

"Don't be silly. It's late and you—"

"You need a shoulder to cry on, honey," Carrie interrupted and hung up. Twenty minutes later, the doorbell rang and she was standing on the step outside surveying Eddie's handiwork. "Hey, I like the new garden," she said. Miriam peered over her shoulder seeing it for the first time, a look for surprise on her face.

"Oh yes," she said. "Nice isn't it?"

They went inside. The American handed her a bottle of red wine. "Get to it, bartender. Where's the bottle opener?" she said. She was wearing an old pilot's jacket with a fur collar over a black tee shirt and tight blue jeans tucked into leather cowboy boots. As always dozens of bangles jangled on each wrist, and big colourful earrings on each ear. Her eyes were heavily mascaraed and her lips a glossy red. She might just as well have been carrying a placard saying 'Look. I'm an American'.

Oh God, Miriam thought. *I must look so drab*. She went in search of the bottle opener.

Carrie planted herself down on the settee and eased off her boots. "Are you sure Romeo is out for a while?" she said.

Miriam was struggling to extract the cork from the bottle. "Yep." I won't see him till tomorrow morning." She filled two glasses and sat down on an armchair facing the settee... "And when I ask where he's been he'll say oh, just out with the dog."

"What a jerk," Carrie groaned.

Miriam clinked Carrie's glass with her own.

"Cheers," she said.

"Skol," Carrie countered.

"What happened to you?"

"My marriage?"

Miriam nodded.

"Aw. The guy was wrecked most of the time. He had the looks of a god and the brains of a walnut. Was a bit-part actor for years then got a chance of a screen role. The asshole turned up at the audition pissed out of his mind. He was too stupid to realise he had a problem. It ended up with him sitting on his butt at home clutching a whisky bottle and me paying all the bills. I got the hell outta there." Carrie raised her glass. "Here's to you, Bradley. Thank the fuck you're out of my life."

Miriam smiled.

"Totally different problem," she said. "Eddie hardly ever drinks."

"Have you thought of following him when he's out on his late-night jaunts?"

"Thought about it but haven't done it. With the streets so deserted at that time in the morning, he'd spot me a mile off."

Carrie peeled off the pilot's jacket and lay back on the settee. She had a tattoo of a snake around her well-muscled left arm coiling round from her bicep and ending at her wrist. "So do as I did," she said. "Leave the shmuck."

"This is his house," Miriam replied. "If I walk out I'll have to go back and live with my parents. No way!"

"He'll have to give you half plus maintenance."

"Maintenance? " Miriam scoffed. "He earns peanuts. I'd probably be granted two of them a week."

Carrie leaned forward and patted Miriam's knee. "Listen sweetheart," she said. "If it ever gets too much, remember I've got a spare room."

Miriam smiled. "Thanks. You're a good pal."

She picked up the bottle. "More wine?"

"Why not?"

Miriam's head was starting to swim. She'd been drinking wine with her father and was now hitting the bottle again. She felt a warm rosy glow radiating through her body. A miserable evening had been unexpectedly transformed into a very pleasant one. She topped up her glass. One more wouldn't hurt.

An hour later Carrie stood up, put her jacket on and thanked Miriam for a lovely evening. She called for an Uber on her phone and they waited in the hallway for the two minutes it took to arrive.

"Well I feel a whole lot better now. Thanks for cheering me up," Miriam slurred. The room seemed to be spinning around and she had to lean against the wall to steady herself.

"Let's do it again soon," Carrie said. Her phone pinged. The car had arrived. She stretched forward and wrapped her arms around Miriam's waist. "Thanks again," she said. Miriam looked up at her. Their faces were almost touching. For a long moment they just stayed that way, staring at one another, not speaking then Carrie cupped Miriam's face in her hands and kissed her full on the lips. It lasted only a few seconds before she pulled away, then "night, night" she said, smiled and walked out to her taxi.

CHAPTER FIVE

The Reckoning

I wanted to stay asleep but I had entered that brief period between dreamland and reality. It was the cold that had woken me up. I was trembling and my head felt as though it were being squeezed in a vice. Had I been drinking last night? Had Miriam grabbed most of the duvet again? I opened one eye and saw another eye staring at me only an inch from mine. I felt vaguely irritated. Miriam sometimes did that. Came too close in bed so that we were breathing each other's exhaled air, but for once I didn't care. I was too tired to move so I shut my eyes again and tried to get back to sleep. Just then I became aware of voices, harsh, strident, angry voices. Some people had no consideration. It sounded like my father-in-law in triplicate. What was *he* doing here? I opened my eyes again. The other eye was still there an inch away, staring at me. I lifted my head to move away and a red-hot searing pain crashed violently around inside my skull. The eye, now six inches away, winced and I realised that I was looking at my own reflection in a pool of dirty water. The loud voices stopped abruptly and a thick brown arm appeared in my line of vision and a hand closed around the lapels of my coat. The ground fell away and I felt myself jerked up like a puppet into the air. My head seemed to explode and I gave a loud yelp of agony. Then something came up beneath me with bone-shaking force and I realised that I had been thrown down on to a chair.

"C'mon you little bastard!"

Somebody was yelling at me from close range. I could feel spittle hitting my face and there was a strong smell of garlic. I badly wanted to see what all the noise was about but I'd screwed my eyes shut in a vain effort to ward off the pain that coursed through my body and somehow my eyelids wouldn't open. A massive, calloused hand slapped me hard across the face and the red-hot agony in my skull reached new levels. Then I heard my own voice as though it was coming from somewhere else whimper.

"Please, please! No more."

Another voice spoke from somewhere further away and there was silence for a while. Gradually the violent hammering in my head subsided to a dull pounding and to avoid being slapped again I squinted through the slits of my eyes at the surroundings. Directly in front of me stood the towering bulk of the grinning West Indian, although he wasn't grinning now. His lips were turned down in a grimace of hate and his eyes were bloodshot and angry. Behind him was the man they called Smalley and sitting on the edge of a wooden table beside the wall sat Baseball Cap sullenly picking at his teeth with a match.

Strangely, I didn't feel frightened. I was trying to cope with such a clamour of different aches and pains my mind could only focus on them. There was no room for fear—yet! I kept thinking, *What have I done? Why did I go snooping around? Look where it's got me.*

The West Indian crouched down and breathed more garlic into my face.

"Who are you, Wheatley?" he said. "You the Bill?" I wondered how he knew my name then saw my wallet and its contents scattered on the floor at Baseball Cap's feet.

"The Bill?" I said.

"Police."

"No, no. I'm not the police."

He bunched his hand into a huge fist and held it under my nose.

"Don't you fucking kid me!"

"Please don't hit me again," I whimpered pathetically.

"I'll rip your sodding head off," he roared. "You're plain clothes aren't you?"

The fist pressed hard against my nose.

"No, honestly. I'm not the police. I swear it. I'm… I'm a shop assistant. I work in a shop!"

"Don't give me that crap, you little shit!" he bellowed and raised his fist to hit me again.

Baseball Cap suddenly appeared beside the West Indian. "'Ang on Winston," he said, "let me 'ave a word." He shouldered the big man out of the way and crouched down beside me, his face almost touching mine.

"You was in the pub, weren't you?" he said.

I nodded.

"Now why would a nice law-abiding shop assistant go followin' people out of pubs?"

I couldn't think of an answer. He waited then grabbed me by the throat.

"I asked you a fuckin' question," he roared.

"I wasn't following you," I wheezed. He had such a tight grip on my neck I could hardly breathe.

"Bollocks!" he screamed, then released my throat and slapped me hard across the face. "Now I know you're lying. You're a fucking cop aren't you?"

"No, please. I'm not a cop."

He grabbed my throat again.

"Then why was you followin' me?"

I tried to speak but found that my vocal chords had gone into a kind of spasm. Fear had arrived with a rush and clutched my insides with a vice like grip. My whole body was trembling and I couldn't tell whether it was from the cold or dread. These men were hard and ruthless and I knew this torture would go on until they'd forced the truth out of me. It was futile to lie. I looked up into the cold grey eyes a foot from my face.

"I was here last night," I managed to blurt out.

Baseball Cap waited.

"I was out late… I… I sometimes walk… walk the dog late at night …even early in the morning."

I stared down at my lap unable to look any longer at the three hostile faces glaring at me.

"It started to rain… I sheltered in the alleyway opposite the garages."

"Yeah. Then what?" Smalley growled.

"I… I saw you unloading your truck… I suppose I was just being nosey."

Nobody said anything so I carried on. "I didn't know what you were unloading… still don't." Then pathetically, "I won't tell anyone… I promise."

"So you came back for another look?" said Smalley.

I nodded. The West Indian, who I now knew was called Winston, and Baseball Cap both turned and looked at their leader as though they were waiting for him to make a decision.

He continued to stare down at me then, after what seemed a very long time, he said, "You stupid, interfering prat!" He gestured to the other two to follow him and walked over to the door. Before leaving the room he turned and said, "Was anyone else with you last night?"

I shook my head miserably. "No."

"Have you told anyone what you saw?"

"No."

There was another long pause. I waited for another question but it didn't come. Just that penetrating cold stare. Eventually he shook his head, muttered, "Cunt," and walked out of the room.

The other two men followed.

"Stay put and don't move a muscle, arsehole," Winston said and slammed the door behind him. I heard the sound of a heavy bolt being put into place on the other side. Ignoring Winston's order I staggered painfully to my feet, crossed the room and pressed my ear to the door.

The three men seemed to be walking away down a hallway. Their footsteps echoed slightly but their voices were amplified enough to reach my ears through the thin wooden door. I heard Winston say, "What now, Smalley?"

"Hang on," Smalley said. "I'm gonna call Haslitt."

There was a long silence then I heard him say, "Haslitt? ... Yeah, it's me." Then he lowered his voice and I could only hear some of what he was saying. "Yeah... nosey blood dog walker... no, not a cop... what? ... Okay, will do... when're we movin' out? ... Yeah, sooner the better... hurry up will ya? ... Bye."

Then there were shuffling noises and I heard what sounded like a drawer being opened then banged shut. More mumbled voices then Smalley again.

"Here, take this," he said. "Go and do the business." I sprang away from the door. 'Go and do the business?' What did they mean? Were they going to kill me? I felt my heart lurch and I struggled to get my breath, panic rising like bile in my throat. For a while I stood paralysed with fear. I looked around the tiny room for some means of escape but apart from the locked door there was no other exit from the room, no other doors or windows. The walls were covered in dirty yellow flaking distemper and the room was lit by a solitary naked bulb which hung from a cobweb-festooned flex in the centre of the ceiling. The old brick floor was covered with puddles of water. Apart from the chair that I had been sitting on, the only other furniture in the room was a rickety wooden table standing near the door and three wooden shelves resting on old and broken brackets on the opposite wall. A bottle and three dirty jam jars stood on the top shelf.

I reached up with trembling fingers for the bottle. It seemed to be my only chance. Maybe I could hit whoever came in through the door with it. But the shelf was high up under the ceiling and I couldn't reach. Footsteps sounded in the hall. I turned and lunged at the table and tried to drag it across the room so that I could use it to reach the bottle, but it had been screwed tight to the wall. I heaved frantically, sobbing with fear and frustration, but it wouldn't move. The bolt on the other side of the door was drawn back. I flung myself across the room and tried, with a final despairing leap, to reach the top shelf, but I was well short and fell sprawling against the lower shelves bringing them crashing to the floor.

A voice from behind said, "Turn round, arsehole"!

I turned round and as I did I swung the heavy middle shelf round in a long hissing arc of dirt, debris and desperation. There was a soft 'phut' noise and something stung against my rib cage. I saw Baseball Cap's face and the sullen expression change to one of stark horror then the edge of the shelf hit him in the throat with a sickening crunch, sending the man flying against the door frame, eyes bulging from his head and blood spurting with a horrific gurgling noise from his mouth. He slumped against the wall for a second or two, his head at a grotesque angle, staring down at the gun in his right hand and then slowly slid down the wall into a sitting position on the floor.

I dropped the plank of wood and stared in horror at the bloody corpse, then fell to my knees on the floor, retching violently. My heart seemed to be pounding its way out of my chest and a pulsating pain emanated from somewhere just below my rib but there was no time to feel sorry for myself. I heard footsteps coming down the hallway and was instantly on my feet again, grabbing the gun from the dead man's hand and backing away from the door. Winston appeared, his frame filling the whole of the doorway. He stared down in disbelief at Baseball Cap's body.

"Fucking hell!" he muttered to himself, then looked over at me with an incredulous expression. "You bastard!" he roared and charged across the room. I felt the gun kick in my hand and then his huge paws were round my throat and we crashed on to the wet floor, his head crashing painfully into mine. It felt as if I was being trampled on by an elephant. Twenty stone of solid muscle was pinning me to the ground.

Smalley's face appeared over Winston's shoulder.

"Kill the little shit!" he yelled. "Kill the bastard!"

The gigantic black body suddenly reared up with an agonising moan and sat across my hips. Smalley charged in like a maddened bull and started flailing at my face with his fits.

"Die, you little bastard!" he screamed.

Finding my arms free again I raised the gun and pulled the trigger. A small round hole appeared in Smalley's forehead and he sat down on the floor with a thump, an astonished expression on his face. Then slowly, as though he was making himself comfortable for the night, he slid down on his back, a small fountain of blood falling back on his face and running down into the puddles on the floor.

I turned the gun and pointed it at Winston's face.

"Get off me!" I screamed. "Get off. Leave me alone!"

But Winston had his hands on his knees and his head bowed. He swayed slowly back and forth, making a deep groaning noise which rose and fell in pitch, almost as though he was humming a tune. Then he looked down into my face and said softly, "Oh shit man. Look what you've done."

Like a building falling in slow motion, he crumpled forward and fell on top of me, once again cracking his head against mine and ramming the gun painfully into my stomach. I couldn't breathe. I turned my head and looked into his face, only inches from my own. The man's eyes had rolled up until only the whites were showing and his mouth was open and slack. Winston was dead.

With enormous effort I pulled an arm free of the crushing weight and pushed with all my strength on one massive shoulder. Slowly the man rolled off me and flopped on his back on the floor. A large patch of blood had appeared on his tee shirt just below the rib cage.

Scrambling frantically across the floor, sobbing and gasping for breath, I curled up on in one corner of the room and stared with horror at the carnage that surrounded me. Baseball Cap had slipped further down the door frame with his head tilted slightly so that the bulging dead eyes seemed to be staring straight into mine. Smalley was on his back with one arm stretched across the floor, his face a mask of blood, and Winston lay like a beached whale on the wet floor, his eyes white and protruding from his face like two halves of a ping-pong ball. I put my head in my hands and sobbed. My body was trembling uncontrollably and I was taking great breaths like a goldfish out of water and whimpering at the same time. It seemed that every part of me was in pain. I felt bruised and cold and still very frightened, but a feeling of enormous relief that I was still alive surged through my veins. I screwed my eyes tight shut and waited till my heart stopped its painful hammering at the base of my throat and settled down to a normal beat in its proper position.

Gradually my mind started to comprehend the horror of what I had done. Three men had died. I had killed three human beings. In all of my life I had never as much as slapped another person, but now, in one night, everything had changed. I was a killer, a triple murderer. I groaned loudly. "Oh God. Oh God. What am I going to do?"

The police. I would now go to the police. They would sort everything out for me. After all, it was self-defence, wasn't it? I'd heard Smalley say, "kill him" and Baseball Cap had come into the room with a gun.

I looked down at the gun where it had dropped when I crawled out from beneath Winston. It was longer than I expected a proper gun to be and had a strange cylinder attached to the end of the barrel. This would be a silencer, I guessed. Of course, they would have had to use a silencer otherwise the whole neighbourhood would be awake and banging on the door wondering what had happened. These three cold-blooded, callous men had just calmly fitted the silencer to the gun and decided to snuff my life out with as little thought as if they were swatting a fly. They would have dumped me somewhere and tomorrow would have been able to carry on with life, consciences completely untroubled. I shuddered when I thought how near to death I had been.

After a while I stood up unsteadily and walked painfully towards the door. My whole body felt stiff and sore and I had to hold on to the wall to support myself. Stepping carefully over Baseball Cap's body, I walked out into the dark hallway.

The floor was made of old, badly worn stone slabs and the walls appeared to be covered with the same flaky, yellow paint as the room I had just left. The corridor receded into complete darkness but I could see a line of yellow light indicating a door and a well-lit room the other side. I crept back into the first room and picked up the gun. After all, there was a possibility that the gang was larger than three in number and a fourth or fifth man could still be in the house. I tiptoed warily back down the corridor and slowly pushed open the door at the far end.

I was in a kitchen. Large and old fashioned and brightly lit. A fire crackled in an ancient black leaded grate and two heavy overstuffed armchairs, strewn with newspapers, sat facing its hearth. A table with a dirty red check cloth, barely visible beneath piles of beer cans, stood against one wall and on the other wall was an old white sink full of dirty paper plates and a wooden draining board piled high with silver cartons from a Chinese takeaway. I stood for a long time listening but there was no one else there. Never in my whole life had I been so pleased to see a fire. I walked in and stood with my back towards it. My clothes were saturated and I was shivering with cold. I wondered why I was so wet then realised that the three men must have been throwing buckets of water over me when I was unconscious. Clamping my teeth in a vain effort to stop them chattering, I stared miserably around the room.

Standing on the floor beside one of the armchairs was Baseball Cap's bottle of whisky. I picked it up gratefully and poured a generous quantity down my throat, steadying myself against the wall as the fiery liquid hit my stomach with a jolt. It was great medicine because, after a few minutes, I started to feel better. The whisky and the warmth from the fire seeped into my chilled, terrified body and I was able to control the violent trembling and panic that had threatened to engulf me.

After another swig from the bottle, I decided it was time to go to the police. But first I had to find my way out. There were two other doors leading out of the room. The first one I opened led directly onto a wooden staircase which spiralled up into the musty darkness above. On the wall directly behind the door was a mirror. I stared at my reflection in disbelief. The figure I saw looked like a tramp after a road accident. My hair was flattened to my forehead and a dried rivulet of blood ran from my nose to my chin. I reached up and touched the swollen and bruised cheeks that I saw reflected and winced with pain.

With a groan I opened the other door. The light in the kitchen showed that I was at the entrance to what must have been the living room. It was completely bare of furniture and fittings but in the centre of the floor was a coffin-shaped mound covered by a grubby sheet. I put my arm around the door frame and found the light switch. A naked bulb dangling from the ceiling filled the room with yellow light. I walked into the room and stared down at the mound, my heart racing.

I knew what was beneath that dirty sheet. Four men had already died for it. Two others were in hospital with shotgun wounds and I had been a hair's breadth from losing my life because I had been unable to contain my curiosity about it. I stopped and with trembling fingers picked up the corner of the cloth, then slowly walked backwards towards the door, pulling the cloth as I went and watching spellbound, unable to breathe as each long, golden ingot was revealed. When I reached the doorway I let the cloth drop to the floor. Thirty million pounds' worth of gleaming yellow metal lay at my feet.

For a long time I couldn't move and stood rooted to the spot, staring at the gold. It seemed to me that the most beautiful sight that I had ever seen was laid before me at that moment. Suddenly I could understand why it was that men were prepared to murder, rob and cheat for it. Strangely it made me feel at peace. My heart was no longer attempting to hammer its way out of my chest and I felt calm and serene and filled with a kind of reverence, as if I had just entered a church and had become aware of some mighty presence. When I did eventually move, it was on tiptoes as though it would be sacrilege to make a noise.

I stepped forward and picked up one of the ingots. It was about eighteen inches long and incredibly heavy. I turned it over in my hands, letting the light from the ceiling play across its surfaces. Five small numbers were stamped deeply into one of the sides and there was a circle with interwoven initials that I could not make out. After staring at it in awe until my arms ached, I put the precious thing down again, pleased with the dull clunk it made as it rejoined the pile.

Sitting on top of the gold was a black plastic dustbin bag, tied at the top by a piece of string. It was fairly heavy and the knot in the string was tight and difficult to undo. After a minute or two, however, I was able to open the top of the bag and peer inside.

A miniature Aladdin's cave lay at the bottom of the bag: a sparkling assortment of exquisite jewellery studded with sapphires, rubies and diamonds. I delved my hand in and pulled out a fistful of rings, necklaces and bracelets which flashed and shimmered as I let them trickle through my fingers back into the bag.

It was at that moment that I knew I was not going to go to the police. Surely it was fate that had guided me to shelter in the alleyway the previous night. And why was it that I, a small fairly insignificant person, had been spared when attacked by three violent men intent on killing me and had turned the tables on them and taken their lives? It seemed to be ordained; it was meant to happen.

I smiled and walked out of the room. Now that I had made my decision I could feel a stab of excitement deep down in my stomach and as I passed through the kitchen and down into the dark hallway, I felt as though I had grown three feet taller. I'd show them who was the weak, insignificant little man now.

CHAPTER SIX

Mike Paterson and Frank Thomson

Mike Paterson was dreaming about Sally. This wasn't unusual. Sally had been on his mind since that chance encounter three months ago when he had finally decided to learn to drive. She was the one who had taken down his name and address in a large brown ledger and had booked him in for an hour's tuition at five thirty p.m. each Wednesday for the next six weeks. He had hoped that she would be the person who did the teaching. But no, she just worked behind the desk doing the bookings.

It was uncanny how much she resembled his late wife, Cathy. So much so that the shock had been like a physical blow when he first walked into the driving school office. Same brown eyes, same short black hair. Same small, high-cheekboned face and that familiar readiness to smile. But she was much smaller than Cathy had been and her voice had a trace of an Irish accent which he found incredibly beguiling.

Almost immediately they had become good friends and for the past two Wednesdays had gone together to a small wine bar for a drink after his driving lesson. She was, he found out, widowed with two grown-up children and the owner of a half share in the driving school. He guessed that she must be in her early forties. Young enough to be his daughter. He was seventy-three. A stupid, ridiculous old fool to hold out any hopes. She was probably just lonely, thought of him as a father figure, felt sorry for him. Not much to offer a beautiful woman was it? False teeth, arthritic hip, a history of heart problems. Oh God, if only it were possible to turn the clock back...

Paterson had lived alone for six years. His beloved Cathy, whom he had adored, had died along with her mother and father in a fire which had engulfed her parents' house when she was paying a weekend visit. There had been no children, so he was on his own.

In tonight's dream they were walking along a sandy beach. Sally was carrying a picnic hamper and a pair of rolled-up beach mats were tucked under one arm. Her children were somehow small and young again. A little tousled-haired boy and a girl of about six wearing a flowered dress and a huge ribbon tied in a bow at the back of her head. There was a white dog. A West Highland terrier which Paterson recognised as the one which his parents had owned when he was young.

Eventually Sally stopped and threw the beach mats on the ground. He helped to flatten them out while she and the children unpacked the hamper. The dog started to bark and turning, Paterson saw a man approaching with a spade and a large plastic bucket. Behind the man, near the sea, the sand had been disturbed. Large holes had been dug out at the water's edge and Paterson assumed that the man was digging for lugworms to use as bait for fishing.

The tall figure in an oilskin coat and wellingtons walked nearer until he was only a yard away from the picnic. He stopped and started to dig and, to Paterson's horror, shovelled the sand all over the food that Sally was unpacking from the hamper. She shouted out in annoyance but another heavy spadeful fell amongst the plates, spattering sand all over her white dress. Paterson tried to protest but strangely no sounds would emerge from his throat. The man didn't seem to notice that they were there. He just kept shovelling more and more sand in their direction and Sally was looking at Paterson with a pleading look, begging him to do something… and although he strained till the tendons stood out on his neck, he still couldn't make any sounds… and worse, he couldn't move. He opened his mouth wide in despair and at last forced out a wail of anguish… the sound woke him up and he found himself sitting upright in bed, perspiration sprinkling his forehead and the duvet in a knot around his legs.

He sighed and slumped back on to the pillow with relief. Thank God. Only a dream. He stared at the ceiling for a second or two until the panic subsided, thinking what a pity it was that a stupid bloody fisherman had to go and spoil a damned good dream. It could have been a really nice picnic. He kicked the duvet free from his legs and turned over on his side. A second later he sat bolt upright again in a state of confusion. Part of the dream hadn't ended… he could still hear the shovelling noise.

He sat perfectly still, holding his breath and straining to hear. Away in the distance he heard the shrill blare of a police car followed by silence, and then, just when he was starting to think he had imagined it, there came the unmistakable sound of a spade digging deep into a pile of earth. Paterson swung his legs over the side of the bed and reached out to the bedside cabinet for his spectacles. He squinted at the luminous dial on his wrist watch. Ten minutes past five. What the hell…?

He stumbled out of bed and crossed to the window. Outside it was still dark but the faint glow of the new morning was starting to appear behind the black silhouettes of the high buildings across the street. A solitary streetlamp further down the road was still lit and in the dim light, Paterson could see the slight figure of his next-door neighbour, Eddie Wheatley, working on his new wall. He was filling the gap between the two rows of bricks with earth. Paterson checked his watch again incredulously. Ten past five! What was the idiot doing? He opened the window and in a hoarse whisper said, "Eddie, in God's name, what the hell are you up to?"

Eddie spun around as if he had been shot. The spade fell from his hand and landed on the path at his feet. Paterson was astonished at the man's appearance. His face was puffy and appeared to be bleeding. His clothes were covered in dirt and his eyes were wild and staring. He looked exhausted and scared to death. For a long time he said nothing but just stood there, swaying and staring up at Paterson's window, and then… "Oh… Hello Mr Paterson." He swung his arm out and gestured weakly at his handiwork as if no explanation was necessary.

"Do you know what time it is?"

There was no answer. It seemed as though the man was too tired to speak.

"For God's sake, Eddie. Are you all right?"

His neighbour sat down on the wall.

"Fine," he said eventually. "Just fine."

"It's ten past five in the morning!"

Wheatley nodded and continued to sit slumped, staring at his feet until after a few seconds he seemed to make a great effort to pull himself together. He looked up.

"I'm sorry," he said. "I couldn't sleep… insomnia I suppose… thought I'd come out and finish this. Tried to be quiet. Didn't mean to wake you."

There was a long pause, then eventually Paterson said, "Eddie, if you'll take my advice, you'll go in now, have a hot bath and then get some rest. You look all in."

There was no reply.

Paterson added, "And Eddie, see a doctor. It isn't right this insomnia of yours. You're going to crack up."

Wheatley nodded. He stood up and raised his head to stare at Paterson with those tired, dark-rimmed eyes.

"You're right… thanks Mr Paterson. I'm sorry I disturbed you." He hesitated, then picked up the spade and threw it into the pile of soil. "I'll finish this off tomorrow."

"Good man. Now get some sleep, you look terrible."

"Goodnight Mr Paterson."

"Good morning, Eddie."

Paterson closed the window and climbed back into bed. He lay staring at the ceiling, a worried frown creasing his forehead. What on earth was the matter with the poor little fellow? The man was obviously heading for a nervous breakdown. It was all very well being an avid do-it-yourselfer, but at five in the morning? No, there must be something wrong. Paterson turned over on his side. He had a feeling that Wheatley would not seek the advice of a doctor. Perhaps if he were to have a word with his wife... what was her name? Miriam. Maybe she would be able to persuade him. He contemplated this for a second... On the other hand it may be from her that he was trying to escape. Paterson had overheard a few snatches of conversation between his next-door neighbours from time to time when they were together in the garden. And he remembered feeling relieved that it was Eddie Wheatley and not himself on the receiving end of her non-stop talking. It was obvious that she was the kind of woman who was used to getting her own way. He couldn't remember ever hearing her shout or get angry but she could somehow imply in the most pleasant and sincere manner that if she did not get her way then there was a heap of trouble just about to land on the person to whom she was talking. He recalled meeting her outside the post office one day and she had asked him in the sweetest way if he wouldn't mind cutting back the weeds on his side of the fence which divided their two properties because they were growing through on to her side. Adding before he could reply, and again with that friendly, well-meaning smile on her face, that if he would be so kind it would save her having to put down weed killer which would probably spread and make the edge of his lawn go brown and could possibly kill off his cat. And hadn't the weather suddenly got cold and how nice it was to see him again looking so well and it had been so nice to stop and have this chat but she must go now and make Eddie's tea.

It was funny really but perhaps not very funny if you had to live with it all the time. Paterson quite liked Eddie Wheatley even though he hardly ever said a word. He was so quiet and unassuming. Painfully shy. Probably didn't have a friend in the world that he could confide in. All his thoughts having to stay locked up inside his head. His only refuge from a domineering wife was to escape into his obsessive repairs and improvements around the house.

Paterson decided that what Wheatley needed was a friend. Somebody he could have a chat with other than his wife… and since there didn't seem to be anybody else around he supposed it had better be him. Yes, that's what he would do. Tomorrow he'd call round, see the poor little beggar, and try to cheer him up a bit.

His thoughts were interrupted by the sound of a vehicle being started up immediately outside the house. He frowned and got out of bed again, screwing up his eyes and staring out of the window into the dim morning light. There was no sign of Eddie Wheatley. He had probably gone to bed. But a builder's truck that he hadn't seen parked there before was just moving out from the kerb. It trundled very slowly up the road keeping its revs slow until it was well down the road and then the accelerator was pressed down and the truck sped away until it was out of sight.

****

I parked the truck on the same spot that I had found it at the end of the lane. With a wet handkerchief I carefully wiped any traces of fingerprints from the steering wheel and gear stick, then gave the same treatment to the outside door handle when I got out.

I let myself in quietly through the garage entrance to the house and spent the next hour removing any traces of ever having been there. Before leaving I wiped off the ignition keys to the truck and replaced them in Baseball Cap's pocket. The three bodies were stiff and cold now and their skins had turned incredibly white. Even Winston's face seemed to have grown three or four shades paler.

As I left the room I turned and looked down at them. I smiled and moved my hand, priestlike, in the sign of the cross. "Bless you, my children," I said. "You've made a fellow human being extremely happy." Then I closed the door gently with the handkerchief and walked out of the house.

By the time I reached home it was daylight. Much to my relief I didn't meet a soul on the way and managed to scurry as fast as my exhausted body was able, unseen into the side entrance of my house and around into the back garden. I let myself into the garden shed and stripped off all my filthy, wet outer clothing, dumping them in the corner behind the lawnmower, then wearing only my underpants and socks I crept into the house and upstairs to the bathroom. It was in a bath full of cold, very dirty water that Miriam found me two hours later, fast asleep.

*****

Frank Thomson liked Sundays. Say what you like, they were different. It was hard to define why. That ancient idea of six days shalt thou labour was long forgotten. People were still willing to beaver away out there as they'd done for the rest of the week. Football matches would be played, shops would be open and the pubs would soon be packed out. Yet a certain tranquillity seemed to him to settle over the world on Sundays like a well-loved and comfortable jacket. This hillside, these woods, were peaceful every day of the week, yet on a Sunday it was doubly so. So, Sundays, even to atheists like Frank Thomson, were special days.

He whistled and an old brown spaniel came trotting out of the bushes where it had been searching optimistically for rabbits. Thomson stooped and lifted the animal over a stile and then clipped a leather leash on to its collar. They had arrived at a narrow country lane. Sunday or not people still drove far too fast along here and the dog, he knew from past hair-raising experiences, had no road sense whatsoever. They walked a hundred yards down the lane and then crossed over to where a concrete sign beside another stile indicated the continuation of the public footpath. Parked on the grass verge beside the sign was a long black Jaguar F-Type sports car. As Thomson approached the window of the car was wound down and a big, square-jawed man of about forty with a mass of very curly blond hair, put his arm on the edge of the door and rested his chin on his elbow. He said nothing but a faint smile was on his face as he watched Thomson tie the dog to the signpost then clamber up and sit on the top rung of the stile. Neither of the men spoke for quite a while, then the man in the car let out a low chuckle of laughter and said, "Thomo, you're a bloody genius!"

Thomson shrugged, "Just a matter of doing one's homework."

"Have you read the papers? They haven't a clue."

Thomson pulled a packet of cigarettes from his pocket and lit one. "Shame about the security guard."

"Eh? Oh yeah... well..."

Thomson said, "Oh yeah... is that all you've got to say? You know how I feel about guns. Was there really any need to shoot the security guard?"

The curly haired man got out of the car and leaned against it, propping himself up by his elbows on the roof. "Smalley had to do it, Thomo, the silly bugger was coming at him with a pickaxe handle!"

"And what about the policeman?"

The man hung his head. "That was me," he said. "What the hell could I do? The bloke was lying across the bonnet of the car. We tried to shake him off."

Thomson got down from the stile and untied the dog, then reached into the inside pocket of his jacket and pulled out a thick brown envelope.

"I'm not very pleased with you or Smalley. You know that don't you, Haslitt?"

The man called Haslitt pushed himself away from the car. His face was flushed with anger.

"Hang on a minute, Thomo," he said. "While you were sitting on your arse at your club, us four were out there riskin' life sentences. So what if there was a bit of shootin'. We got the stuff, didn't we? I thought you'd be pleased for Christ's sake!"

Thomson held out the envelope. "This is a small advance," he said, ignoring the other man's outburst. "I've decided to postpone the pick-up a little while longer. London is probably swarming with eager plain-clothed policemen. It's too big a risk just now." He saw the dismay on Haslitt's face. "I'm sorry, I know it must be frustrating now that the main work's done but I don't want anything to go wrong at this stage. It won't be long, I promise you. How are the other three?"

Haslitt took the envelope sulkily. "Oh, wonderful," he said. "We're just like one big happy family back there in that stinkin' house. Munroe does nothin' but get pissed and moan all the time. Winston smells and Smalley is probably the most miserable, sadistic bastard I ever met. Oh yeah, we're ever so happy."

"I expect they speak well of you too," said Thomson.

He stared at the other man for a while and then said, "Look, you've only had to put up with it for two days so far. I promise it won't be more than seven."

The big man nodded dolefully and started to climb back into the car. Thomson said, "By the way, apart from the unfortunate injuries to the security man and the policeman, I think you did a grand job." He thought for a moment then said, "Several grand in fact." He laughed at his own joke, picked up the dog and climbed over the stile. "Meet me here at six o'clock on Tuesday night," he said, then walked off down the footpath.

The other man watched him until he was out of sight then turned his attention to the brown envelope. It contained four thousand pounds made up of twenty- and ten-pound notes. Haslitt counted them carefully then stuffed them back into the envelope. He sat frowning for a while and staring out of the window, tapping the envelope absent-mindedly on the steering wheel, then reaching forward he pressed the ignition and eased the car slowly off the grass verge and pointed the bonnet in the direction of London.

CHAPTER 7

Lunch With the In-Laws

Miriam finished setting the table and stood back to admire the layout. She ticked off each item, muttering under her breath as she did so. "Knives, forks, spoons, wine glasses, serviettes, place mats..." There was something missing. The toothpicks!

She hurried through to the kitchen and found the little pottery egg cup shaped like Humpty Dumpty filled with wooden toothpicks, then took it back into the dining room and placed it on the table where her father could easily reach it. He always had such a lot of trouble with his dentures after meals.

She smiled down at the table. Yes, it was complete now. Presentation was the thing. A good meal could be totally spoilt by a badly laid table. Miriam prided herself on being a good hostess. In the kitchen, amongst her cookery books, were other books on how to lay a table, how to dress, how to set the lighting of a room and conversational opening gambits when entertaining guests in one's house. It didn't matter to her that the only people they ever did entertain were her parents. She still went through the whole rigmarole of dressing properly, setting the table as though it was a Lord Mayor's banquet and selecting discreet background music for the occasion.

Having satisfied herself that the table was set to her liking, she moved over to the music centre on the sideboard and placed a Sinatra CD in the slot so that it was ready to play as soon as the guests arrived.

The kitchen was full of the delicious smells of roast beef cooking on a bed of onions. She glanced up anxiously at the clock. Twelve fifteen. Her parents were due at one thirty and

Eddie was still in bed. Him and his stupid insomnia! She guessed that as usual he would probably sit all the way through the meal looking as though he were at death's door, too tired to say a word, leaving her and her father to make all the conversation.

She started to peel the potatoes. She'd give him another fifteen minutes then he would have to get up, tired or not.

Miriam felt angry and frustrated. Why on earth couldn't she have married a man who was content to stay home at night? What did he get up to, for heaven's sake? It wasn't just to walk the dog, she was sure of that. After all, last night he went off on his own despite his denials. Could it be another woman? She laid the potato peeler down and stared out of the window. Surely not. Eddie was probably the least sexual male she had ever met. He would most likely be perfectly happy to remain celibate for the rest of his life and probably would if she didn't take the initiative from time to time. But she felt sure that there had been the smell of whisky on his breath when she helped him out of the bath that morning. Eddie never drank, apart from the occasional wine at Sunday lunchtimes or on special days like Christmas or birthdays.

She picked up the peeler and attacked another potato with it, then dropped them both back into the sink with a clatter as another thought occurred to her. What if it was a man? Could it be…? Was it possible that her husband was homosexual?' Now *that* was a real possibility. She sat down at the kitchen table and rested her chin in her cupped hands. The more she considered the idea the more it seemed to her that she was near the truth. These late-night, early morning walks of his were to meet another man. His obsession with doing jobs around the house was just to convince himself that he was a man. Desperately tackling the heavy, manly tasks in order to fool himself that he was what he was not. All the unnecessary scraping at his chin with a razor every morning when there was no need to. Surely it wasn't natural for a man of his age to have such a smooth babylike skin? Miriam moved to the sink again and hacked angrily at a potato. It was all starting to fit into place. She remembered how much of a mummy's boy he had been when they first met. His reluctance to have any sexual contact with her... a reluctance which persisted. If it was true then... he was gay! Oh the little bastard!

She moved quickly across to the Welsh dresser and flicked through the pages of her diary to find out when it was that they had last made love. She always kept a record of such things by marking the page with a large red asterisk. Three months ago! If he had passed anything on to her would it have shown itself by now? Oh God! She didn't know! Maybe a discreet word with the doctor tomorrow morning...

Her anguished thoughts were interrupted by a frantic barking coming from the hallway. She opened the kitchen door. Rufus was hurling himself hysterically against the front door. A shadow appeared against the frosted glass panel at the top and somebody pressed the doorbell. Miriam bundled the dog into the front room and opened the door.

Mike Paterson was standing smartly to attention on the doorstep. Unusually for him he had dispensed with a jacket and was wearing a bright green, short-sleeved shirt with a red spotted cravat. He flicked his walking stick up under his arm as Miriam opened the door and smiled down at her through his luxuriant moustache.

"Good morning, Mrs Wheatley," he boomed. "Or should I say afternoon?"

Miriam put her hand to her hair and patted it awkwardly.

"Oh, hello Mr Paterson," she said. "What a surprise." She wished she had had time to straighten her hair and take her apron off. "What can I do for you?"

"Well, actually, it was Eddie I wanted to see."

"Eddie?"

Paterson laughed. "Yes, you remember Eddie. Small chap, fairly shy, used to live here."

Miriam was taken aback. This was the first time that she could remember anyone calling and asking for her husband. She was the one who always had to deal with callers.

"I'm sorry," she stuttered, "he's busy just now. Can I give him a message?"

"Oh, it's nothing important," Paterson smiled. "I was just calling on the off-chance that I might drag him out for a lunchtime pint."

Miriam's mouth had dropped open. Paterson waited but she just stared at him without saying anything. He leaned towards her.

"Is there anything wrong?"

Miriam closed her mouth and folded her arms. It seemed to Paterson that her whole attitude had suddenly changed. She glared up at him with an expression on her face of deep and hostile suspicion. Without meaning to, he took a step backwards.

"Did you see my husband in the early hours of this morning?" she said in almost a whisper.

He nodded. "Why yes," he said, "that's why I—"

"You pervert!" she snapped.

This time it was Paterson's mouth that fell open. "I beg your pardon?" he stammered.

"Don't fool yourself that your activities have gone unnoticed!"

"I don't understand. I—"

"My God. Your sort make me sick!"

The old man stared at her in shocked disbelief. It was obvious to him that the woman was mentally unbalanced and needed treatment.

Miriam prodded him in the chest with her forefinger. "Take yourself and your pretty shirt off my property," she hissed. "Your little late-night meetings are over until the divorce."

She turned angrily, stepped back into the hallway. "Then you're welcome to him," she screamed. The door slammed shut with such force that a small pane of glass which was one of nine similar panes set just above the letterbox, shattered, sending tiny, red-tinted shards of glass flying onto the doorstep.

Miriam stood for a while breathing heavily, trying to control her anger, staring at the hole in the window and listening to the sound of Paterson's footsteps as he retreated down the path to the front gate. After a moment or two, she turned and started towards the kitchen, stopping suddenly with a sharp intake of breath. Her husband was standing at the foot of the stairs. He was dressed in casual grey slacks and a short-sleeved blue shirt. His hair was combed and a small piece of Elastoplast had been placed on one side of his forehead. She thought his face looked even more puffy and bruised than when she'd found him asleep in the bath before dragging him to the bedroom. One of his eyelids was so swollen that it almost closed the eye on that side.

*****

I would happily have spent the whole of that day in bed but Miriam must have pulled back the curtains and the fierce sunlight woke me up. My head was still pounding and I didn't want to open my eyes, so I lay for a long time trying to ignore all the aches and pains which seemed to affect every part of my body and to concentrate instead on the events of the previous evening. Had it really happened? Was I waking from a vivid dream? I touched my face and winced. No, not a dream. It had all taken place and somehow I'd survived. My stomach knotted when I recalled that I had killed three men. Okay, it was kill or be killed but what the hell had I been thinking? Why hadn't I gone straight to the police and told them the whole story? I groaned. How was I going to explain that I'd moved the gold? Maybe I should take it back to where I'd found it, then ring the police. But how? My muscles ached so much I didn't think I had the strength to shift all that heavy metal again. Well, not for a couple of days at least. I turned and squinted through my one good eye at the bedside clock. Twelve thirty. I'd better get up. Miriam was cooking her weekly lunch for her parents and I was duty bound to be in attendance. I groaned even louder at the prospect but got out of bed and hobbled into the bathroom. Half an hour later I had had a shower, swallowed two paracetamol tablets and felt decidedly better. I had placed a large sticking plaster over the gunshot wound on my side which hurt but luckily was only a graze and another smaller one over a cut on my head. I was climbing painfully into some fresh clothes when I heard Miriam shouting downstairs. Mildly curious, I combed my hair. Was she yelling at me to get up and help? It wouldn't be the first time she'd raged at me for sleeping on too late. Then I heard the front door slam loudly, followed by the tinkle of glass. This was unusual so I decided to investigate.

When I got downstairs, I found Miriam in the hallway staring angrily at some shards of glass that had fallen from the door and lay scattered at her feet.

I pointed at the door. "Who was that?" I said.

She jumped when she heard my voice, whirled around and tried to brush past me. I placed an arm across the gap between the staircase and the passage to the kitchen.

"I said, who was that?"

"Get out of my way!" she snapped.

I didn't move and she stared at me with an expression of contempt and disbelief.

"How dare you," she hissed. "Get out of my way!"

I stood my ground and there must have been something so unusually uncompromising in my attitude, such an unfamiliar resolute anger in my gaze that Miriam, for once in her life, was for a moment or two at a loss for words. We glared at each other for a long time then she pulled herself together and pushed roughly past me in to the kitchen shouting as she did so, "Your fancy man, that's who!"

I followed her to the sink. "Fancy man?"

Miriam had busied herself, throwing saucepans into the sink and scrubbing furiously at them with a Brillo pad. "Don't play innocent with me," she said. "You've been rumbled m'lad. Walking the dog indeed."

She turned so that her angry face was close to mine. "It was your boyfriend, pretty boy Paterson at the door, that's who!" she shouted.

I glared at her. "Mr Paterson?" I said. "What did he want?"

Miriam grasped my chin roughly in her hand and turned my head from side to side, peering with mock curiosity at my swollen face.

It hurt. My face had been through enough rough treatment.

"Had a little lover's tiff, have we?" she snarled. "Did he beat you up then? Well you'll be pleased to hear he's feeling remorseful and came round wanting to take you out for drinkies so that you can kiss and make up!

I backed away from her, my anger rising. "Are you telling me that Mr Paterson called to ask me out for a drink?"

"Mr Paterson? Is that what you call him?" She snorted turning back to the sink. "I thought it would be Patty or Pat."

"Hang on a minute," I said. "… and you took it upon yourself to say no on my behalf?"

"You're busy."

"You had no right to do that, Miriam."

She turned to face me again.

"Oh, really?" she said scornfully. "Well I really am most sorry to come between you both and perhaps you might have forgotten that we, that is you and your heterosexual wife have guests arriving at any moment now and your absence just might be noticed."

"Right!" I said and walked towards the door.

"Where are you going?" she said following me, an edge of panic in her voice.

"I'm going out for a lunchtime drink."

She came up beside me in the hallway and grabbed me with a soapy hand.

"Have you gone out of your mind? We've got guests coming." I pulled myself free and opened the front door.

"Guests?" I said. "What guests? You've got your mother and her pet warthog coming to gorge."

"Edward, come back," she ordered.

I walked out and stopped beside my new wall and smoothed down the topsoil between the bricks with my hand.

"I'll see you later dear," I smiled. "Please feel free to start without me."

Miriam's face was crimson with rage.

"You filthy little poof!" she roared. "You're a pervert!"

A couple of men from the building site next door stopped and were watching the scene with ill-concealed curiosity. Miriam's face flushed an even deeper shade of red. "You'll regret this," she hissed through gritted teach, and closed the door.

Feeling high with elation, I marched round into Paterson's garden and knocked on the front door. I felt that I had crossed a new frontier, fought a mighty battle, shed an old, shrivelled unwanted skin, revealing to the world and myself, the new, confident Eddie Wheatley. Apart from my walkout the previous evening, this was the first time that I had ever stood up to my wife—in fact, it was the first time that I could recall that I had stood up to anyone, and having done so, I liked the feeling. Consequently, when Paterson opened the door, it was to a beaming and smiling next-door neighbour, which was a new experience for Paterson too.

However, Paterson's normal good humour had been shattered by Miriam's earlier behaviour and he was no longer in the mood for neighbourly chit-chat.

"Eddie," he said. "What the bloody hell's going on?"

I dropped the smile.

"Going on," I said. "I thought you'd called at my place to take me out for a drink... Miriam said—"

"Do you know what your wife just insinuated?"

I suddenly felt my new confidence starting to slip away. "Oh dear," I said, feeling my swollen cheeks flush with embarrassment. What had Miriam done? I had only heard the door slamming and seen her annoyed face. I started to back away from Paterson's step. "I... I'll find out what's happened. I'm sorry... I..."

Paterson stepped out of the house and closed the door behind him. He caught up with me midway down the path retreating fast and grabbed me by the arm.

"Come on," he said. "We'll discuss this on the way to the pub."

He put his arm around my shoulder and marched me past my house. The curtains twitched and I could see Miriam's angry face peering through the glass. I gave her a cheery wave then when we were well past the house he released his grip and said, "Now, Eddie. What goes on between husband and wife is none of my business. I appreciate that but I think I'm owed an explanation."

I shrugged. "I can't explain until I know what's happened. What did Miriam say?"

Paterson recounted the scene with Miriam and I groaned loudly. We crossed the road and walking through the market square.

"I'm sorry you had to go through all that," I said. "It's me who should take the blame. It's not her fault. I can't be easy to live with." We were approaching the car park of the Rose and Crown. "In fact I'd hate to be married to me." Paterson pushed open the door of the saloon bar and we squeezed in to the packed interior. As before the familiar aroma of furniture polish hung in the air but mercifully the usual deafening thump, thump of music had been turned down to a tolerable level. The landlord faced with a full pub and a rapidly filling till was animated and smiling and managed a "Good morning, gentlemen," as he poured two pints of bitter which we carried through the jostling crowd to a table on the far side of the room which had only that second been vacated.

We sat down, pushed the previous occupants' empty glasses to one side and I took a first sip of my beer.

"I'm never very sure what to call you. Should it be Mike or do you prefer Paterson?" I asked.

"Och," he said. "It's ridiculous. We've been neighbours for ages now. You shouldn't have to ask. It's Mike."

"Okay, Mike. Cheers," I said and clinked his glass. The beer was deliciously cool and I enjoyed the taste. But most of all the new experience. It had been some years since I'd done something like this. I looked across at Paterson. The man was obviously waiting for an explanation.

"Prepare yourself for an unburdening," I said.

"No rush," he smiled. "Go ahead when you're ready."

I took a deep breath. This was difficult. I'd always been a very private person and not used to discussing intimate or personal details with others, but on this occasion it didn't seem that I had any choice.

"I think I've been a bit of a let-down to Miriam," I said. "Miriam should have married someone more assertive. Someone who could dominate her or perhaps be on an even par at least." I glanced up at him and smiled. "I suppose you'll think that this is that old 'my wife doesn't understand me' story getting trotted out again. Maybe it is. I don't know. I just know that her personality is… well, so all-embracing, so powerful, it seems to suffocate me at times and I've got to get out… to escape. I'm not much good at arguing with her anyway, like I said, it's not her fault. She needs someone stronger than me." I stopped for a moment, feeling slightly embarrassed. "Am I boring you to death?"

"Not in the least," Mike said. "It'll do you good to get it off your chest and I promised you that it'll go no further than me."

I sipped again at my beer. "Well, it'll probably sound daft to you but the only time I can be alone, truly alone, is at night. I've become a bit of an insomniac I suppose. I walk the dog at all hours of the night. I love it. I feel safe. That's my escape."

"But what about last night?" he said. "What on earth made you decide to work on your wall in the early hours of the morning?"

I felt the hairs on the back of my neck rise.

"How long were you watching me?" I asked.

"Only a wee while," Mike said. "But Ed, walking the dog is one thing but building walls and crashing around with shovels and trowels at five in the morning is another. You'll crack up man!"

I shook my head. "You're right. Not very neighbourly. I'm sorry. I'd been out for a walk and I just wasn't tired. I didn't want to disturb you."

"Not tired? Good God. Look at you. You look all in… and what happened to your face?"

I touched my face gingerly.

"Oh," I said, thinking desperately for a reasonable explanation. "I… I got mugged." The lie slipped off my tongue so effortlessly I almost believed it myself.

Paterson put his glass down with a thump.

"Och, you poor devil," he said. "Why on earth didn't ye say last night? What happened? Have you told the police?" He stood up. "Hang on, I'll get another drink in. I expect you could use one." He disappeared into the crowd and returned a minute later with brimming glasses. "Okay, Eddie. Let's hear it."

I was grateful for the interruption. It had given me time to concoct my story. "I think there were three of them," I said. "It was dark, I couldn't see. It was miles away from here… up near the old cinema just past Argyle Street. You know how dark it is up there… Well it was stupid of me, I suppose but I walked right into the darkness. The next thing I knew somebody was punching my face… somebody else grabbed me from behind and I was down in the gutter. I thought I heard three different voices but I'm not sure then I was out cold and lying in a puddle of water, my wallet had gone and my face felt sore as though they'd gone on hitting me after I was unconscious." I stole another glance at Mike's face and was relieved to see the concern there. He patted my shoulder.

"The bastards," he said. "Have you told the police?"

"Yes of course," I said hesitantly.

"The bastards!" he said again. "The thieving bastards!"

"Well I managed to get home," I said, warming to my story, "… and I knew I wouldn't be able to sleep so I thought I'd tire myself out completely by shifting all that topsoil into my wall. I'm sorry I woke you up. Stupid of me!"

Mike emptied his glass and wiped the froth from his moustache. "I still don't understand why your missus was so angry with me."

I looked at my glass, still half full. My neighbour could certainly put it away. I glugged it down, determined to keep up, then picked up the two empty glasses.

"My turn," I said, then "I'm sorry about Miriam. It's not really her fault. It's the way she was brought up by her moronic, charmless father. He's an old dyed-in-the-wool racist and puritanical homophobic. Sadly, the old git has passed on those views to his daughter who believes his every word and dotes on the silly old fool." I laughed. "She called me a few choice words when I left the house to call for you… I'm afraid she's put two and two together and made five." Mike looked puzzled. "So she's decided that the reason for my late-night walkabouts is because I'm having an affair." I hesitated, then added, "… and not with a woman." He still looked puzzled, so I left him to work it out and fought my way to the bar. When I returned a few minutes later he was sitting with a huge grin on his face.

"I've got bad news for you, Eddie," he said.

"What's that?"

"You're not my type matey. I secretly lust after Irish navvies with tattoos and bristly chins."

"Well you're in luck," I said. "There's quite a few of them working on the building site in our street."

He laughed, then leant back in his chair. "You're not what I was expecting, y'know, Eddie."

"Oh?"

"No, not at all. I thought you'd be so shy I'd not get a word out of you, but look at you… big smile, full of confidence."

"If you thought that, why invite me out for a drink?"

He shrugged. "Being neighbourly I suppose… and it was about time."

I looked at Paterson and saw a genuine, untroubled, happy expression on his face. All around me were groups of people who were enjoying and responding to each other's company. People who were not afraid to laugh out loud and could shout and sing without fear of reproof. It was as though a blindfold had been removed and I was seeing for the first time the way that life should be lived. Not necessarily in a pub, but certainly in communion with other human beings. I felt a glow of warmth and companionship and was basking in that euphoric mood when suddenly and without warning, the vision of conviviality was replaced in my mind's eye by a picture of a cold, bare room and the bodies of three men with bleached white skin and staring, dead eyes.

I shuddered violently and the glass fell from my hand and smashed on the floor sending a shower of beer across the legs of everyone nearby. There was a roar of approval from the crowd as though I'd done something clever and Paterson was leaning forward, touching my arm and looking concerned.

"Are you all right, boy?"

I smiled lamely at the people I'd doused.

"So sorry everybody," I mumbled. "It… it just slipped." I bent down and started picking up the slivers of glass.

The landlord bustled up with a dustpan and brush plus a frown. "You're supposed to drink it, not chuck it on the floor," he said, elbowing me out of the way and scooping glass and beer into the dustpan.

I apologised again.

"Just take care next time," he said and disappeared amongst the crowd.

Paterson, who was becoming more and more Scottish with every beer, patted my shoulder. "Don't worry laddie," he smiled. "Happens all the time in pubs. It's not the end of the world."

I forced a grin and got to my feet. "Yeah, you're right," I said, "… but I've got to have a pee. Won't be long." I pushed my way through the drinkers and headed for the gents. I did need that pee but even more urgently, I had to make a phone call which was difficult. I didn't want the call I was about to make to get traced, so I couldn't use my mobile. There was no public phone available in the bar so I turned and was about to make my way to the toilets when I spotted a group of youngsters yelling at each other over the banshee wailing of the pub's loudspeakers.

A lad wearing a vest and an armful of tattoos was leaning forward and pointing out something to his group on the TV. On the table beside him was his mobile phone. Everyone at the table was staring up at the TV. I picked up the phone and hurried into the gents. There was only one other occupant. I unzipped and emptied my bladder at the urinal then waited until the other man had washed his hands and left the room. I checked the phone and gave a sigh of relief to find it unlocked. Then I dialled emergency services.

The voice on the other end was polite and female.

"This call is about the Fletton Stewart bullion robbery," I said as quietly as I could. I lowered the pitch of my voice lest by chance in a million it might be recognised. The other voice asked for my name and address but I ignored her and hurried through with my message.

I described the location of the house where the bullion had been hidden, asked if she'd got the message and finished the call.

Nobody had come into the toilet whilst I was speaking but I found that my heart was beating fast and a cold sweat had broken out on my forehead.

I wiped the phone clean, walked back to the bar, put the phone, which hadn't been missed, back on to the table, ordered a large Scotch, drank it and carried two more over to where Mike Paterson was sitting.

"Good grief, Eddie. What are we celebrating?" Paterson laughed.

I raised my glass. "To good neighbours," I said.

"Yes, very good idea." We clinked glasses. "Especially to neighbours who let their neighbours sleep at night."

We emptied our glasses and within the hour, had emptied several more. During that same period, my marriage problems had been sorted out. Paterson's photographs of his late wife, Cathy, had been scrutinised and discussed, the intricacies of corner building in brickwork had been explained, the secrets of good begonia growing had been passed on and a complete cabinet reshuffle had been arranged.

Eventually we steered our way out of the comfortable gloom of the pub into the cruel, bright sunshine outside.

Almost immediately I made an amazing discovery. An astonishing revelation which became more and more apparent as I squinted around at my surroundings.

Intoxication was not caused, as I had always believed, by alcohol. It was caused by fresh air and sunlight. Inside the pub everything had stayed in its allotted place. Tables, chairs, horizontals and verticals all had behaved exactly as they were meant to. But only a few seconds' exposure to sunlight and two or three lungsfuls of fresh air were enough to tilt the car park to a crazy angle and make the wall of the pub move sideways and crash violently against my shoulder.

A retreat back to the safety of the pub was denied me because, for some reason, the door had disappeared. I leaned against the wall and giggled quietly to myself. Then put my hands on my knees and stared intently at the cracks and paving slabs at my feet, trying to bring them into focus.

I gave up and grinned sheepishly up at the two Mike Patersons standing before me.

"Well, here it is," I slurred. "This is what it's like to be drunk then."

Mike laughed. "I'm sorry. I had nae idea ye'd had too many." He grabbed my arm. "Come on, a'll help you."

I stood up. "How many of me can you see?"

"Just the one."

"Damn," I slurred. "I can see two of you." I lurched forward. "Maybe you should take an arm each."

He laughed again.

"Come on, Eddie. I think some strong coffee is called for at my house before ye face your missus."

We moved slowly down the street. Me lurching slightly and probably looking like the victim of a car crash being helped away from the scene of the accident.

But there was a smile on my bruised face and a massive, glorious exuberance welling up within my body that made me want to shout and sing and tell the world that a new Eddie Wheatley was born, that the old timid, dominated nonentity that used to be Eddie Wheatley was no more and had been shed like an unwanted skin.

But what had caused this transformation? Although my tongue and limbs were acting as though separated from my brain. My mind was functioning in overdrive. Could this new-found confidence and happiness be because I had suddenly become richer by thirty million pounds? I wondered, was that what it took to make happiness? Or was it because the gaining of it had allowed me to think of myself as a man. Accidentally or not, I had achieved something that I had never fully possessed before: my self-respect. The remorse and fear that I had experienced earlier that morning over the killing of three men I realised now was completely false, a delayed nervous reaction. I had killed three fellow human beings and now I didn't give a damn! The world was a better place without them. I knew with absolute certainty that by now I would be dead and forgotten about if those three thugs had had their way. But I had turned the tables on them, so thank you guys for giving me back self-respect and good riddance! I gave a great "Yahoo!" I felt great. What an incredible change to a person's life in such a short period of time. Here I was, gloriously drunk, happily wending my way home from the pub in the company of a friend. I glanced up at Mike. It was unheard-of. Impossible. Wheatley at the pub with a friend? Never! Eddie Wheatley stayed at home and went to work and did what he was told, not communicating with anyone apart from himself within the protective, invisible shell, in which he had chosen to live. Well, no more. The chicken had hatched and the shell was broken. From now on there would be lots of friends and good times. My door was open to all and sundry.

"You feeling okay, laddie? You've gone awfully quiet." Paterson was staring down at me anxiously.

I snapped out of my reverie, glanced around and realised we were only a few yards from my house.

"Sorry Mike," I said. "My mind was far away."

"You're not feeling ill?"

"No. I'm fine. I was just thinking how much I've enjoyed myself. How long have we been neighbours?"

"A year."

I stopped and turned to face my new-found friend.

"A year? Crazy isn't it. We've been living next door to each other all that time and not been out for a drink, or socialised, or, or... well hardly spoken more than a few words in passing." I frowned down at the pavement, trying to find the words. "It's terrible! What a waste of time!" I looked up at him. "You've never even been through my front door. What a rotten neighbour I've been." I weaved across the pavement towards my house. "Come on in an' have a drink."

Paterson followed and put his arm across my shoulder to restrain me, noticing as he did so another movement of the curtains in the house windows.

"Another time," he said. "Don't you think it would be a good idea to have a coffee at my place before you... er, see your wife?" He took his arm away, suddenly aware of the possible implications.

I peered down at my watch and a chill feeling of apprehension crept over me. It was extremely late and Miriam and her parents had to be faced. A little of my new-found confidence suddenly slipped away.

"No," I said. "Thanks all the same but I'd better get in." I hesitated then said almost pleadingly, "Can we do it again? I'm sorry I didn't mean to get squiffy. I hope it hasn't embarrassed you... I've really enjoyed it... really."

Mike smiled. "I have too," he said. "It's been good fun. You're a bit of a dark horse really, aren't you, Eddie?" He started walking way towards his own front gate. "Give me a call when you're free; we'll have a game of pool next time." He opened his front door and just before he disappeared inside said, "I hope you're not in too much trouble with the missus."

I waved at him and stood for a second or two staring down at my new wall, leaning forward and patting the earth between the bricks. Once again I smiled, took a deep breath and walked as steadily as I could up the path and round to the side entrance of the house.

They were all in the front room. Miriam, as usual, had turned the central heating up and the house was far too warm. Sinatra was crooning away quietly in the background accompanied by the demented barking of the dog. A deep sense of foreboding hung almost tangibly in the air.

I walked slowly up the hallway and paused for a second outside the sitting room door. Apart from the dog and Sinatra, there was complete silence within the room. I guessed they were just sitting there, waiting for me to make my entrance. I turned the handle and pushed open the door. I was right.

They were grouped around the fire. Three hostile faces were turned my way. The dog, realising that the house was not being invaded by Martians, yapped a few more times and then was silent. The three hostile faces continued to stare. Nobody spoke. The clock above the fireplace chimed three o'clock and Sinatra finished his song about the moon, then launched into one about facing the music and trouble lying ahead. I smiled sweetly at my relatives. They scowled at me. For a long time the silence continued. Then …

"Mafekin has been relieved!" I announced loudly. Five thousand dead, sixty-five injured and one with a badly bruised thumb." A brief flicker of amusement crossed my mother-in-law's face then was gone again. Miriam made to speak but her father held out his hand and stood up.

"Have you gone completely off your head, Wheatley?" he barked.

I entered the room and leant on the back of the settee.

"How nice of you to ask," I said. "I'm feeling very well, thank you. How are you keeping in the old brain box department?"

"Eddie!" Miriam squawked.

Hislop's eyes bulged and he stepped around his chair until he was standing face to face with his happily intoxicated son-in-law.

"How dare you! Don't be impertinent to me, young man. Where the hell have you been?"

"If it's any business of yours, I've been down to the pub and had a very pleasant lunchtime drink with a good friend. Having done so, I'm feeling rather peckish, so if you'll excuse me…" I turned to Miriam. "I assume lunch is in the oven? If your daddy has left me any, that is." I swayed slightly and turned towards the hallway again, but Hislop caught up with me and swung me around till we were face to face again.

"You're drunk, you disgusting sot. There'll be no food for you in this house, my lad. You've got a few questions to answer."

I felt the blood rush to my temples and a red wave of fury swept over me.

"No food? Questions to answer?" I shouted. "Do you realise where you are? This isn't the shop you know. This isn't your house." I grasped him by the tie and hollered, "This is *my house*. It was *my* food you stuffed into that hole you call a mouth. It's *my* furniture your bum has been sitting on. *My* heating. *My* lighting. *My* air you're breathing." I pushed him violently back against the settee. Mrs Hislop gave a frightened yelp and Miriam rushed forward like a referee to part the two of us.

"Eddie, what are you doing? Have you gone mad?" she screamed. I clung on to Hislop's tie and pulled him roughly towards me so that our noses were almost touching. The old man's eyes were almost popping from his head with a mixture of astonishment and fear.

"Well, this is the last time, d'you hear? This is the last time you'll be stuffing your face at my table!" I bellowed

Hislop managed to extricate himself and we stood facing each other, panting slightly. Miriam started pummelling my shoulder with her fists.

"This is my house too," she cried. "Daddy is welcome any time he likes."

I pushed her away angrily.

"Let me get one thing straight, Edward Wheatley," Hislop panted, trying desperately to regain his position of authority on all matters. "I have to know this for my daughter's sake... are you a... a practising homosexual?" He spat the words out in disgust as though they made a foul taste in his mouth.

"I don't need to practise," I roared. "I'm an expert at it!"
I wanted to laugh at my own joke and the effect it had on the
other three people. But the room seemed to have become
oppressively warm, my head was spinning and a wave of nausea
crawled upwards from the region of my solar plexus.

The faces of my three relatives swam back and forth
across my vision, white blobs, contorted into expressions of
disgust and loathing.

"My God!" I snarled. "You three make me sick."

And then, as though I was determined to prove the point,
I was. In glorious Technicolor with stereophonic sound. In the
midst of which, way off in the distance, a noise, like a howling
banshee, reached my ears followed by a crashing sound. It was
a noise that normally would have aroused my curiosity, but
somehow now it didn't seem to matter. It was time for a sleep
with my head comfortably tucked under the sideboard and my
legs spreadeagled across the remains of Miriam's best tea service.

CHAPTER 8

Smart Removals

Haslitt drank the last of his coffee and put the empty cup into the sink. He poured some water into the cup then switched the overhead light off. It was time to go. On the far side of the room, his private bar with its rows of bottles, each one with its own optic dispenser, beckoned enticingly. Too risky. There was still a bit of driving to do and it would be catastrophic to be picked up by the police at this stage. He wandered across to the big sliding window. Outside he could see the balconies and windows of the flats owned by the other occupants of the Barbican. People were settling down to their Sunday lunches; a smell of roast beef reached his nostrils and somewhere in one of the flats surrounding the square, someone was playing a recording of Beethoven's Pastoral Symphony. Down below he could see a group of young people setting out music stands and chairs outside the Guildhall School of Music in readiness for one of their lunchtime open-air concerts. Haslitt did not want to leave. The thought of vacating his comfortable bachelor flat and spending any more time cooped up in that dingy house with Smalley and company filled him with dismay. Breaking the news to them that they had to stay put for another week and not move the gold bullion was something he wasn't looking forward to either. He picked up his jacket from the settee and put it on, patting the pocket as he did so to check that the envelope of money Frank Thomson had given him was still there.

He had been unable to resist the temptation to call in at the flat after his meeting with Thomson even though it had only been for one brief hour. He loved this place. It was a haven from the normal frantic activity of his life and paid for legally too. His partnership in a small drinking club in Holborn had been more lucrative than he could ever have imagined. City workers flocked there at lunchtimes to drink, to eat and then stagger back to their offices, sometimes in the early evening. A few actors and actresses had discovered the place and the *London Evening Standard* had published a glowing report on the pleasing ambience and the delicious food available. They had named the club 'The Parrot's Perch' because the man from whom they bought the club had owned a scruffy cockatoo which could speak only three words. These it had picked up from the big-screen football matches shown in the bar. It used them when Haslitt and Sam Joplin, his partner, sat in the dingy back office deliberating over whether or not to take the plunge to join forces and buy the place.

"Go for it," the bird had squawked and that had been the clincher.

Sam Joplin had done some time too. The two men had shared a cell at Norwich Prison for six months. Joplin was serving six years for having printed and distributed the most exquisitely accurate forgeries of ten-pound notes that Scotland Yard had ever come across, whilst Haslitt was only doing six months for petty larceny. They had become good friends during their enforced stay together, but it was at least eight years after Joplin's release that the two had decided to pool their legitimate resources and buy The Parrot's Perch. Sam had not been invited in on the bullion raid and had been furious when Haslitt had accepted the offer to take part. His argument had been that the club was doing very nicely for them both legitimately. The money was rolling in. They both had healthy bank accounts. Life was good without having to look over their shoulders all the time. Why spoil it by taking chances and going back off the rails? Haslitt could see the sense in Sam's argument but the rewards offered if the raid was successful were so great that the temptation had been too much. The three million pounds which was his share was not something that could easily be turned down.

He grinned, closed the door and walked down the corridor to the lift. The raid had been successful. He was three million quid better off so why the hell was he getting upset about having to spend a few more days with dear little Smalley, Winston, and Munroe?

Lovely chaps, all three.

He changed his mind about driving and left the Jag in the basement car park of the Barbican, walking instead towards Liverpool Street Station where he managed to get a cab which dropped him off near the Elephant and Castle pub. Twenty minutes later he was walking fast towards the archway which led into the scruffy little lane, serving as garage and storage space for the shops on the street running parallel with it. He was almost into the lane before he saw the policeman, standing a couple of yards in from the pavement in the shadow of the wall. Haslitt felt a cold sweat instantly break out on his body and a clutch of fear grasp at his insides. To change direction would be certain to arouse the policeman's suspicions so he walked straight up to him as though delighted to see him and said,

"Thank heavens for a policeman. You've no idea how glad I am to see you. I've been wandering up and down for ages looking for Belton Road. Can you help me?"

The young policeman looked puzzled. "Belton Road? Are you sure you've got that right?"

Haslitt took Frank Thomson's envelope from his inside pocket and pretended to read the back of it.

"Yes," he said. "53 Belton Road. It's above a laundrette." He put the envelope back into his pocket and wiped his forehead with the back of his hand. "At least, that's the address she gave me. I'm beginning to feel I've been stood up and given a bum steer."

The policeman produced his phone from his back pocket.

"I think you have, chum," he said. "But let's just have a look see."

Haslitt glanced down the lane. Two police cars were parked outside the house and he could see what looked like an ambulance standing behind them. Two more policemen were standing by the back door. His heart sank.

"You're out of luck round here," the policeman said. "There's a Belton Road in NW3 and another up Romford way but nothing round these parts."

Haslitt looked up to heaven.

"Shit!" he said. "Bloody women!" He thought for a minute. "I suppose I'd better try NW3 then. Thanks a lot." He started walking away.

"Ask again when you get to Belsize Park Tube station," the policeman said, then merged back into the shadow. Haslitt's mind was in turmoil. He had to force himself not to run. What the hell had happened? The police were obviously onto them. But how? Shit! Nobody knew of the safe house apart from the team and Thomson. He turned the corner and started to run. 'Oh God, Oh God!' he muttered to himself. 'Three million quid. Three million fucking quid!'

A taxi came around the same corner and had to brake hard as he jumped out from the pavement with his arms outstretched to stop it.

"All right, all right mate, I saw you. I'm not bloody blind."

"Gilbert House, The Barbican," Haslitt shouted.

He slumped into the back seat and covered his face with his hands.

"Munroe," he moaned to himself. "I bet it was that drunken bastard Munroe, blabbing his mouth off!" He slammed his fist down on his knee. "I'll cripple the bastard. I'll kill him."

The taxi driver saw the angry, contorted face of his passenger in his rear-view mirror and was glad that this one was a short fare.

*****

Back in his flat, Haslitt, poured himself a generous measure of whisky with trembling hands. He gulped it down, refilled his glass then walked with it up and down the room, trying to untangle the confused whirlwind of thoughts that were racing around in his head. He glanced at his watch then switched on the television set. An old black-and-white film starring Spencer Tracey was just nearing its end. Haslitt continued to pace while the credits, which seemed to take forever, rolled down the screen. Then the announcer read out an interminable list of forthcoming attractions before, at last, the six o'clock news came on. There was no mention of the robbery. Haslitt switched off and resumed pacing. The trouble was that he didn't know what to do. If the three men back at the house had been arrested and one of them started squealing... on the other hand he had seen an ambulance outside in the lane. Perhaps the police had somehow found out about the safe house and there had been a shootout. Oh Christ! If one of those ignorant buggers has shot a policeman and then gets caught, we've had it. Twenty years apiece at least.

Haslitt refilled his glass. If only he could contact Frank Thomson, he'd know what to do but nobody knew Thomson's address or phone number. He was a cagey devil, that one. A mastermind at planning robberies but always from a distance. Never getting involved with the hard graft or the danger. It was probable that Frank Thomson wasn't even his real name. So if any job did get bungled there would be no trace back to him, no trail leading to his door.

The whole operation had been planned and co-ordinated by telephone calls to a place with the apt title of 'Smart Removals Co'. Haslitt didn't know if it had another name or even whether such a place existed at all, but any messages to or from Frank Thomson were always via the one telephone number that he had been given when first approached about the bullion snatch. The voice at the other end of the line was always cheerful, friendly and straight to the point. It had a slight Italian accent and Haslitt always pictured a dark-haired man of about thirty-five with a drooping moustache. There was never any background noise. No phones ringing or other voices that would be normal for a busy office. Just this young man who spoke to Haslitt as though they were old friends. He said his name was Julie.

Two meetings that Haslitt had had with Frank Thomson had been arranged via the Smart Removals Co. Both times had been at the same spot near the stile in a country lane close to Colchester. No mention was ever made of where Thomson lived and Haslitt suspected that after their brief meetings Thomson had a car waiting which drove him to his home in a completely different vicinity.

He picked up the telephone. It was as though Julie had been sitting right beside the telephone at his end.

"Smart Removals," said the familiar voice after the first ring.

"Julie?"

"Oh, hello Mr Haslitt. What can I do for you?"

Haslitt wondered how the man could recognise his voice so quickly.

"Has Frank Thomson been in touch?"

"Well, no, not since the last message."

"I need to talk to him urgently, Julie."

"Okay," Julie said brightly. "I'll pass the message on."

"I can't wait that long," Haslitt almost screamed into the phone. "You must have his number. Let me call him."

"Like I said, I'll pass on the message. Cheerio Mr Haslitt." The line went dead. Haslitt slammed down the telephone, paced a few more times, then rang his partner, Sam Joplin. Sam sounded agitated.

"Jesus! Where've you been? Why didn't you get in touch before?"

"You know why, Sam. Listen, have there been any messages for me?"

"No, but—"

Haslitt cut him off. "I'll be in touch," he said and put down the phone.

It was not until the 10 o'clock news that there was any mention of the item Haslitt so badly wanted to hear. Though brief, it was the lead story.

Three men had been found dead in a house in East London. Police suspected that there was a connection with the massive bullion robbery of a few days ago and that the murders were probably the result of a gangland feud. No gold had been found at the house.

There followed a short footage of film showing the outside of the house. A stretcher covered in a blanket was seen being carried to an ambulance and a Chief Superintendent mouthed a few words into the camera about gangland warfare and how the police were following certain leads in their search for the missing gold bullion. The picture cut back to the newsreader who started to talk about an atrocity in the Middle East. Haslitt switched off. He slumped back into the soft cushions of the settee still staring at the blank television screen, unable to believe what he had just seen and heard. For a full five minutes he sat unmoving, his mouth slightly open and a half glass of whisky dangling from his fingers, then slowly he stood up and walked over to the telephone. He dialled a number.

"Smart Removals."

"I want to talk to Frank Thomson."

"My, my, Mr Haslitt, haven't we had this conversation before?"

Haslitt threw his glass of whisky savagely against the wall and bellowed into the phone. "You heard me. Get me Frank fucking Thomson!"

"I am but a humble carrier of messages, Mr Haslitt."

"Don't give me that crap! You know where the bastard lives. Now give me the number." Haslitt was screaming with rage.

"I'll pass on the message, Mr Haslitt," Julie said and the line went dead.

"You greasy little wop. Answer me." Haslitt roared.

The big man threw down the handset with all his might onto the wooden table, then kicked the whole table and telephone savagely across the room. Small shards of grey plastic fell from the phone and a leg from the table shattered and rolled into one corner. He followed after the wreckage, roaring like a maddened bull. For a brief instant, the base section of the telephone became Julie's face and Haslitt stamped and crunched it under his foot until the instrument lay shattered at his feet.

He stood staring down at the mass of plastic and coloured wires for a second or two, breathing fast and filled with a pent-up fury that threatened to erupt into an orgy of destruction. Then he turned and gripped the back of the settee with his massive hands, fingers gouging into the soft material, his face contorted and red as though in pain.

"Thomson," he hissed. "Thomson you bastard! You thieving bastard! You've conned us."

After a while he managed to control his boiling rage and tried to assess the situation in as cool a manner as possible. Five minutes later he had decided on his course of action. He walked into the bedroom and opened the door leading into the airing cupboard. Leaning in, he removed a loose board which lay underneath the copper water tank, put his hand into the exposed hole and withdrew a Walther '38 pistol in a soft leather holster. He checked the clip, then slipped the gun back into the holster and buckled it firmly around his left shoulder. Then he put on his jacket and strode purposefully towards the front door. Two could play at Frank Thomson's game.

*****

Sir Arthur Freeman took a long pull on his cigar and stepped away from the table. He picked up a small square of blue chalk from the polished mahogany and stroked it thoughtfully across the end of his cue. The yellow ball was hidden in a cluster of the blue, green and black balls, with the white ball resting firmly against the side cushion. He glanced across at his companion.

"Y'know, it's just not done to come to another man's house, eat his food, drink his drink and then thrash him at snooker," he said with a mock frown. The other man sitting down on one of the sumptuous leather settees that lined the walls of the room smiled.

"Come now, Arthur. I'm sure you can get out of that one."

Freeman grunted and leaned his corpulent frame over the green baize. The white ball rolled slowly across the table, rebounded from two cushions and gently clipped the yellow ball before coming to a halt. Freeman's cheerful red face lit up into a delighted grin and he walked across to a small table that stood in the great empty fireplace at the end of the room.

"I think I'll celebrate that shot with another brandy," he said. "How about you Frank?" The other man stood and crossed to the table. He was of medium height but whose beautifully tailored clothes and thin, elegant frame, gave the impression that he was much taller. He had a thick mane of wavy, grey hair swept back and over his ears, and by contrast, very black eyebrows. Although approaching sixty he was still a very handsome man. Almost gypsyish, Freeman thought, with that thin, hooked nose and hard, full mouth. "I'll have the brandy when I've got something to celebrate too," he said. Then leaning forward he proceeded to clear the table. "Yellow, green, brown," he murmured confidently, as each ball dropped into a pocket "... blue, pink, black." He laid his cue on the bare green cloth, picked up his empty brandy glass and walked across to his host. "Celebration time," he said.

"You're an arrogant devil," said Freeman. "I've a good mind to set the dog on you and see you off the premises." He poured brandy into the empty glass. "Why on earth I ever bother to invite you and Janet to dinner, I'll never know. Next time, I'm only going to invite Janet. I might just beat her!"

"Don't be too sure," his companion said, laughing. "She's a bit of a hustler herself." He clinked Freeman's glass with his and the two men walked slowly around the snooker table to the doorway. When they got there the thin man turned and looked back at the room. "My, I do envy you this though," he said. It was a truly beautiful room. The walls were panelled in finely carved mature oak which in wintertime, when the huge inglenook fireplace was ablaze with logs, the glow of the flames reflected and transformed the colour of the dark wood nearest the fire to that of honey. The leather settees that encircled the room were of a rich, red hue and against one wall stood a massive glass-panelled and heavily carved bookcase, filled with leatherbound books. Above the fireplace was a large glass case surrounded in carved wood and containing a display of old clay pipes. There was an original Cezanne, a couple of Utrillos, and a small sculpture by Epstein decorating the far end of the room. And high in the ceiling, almost wasted because it was partly hidden by the snooker table lights, hung a magnificent and huge cut-glass chandelier. This was only one small facet in the beauty that was Raydon Manor, an elegant, small country seat set in the undulating green slopes of North East Suffolk. It had been built by Sir Hugh Passingham Freeman in 1825, and passed down through generations to the present incumbent, Sir Arthur Freeman. Friendly, popular, slightly eccentric Sir Arthur Freeman. Peer of the realm, director of the largest and most prosperous frozen food factory in East Anglia. The last of the line. Sixty-six and childless. He beamed at his friend, pleased with the admiration that showed on his face.

"Having been to your house, my friend, I know that there are a lot of people in this land that would envy your ownership of it." He put his hand on the other man's shoulder and guided him through the doorway into the hall. "And let me say that their envy is a greater tribute to you than yours is to me."

"I don't understand."

They walked across a large circular hallway with a stone fountain shaped like a shell, spouting cascades of silvery water high into the air. The older man paused with his hand on the handle of the door leading into the drawing room.

"Because what you own Frank, you have acquired by your wits. What I own I have to thank great-great-granddad for." He raised his glass and led the way into the room where their wives were sitting. "Janet," he said gruffly. "Would you kindly take this man home and not bring him back again!"

"I take it you lost," Janet said, turning in her chair and smiling up at Sir Arthur. She was a small, dark-haired woman in her late fifties, with an attractive smile and large brown eyes.

"I think he lets me win," said her husband.

"Oh go on," she scoffed. "You hate to lose at anything." Sir Arthur sat next to her and patted her hand.

"That's why he's such a successful businessman," he said. Lady Freeman spoke, "Drat it, Frank. I wish you'd let him win once in a while. He'll be inconsolable when you've gone." She was a tiny little bird of a woman with thick glasses and close-cropped mannish hair. She spoke in whispers as though she were frightened that someone she didn't want to would overhear.

"Sorry we left you so long on your own." Freeman lit up another cigar. "What have you two been up to?"

"Oh, just chit-chat, I suppose," his wife replied. "And I'm afraid I was rather bad-mannered and I switched on the television for the news." She looked apologetically at her husband. "I wanted to find out about the tennis."

"The British girls are all out again," Janet said. "Well, they're playing true to form."

"I expect the two remaining men will follow suit soon."

"Yes."

They all fell silent for a moment then Janet said, "It looks like they've caught the gang who robbed the Fletton Stewart security firm of all that gold."

"Have they, by heaven?" Freeman said.

"Well not exactly caught them," Lady Freeman butted in. "More like shot them."

"Oh, was it all of them?" asked Janet. "I only remember seeing one body on a stretcher."

"Have they recovered all the gold?" Freeman asked interestedly, leaning forward.

"Mmm, I don't know. I was only half listening."

"For Christ's sake, woman! Did they or didn't they?" Frank Thomson was on his feet staring down at her. His face had gone an ashen colour and his bottom lip was trembling.

"Frank! Whatever is the matter?"

"Have the police recovered the gold or not? Who was killed? How many?" Thomson was shouting.

Freeman crossed the room and put his arm around the other man's shoulder.

"Good gracious Frank. Whatever is the matter? Calm down!"

Thomson looked round at the staring faces; his hand were trembling and he realised with horror that he was making a spectacle of himself. He made a desperate effort to pull himself together.

"I'm sorry," he said. "Good heavens, unforgivable of me." He sat down. The others were still staring at him, waiting for an explanation.

He made an attempt at a laugh and said, "Why should I care after all? It's just that a colleague of mine has business interests in the Fletton Stewart Company and because of that connection I've been following the gold bullion story with quite a lot of interest. Good to hear the police are on the scent at last..." He faltered to a stop and said, "Sorry everybody."

There was a short pause then Sir Arthur coughed and said, "Well, my glass is getting low... anyone else need topping up?"

The evening progressed in a somewhat desultory fashion from then on. At eleven o'clock they said their goodbyes and the two guests were driven the six miles to their seaside home in Southwold by Sir Arthur's chauffeur. Once inside, Thomson went immediately to his study and switched on the television set. His wife followed him into the room with a puzzled look on her face. She came up to the back of the chair where he was sitting and placed her hands on his shoulders.

"Darling, what is it? What's the matter?"

He patted her hand.

"Matter?" he murmured. "Nothing's the matter dear, why?"

"Well, you've been so strange. You looked so angry with me at the Freeman's place."

He turned and looked up at her. "Janet, I have apologised about that. I told you. A very dear friend of mine has lost rather a lot of money over that raid at the security firm and I suppose I was upset on his behalf. Forgive me."

She could feel the tension in his body and there was a strange inflection in his voice that she had not heard before. It worried her but she put it out of her mind and bending forward, kissed his head.

"Of course I do," she said, then after a pause, "Are you coming to bed soon?"

"You go up. I'm just waiting for the late news. I want to see whether the goodies got the baddies who stole the gold bullion."

"Shall I keep you company?"

"No, no. Go on up. Get the bed warm for me. What do you think I keep you for?"

The comedy show that was being screened ended and it had been replaced by a commercial. She kissed him again and walked to the door. "Don't be too late, will you Frank," she said but there was no reply. Her husband's attention was glued to the TV screen and he had such a look of anxiety on his face that she climbed the stairs with her mind even more troubled than it had been before. Ten minutes later, Frank Thomson picked up the telephone. The look of anxiety had gone from his face and had been replaced by one of terrible anger.

Julie's voice came on the line. "Smart Removals. How can I help you?"

"Julie? It's me, Frank Thomson. I want you to do a small job for me."

"Sure thing, Mr Thomson."

Thomson gave him his instructions and after he had finished Julie said, "Talking about Mr Haslitt, he was trying to reach you earlier on, Mr Thomson."

CHAPTER 9

Sally Russell

It had been the first time in my whole life that I'd been drunk. I mean really drunk; incoherent, dribbling, rat-arsed, mindlessly drunk. Yesterday it had seemed impossible that my body could absorb any more pain. Every muscle, nerve and bone had been full up, complete, unable to take any more agony. Now, however, just 24 hours later, crashing and banging and elbowing its way to join all the other bruised and tender parts of me a new pain had arrived. A deep, dull, resonant variety that rumbled down in my gut and thundered around inside my head producing a noise between my ears similar to that of a saw being dragged slowly across the bass string of a cello. This was no ordinary hangover, this was the bee's knees, this was the crown prince of hangovers on speed.

I sat staring miserably down at an empty coffee cup on the table; my only consolation was that my eyes could focus again at last and only one cup and one table registered in my befuddled brain. I was still thirsty. Three cups of coffee hadn't helped at all. The kitchen sink seemed a painstaking trek away but I pushed myself to my feet and stumbled the three yards to the tap, not bothering with a glass, holding my open mouth against the cool, liquid pillar then stooping forward and allowing the water to run for a full three minutes against the back of my neck.

It seemed to help a little. I turned and walked very slowly into the hall, leaving a train of water in my wake, then, leaning heavily against the telephone table, I stared at my reflection in the mirror above.

I groaned: the apparition facing me was not a pretty sight. The bruises on my face had blossomed into an astonishing variety of colours, ranging from black, through dark blue, purple and blood-red to a subtle canary yellow. A new cut had appeared on my forehead and a rivulet of dried blood traced an erratic course past my eye and down my cheek. I guessed that this had been caused by Miriam's tea set on which I had spent the night. My hair was blackened with dried blood and was plastered down in wet streaks across my swollen face and on opening my mouth I discovered that a fairly large piece of a front tooth had disappeared. To top it all my jacket and shirt were badly stained and I stank of my own vomit. I closed my eyes and turned away from the mirror.

In the kitchen I collected together a bucket of hot water, some disinfectant, a dustpan and brush and a can of air freshener, then carried them into the scene of devastation which was the sitting room.

One hour and two more cups of coffee later, I pushed open the windows of the room to let in some fresh air and tottered back to the kitchen feeling marginally better. For the first time I noticed a white envelope on the tiled worktop, propped up against the tea caddy. On it was my name written in Miriam's unmistakably large, bold handwriting. It was hardly necessary for me to open it. I knew what it would say:

Eddie

At last you have shown yourself in your true colours. I am shocked and disgusted by your behaviour. Never have I felt such shame and humiliation. How could you? I shall be staying at a friend's place until I have decided what is best for my future. Please do not try to get in touch.

Miriam

P.S.   I have taken Rufus.

I felt decidedly better. I tossed the letter on to the kitchen table and started back up the hallway. 'Don't worry about that, Miriam, my angel,' I murmured to myself. 'I won't try to get in touch. I've only just escaped from jail.'

The telephone rang and the headache bounded back into full vigour as the jarring sound scraped across the tender nerve ends in my brain. I picked up the receiver and held it tenderly to my ear.

"Hello."

"Wheatley." Hislop's voice bellowed down the line.

"Yes," I said.

"You disgust me."

I thought what a good day it was turning out to be for disgusting people.

"My daughter's life has been nothing but misery since she married you. I wasn't happy about it from the beginning and you've proved me right." Hislop's voice was rising in pitch as he warmed to his theme. "Miriam is staying at a friend's house and I'll do my damndest to see that she continues to do so. I don't want her living with a pervert. Do you hear me, Wheatley?" He didn't wait for an answer but ranted on. "And I don't want perverts or drunks working for me either. You're finished. Finished! I've done my utmost for you and look how you've repaid my kindness! Well, no more. You're out, do you hear? Out!" There was a pause. Hislop was out of breath, panting. "Well! What have you got to say for yourself?"

"You can come round and kiss my arse," I said. There was a sharp intake of breath followed by a rattling sound as though the phone at the other end of the line had been dropped, then a second later it was slammed down and the line went dead.

I climbed the stairs, a happy smile on my face. The day was getting better and better. I started peeling off my dirty clothes, dropping them on the floor as I went, then as I waited for the bath to fill with water, I sat naked on the edge chuckling to myself and rocking slowly backwards and forwards.

*****

Afterwards I walked to the newsagents and bought a copy of *The Daily Mail*. Resisting the temptation to read it there and then on the street I carried it home, spreading the paper out on the kitchen table, then making myself a cup of tea before settling down as calmly as possible to soak up the news. The item was the lead story on the front page. **GANG WARFARE!** the headline screamed. It then described how the three bodies had been found in a dilapidated house after an anonymous tip-off, that forensic scientists had established the house had been used to store a quantity of gold, and that the police were ninety-nine percent certain the gold was that stolen from the Fletton Stewart security company last week. They also had a theory that a rival gang had found out about the gold and had stolen it after murdering the three men. There were photographs of Smalley, Winston and Munroe, which looked like prison mugshots, and a large one of the house. An artist had drawn a plan of the house with little silhouetted figures of the dead men lying together in one room while a different set of figures were unloading the gold through the front room window into a waiting truck. So far the police did not know where the gold was but they were continuing their enquiries and hoped to make an arrest soon.

I looked again at the artist's silhouetted drawings. Once again the real images surfaced in my mind and I saw the three grotesque, dead faces staring back at me. I threw the newspaper down on the table and covered my eyes with my hands, stomach knotting and the recently swallowed warm tea rising and filling my mouth with the taste of bile.

"Damnit." Why did they have to print those photographs? Ugly, sullen faces staring out from the newspaper, tormenting and reminding me. Hard, uncaring faces but living and breathing, hair and bone, all lying in a mortuary thanks to me.

I stood up and started to pace the room. Visions of grieving families flitted across my mind. Somebody must have been close to Smalley and Winston and maybe even the repulsive Baseball Cap. The image of the man's distorted face, eyes popping, head twisted round at an impossible angle against the door frame in that damp little room was one that would stay with me for the rest of my life. That and the knowledge that I had killed three fellow human beings.

I stopped pacing and leaned my head against the wall. I prayed for the first time in years.

"Oh God," I said through clenched teeth. "Forgive me Lord, I didn't want to kill anyone."

The whole episode replayed itself in my mind. The killing of Baseball Cap. Winston lunging at me, face contorted in a snarl; the kick of the gun in my hand; the feeling of terror as the big man fell on me, knocking the wind from my body. Smalley punching at my head, the gun kicking again in my hand.

I pushed myself away from the wall and started to circle the kitchen table again. It was self-defence, no doubt about it. I'd had no choice. It had been my life of theirs. There had been no intention on my part to kill.

Had things gone as planned, had Baseball cap killed me, would he and the rest of the gang be feeling remorse? Would they be worrying about my grieving family? I picked up the newspaper and walked out of the kitchen, up the hallway and into the front room.

"No way!" I muttered to myself.

I looked out of the window at my new brick wall. Slowly, the nausea was replaced by a flutter of excitement welling up inside my stomach and I felt my heart beat faster. In truth, there had been a strange sense of loss after reading the article in the paper. The reporter had written about the dead men, the gold, the original robbery, but there had been no mention of the person most deeply involved now with the whole affair: *me!* I felt an impulse to cry out, 'No, No! You've got it wrong. There was no rival gang. It was me, Eddie Wheatley. I fought with those murderers, and I killed them and I took their gold. I beat them all!'

An elderly couple walked by. I found myself grinning and wondering what they would think if they knew that only inches away and buried under less than a foot of soil, was a fortune in gold and jewellery.

I badly wanted to rush out and scrape the soil back and feast my eyes on those wonderful yellow ingots. To yell out to the world, 'Look what I've got!' It was such a pity that my monstrous slice of good fortune had to be kept a secret. A secret to be shared with no one. I felt I deserved a few plaudits, would have liked a pat on the back and a few words of praise.

I shrugged and sat down on the window seat. I was being stupid. It was not praise that I needed, it was advice. After all, what did one do with thirty million pounds' worth of stolen gold? How could I set about changing it into real, usable money? And who could I ask? Who would give me the advice? I could hardly walk into a bank with an ingot or two and say, "Please change this into cash."

What a pity Smalley and Co hadn't robbed the security firm of thirty million in used fivers. That would've solved a few problems.

Again that painful pang jolted at my innards. Mustn't think about Smalley and Co, get them out of my mind. It was self-defence. Not my fault.

I wandered back into the kitchen, deep in thought. In films or in books about robberies there was always somebody called a fence. He'd charge an extortionate amount of money for his services but he'd be there to hand out money for stolen goods. No questions asked but again a huge profit to himself. He is happy, the thief is happy (until he gets caught at the end of the story). Everybody is happy. That's business, an everyday transaction in the underworld. But how does one go about finding a fence? You can't just put a card in a newsagent's window. You can't google 'fences'. I sighed. Finding a buyer was going to be a problem.

I unlocked the back door and walked out into my garden. It was a long narrow strip of land with high, interwoven fencing panels all around. The ground had been arranged into three levels, each one about eighteen inches higher than the other, divided by one of my meticulously built low walls. The bottom two sections were mainly laid out as lawns and flower beds but the top level was a patch of rough grass in the middle of which was a metal incinerator. This part of the garden I had discreetly screened off with a high trellis and climbing rose tree. To one side was a brick outhouse—designed as a washhouse probably seventy years ago, but now just used as a shed. It also incorporated an outside toilet. The clothes were still where I had hidden them behind the lawnmower. I took them over to the window and inspected each article carefully. The trousers, jacket and shirt were only dirty and wet but the coat was covered in blood—Winston's blood.

Oh God. The rank smell of the man came back to me immediately: the huge black face pressed close to mine, the eyeballs rolling upwards into the skull till only their whites were showing and the crushing weight of the man's body as his life oozed out through the hole which I had just made under his ribs. It all seemed like a dream now, as though it had happened to someone else in a TV play and somehow I had stumbled on the props. It still didn't seem possible that I was responsible for snuffing out the lives of three other human beings. I was surprised at my own calmness. I ought to be terrified. That's what the old Eddie would be. Trembling like a jelly, waiting for the heavy hand of the law to knock on the door. Perhaps even saving them the trouble by rushing round to the station myself and tearfully confessing all. Perhaps I was suffering from shock and would soon revert to my old self? But even as the thought occurred, I rejected it. I knew the old Wheatley was dead. As dead as Winston, Smalley and Baseball Cap. The new Wheatley was here to stay. I thought about this for a while, bewildered by the change that had taken place within myself, then gave up the struggle of trying to find a solution to it all. Smiling, I shook my head and then immediately wished I hadn't as my headache roared into life again.

The coat didn't burn well in the incinerator. It was too thick and heavy with water. I prodded it with a stick, lifting the wet folds to allow a draught of air to pass between it and the pile of newspapers and sticks I had laid as a base to the fire. I tipped a cupful of paraffin on to the smouldering mound and it flared briefly into life but quickly lapsed once more into a grey mass, spouting forth a great column of dirty black smoke, but with little or no evidence of any flames. There was a discreet cough from the next-door garden. I whirled round. Mike Paterson's grinning face was peering over the fence at me.

"What are ye trying to do, Ed? Smoke the whole neighbourhood out?"

I looked up. The wind had pushed down the column of smoke and it had formed itself into a dark cloud that drifted low across the adjoining garden.

I closed my eyes and said through clenched teeth, "I'm sorry, I didn't think."

Mike squinted down at the incinerator.

"What are ye burning, for heavens' sake? Smells like a camel's Y-fronts."

I looked down anxiously at the smouldering clothing and was relieved to see that there was no sign of the telltale bloodstains.

"Just a few old gardening clothes," I lied. "I found them in the wash-house. They'd gone mouldy and the mice had been using them as a home."

"No matter." Mike smiled. "I want you to meet a friend of mine."

"Friend?"

"Don't sound so surprised. I do have a few friends." He looked down at someone on his side of the fence and then back again at me.

"It's a wee bit difficult," he chortled. "She's not as tall as me..." He looked down again and said, "Stand up on that box. Can you manage... careful."

A second later the face of a woman appeared on Paterson's left. She was grinning broadly and clinging tightly to the top of the fence as though whatever it was she was standing on was not very steady and at any moment she might fall off.

Mike put his hand on her shoulder and said, "Eddie, I'd like you meet a very dear friend of mine—Sally Russell. Sally, this battered and bloodied wreck is not a professional boxer, he's my next-door neighbour, Eddie Wheatley."

I stepped closer, wishing he hadn't drawn attention to my swollen features.

"Hi, Eddie," Sally said. "Nice to meet you."

"For God's sake, don't try to shake hands!" Mike said, "Or you'll be flat on your back in my courgette plants."

She had spiky black hair and a pert, almost impish face. She wore tortoiseshell-rimmed glasses and I noticed that each of her fingernails was varnished in different colours. I thought she had a nice smile.

"Hello," I said lamely, then, "I'm sorry about the smoke."

"We had a horrible feeling it might be a barbecue," she chuckled, "and that we'd get invited around to eat charcoal sausages and drink homemade nettle wine."

Her voice was quiet, with the faintest trace of an Irish accent. I thought desperately for something to say but nothing would come, then Sally said, "I was sorry to hear about the mugging. It must have been terrible for you."

"Mugging?" I stammered. "Oh, yes. Well it's over now. Only a few bruises left."

Mike laughed. "Underneath all those bruises, Sally, he looks just like Robert Redford."

"Have you seen a doctor about your face?"

I shrugged. "No, I didn't think it was worth the bother." She stared at me. I felt a bit like an insect under a microscope. Paterson said, "Didn't the police insist on a doctor's examination?"

"No!"

He looked thoughtful. "How odd," he said.

Sally snapped her fingers. "I've got just the thing for you," she said. She climbed down from her perch and disappeared from view.

Mike watched her go then said in a conspiratorial whisper, "Everything all right, Ed?"

"How do you mean?"

"Well… about yesterday. No trouble I hope when you got home from the pub?"

I smiled and poked my stick into the incinerator, which thankfully had gone out. "Oh that. Gosh no, no trouble, just a perfectly normal day. I had a fight with my boss, my wife left me and I got the sack from my job." I glanced up at the face peering at me over the fence.

"Are ye serious?" Mike asked in a hoarse voice.

"'Fraid so."

He clapped a hand to his forehead. "Oh jings, I'm sorry. This is all my fault."

"Your fault!"

The older man nodded. "Yes, if only I hadn't asked you out for a drink… or if I'd stopped you from having so many …"

I walked up to the fence and put my hand on his arm. "Listen," I said. "I wanted to go out for a drink with you and how many drinks I have while I'm out is totally up to me, not you. I'm a big boy now." He started to say something but I carried on. "Besides, before you start getting emotional about my predicament, I want you to answer me a question."

He looked puzzled. "Question? What question?"

"Look at me. Apart from my beaten-up face, what do you see?" I was smiling.

Mike continued to look bewildered and didn't say anything.

"Do I look happy?" I asked.

"Well, yes… fairly."

"Do I look sad and miserable?"

He stared at me for a while, then a slow grin spread across his face.

"Good Lord. No, you don't."

"Well then, enough said."

The old man continued to grin down at me, then his shoulders began to shake and suddenly a great bellow of laughter burst forth and he had to cling hard to the top of the fence. It was infectious; I started to chuckle.

"Well, it's nice to have your condolences," I said.

"Forgive me. It's so sad," Mike roared, then sank his head into his arms, making little choking sounds. Sally came back up the garden and looked in amazement at us two men who were by now giggling like children up to no good.

"What on earth's got into you two?"

He looked up, his eyes streaming with tears. "Eddie's wife left him," he spluttered.

"What?"

"And I've been given the sack," I said, collapsing and leaning on his side of the fence.

She didn't say anything but the perplexed look on her face was enough to send us into further paroxysms of mirth. Eventually, Mike pulled himself together and said haltingly, "Oh God, I'm sorry. I don't know what got into me."

Sally said, "Men! The more I see of them the less I understand them."

She pointed with her thumb at the house behind. "Come on over," she said. "Nurse Russell is going to have a look at that face of yours."

Two minutes later, I found myself sitting in Mike Paterson's kitchen.

Sally had been out to her car, which was parked outside, and had reappeared with a small blue medical box, complete with a red cross painted on the lid. She produced a bottle of white pills and made me swallow two, then gently started to work on my face with a soft gauze and wonderfully cool cream which stifled the fire on my swollen flesh and immediately evoked within my battered body a feeling of joyous well-being. Neither of us spoke. Paterson had stopped in the kitchen only long enough to put the kettle on and then had wandered back into his garden leaving nurse and patient to get on with it.

I let out a happy sigh and found myself wondering what the amazing ointment was that she was applying to my face. It certainly had remarkable healing powers. I was positively glowing. Sally was leaning over me, dabbing gently at my forehead. She had a slight frown of concentration on her face and was biting her bottom lip. A delicate perfume wafted like a cloud around my head and I was blissfully aware that the ingredients of the healing miracle that was happening to my face was 10% ointment and 90% Sally Russell.

Occasionally she would look down at me and smile and I found myself entranced. There seemed to be a buzzing sensation at the back of my neck and my eyelids felt heavy. The silence between us somehow enhanced the pleasure of the moment and I hoped she wouldn't break the spell by speaking… although had it been possible, just then, I would have purred.

At last she was finished and stood back to scrutinise her handiwork.

"I hope that didn't hurt too much," she said.

"Not a bit," I said truthfully. She started to pack all the bits and pieces back into the medicine box.

"You travel well equipped."

"Oh, I've always carried a medical box around with me. You have to when you run a driving school. I never know when one of my pupils will flatten a pedestrian or put his own head through the windscreen."

I laughed and she continued. "You look a bit shiny at the moment; I didn't want to rub the ointment in too hard because I was scared of hurting you." She turned towards the kettle, which was boiling away on the kitchen worktop. "Shall we have a cuppa?"

"Please."

She switched the kettle on and went to the back door. "Hey," she shouted, "we're brewing up in here. D'you want a cup?"

I heard Mike shout something from the far end of the garden and when she started pouring the boiling water into the cups, I said, "Thanks Sally. Thanks for all you've done."

She turned to face me. "Has your wife really left you?"

I nodded.

"And you've lost your job?"

Another nod.

"You don't seem very upset."

"I'm not really as callous as you might think." I smiled. "Speak to Mike, he'll put you in the picture."

As if on cue, Mike Paterson walked into the kitchen and slammed the door behind him.

"Your tea's on the side," Sally said.

Mike was staring down at me with an incredulous look on his face. She handed the cup to him.

"Well, what do you think of the patient now?"

He didn't answer but continued to stare open-mouthed at me as if I'd suddenly sprouted another head. He was breathing hard and making little gulping noises.

He turned to face her. "What? I'm sorry, what did you say?"

"I said what do you think of my patient?" Paterson stared down at my shiny face again. He seemed suddenly to look pale and old. "Incredible," he breathed. "Just incredible."

All at once I felt uncomfortable. I was irritated that Mike had blundered in and shattered what was for me special moment and I hated being the object of attention, like a dissected frog pinned out for inspection. I stood up and gulped my tea.

"Well, I must go," I said. "Got so much to do."

"You've hardly finished your tea," Sally protested.

I drained the cup, scalding my tongue. "Thank you, that was lovely. Well... er..." I said again, "must go... three's a crowd and all that."

She was staring at me with a puzzled expression and I knew I was being rude after all she had done, but I somehow felt in the way. She was Mike's girlfriend, not mine. Three was an uncomfortable number, somebody had to go. I wished it didn't have to be me.

"Thanks," I said, shaking Sally's hand. "For being Florence Nightingale."

Mike still had that strange look on his face.

"Thanks Mike," I said and walked out through the kitchen door.

Paterson didn't answer back but I didn't notice. I was hurrying to my own front door, a walking bundle of mixed emotions: embarrassment and anger at my own inadequacy but predominantly confusion concerning the turbulent emotions I had experienced in the very short time that I'd known Sally Russell.

*****

Little Peeley heard the car come to a halt way down below in the street and prayed silently that it wasn't another customer. She turned and squinted up at the alarm clock on the bedside table. The luminous hands pointed to twenty past three. It was always awkward getting rid of a new customer if you already had a client staying the night, especially if the new man had had a few drinks. She lay back on the pillow and waited, straining to hear footsteps coming up the stairs. It was impossible. Curly had started snoring again and Hannibal could have brought his elephants up the stairs and she wouldn't have heard. Hell, he'd had a few that night. Hardly able to stand when he found her, searched her out especially like he always did when he came into the club. But it had seemed different tonight. He wasn't the happy, joke-

115

cracking Curly she'd known for the past three years. Tonight he had been tense and irritable, impatient to leave the club and get back to her bedsit. Swallowed half of a new bottle of vodka from her precious store of drinks in the cupboard, then sat staring morosely at the wall, ignoring her when she had enquired as to what was the matter. She wondered why he'd bothered to find her. There had been no interest in sex and little or no conversation. She closed her eyes again and decided not to worry about it. After all, it was a night off for her. Curly never forgot to pay and was always generous. So as he was incapable of anything but snoring for the night, it was money in the bank and a good night's rest for a change. She turned over and laid her head into the crook of the big man's arm.

There was a soft tap on the door. She cursed under her breath and got out of bed slowly so as not to wake him. God, what a business to be in! Three thirty in the morning and she had to be answering the door to some fat slob who'd been on the booze all night and suddenly discovered he's feeling horny. Bad pay or not, she should have stuck to being a stripper.

Putting her mouth to the crack in the door, she whispered, "Who is it?" She didn't recognise the voice that replied from the landing outside. It had a north country accent, it sounded sober and whoever it was either had bad asthma or was out of breath from the climb up the stairs.

"Can I come in Peeley?"

"Sorry, I'm busy for the night. Try tomorrow."

The voice persisted. "I've got to see you, Peeley."

"Yeah, why?"

There was a pause, then, "I owe you money."

The words had the same effect as 'Open Sesame'. Little Peeley fumbled the door chain into its socket and opened the door a few inches. There was a sharp crack as the chain was torn from the woodwork and the door was violently banged open, smashing into her face and flinging her across the room like a rag doll. She flew, screaming and crashing into the dirty dishes on the wooden draining board.

Curly started to move from the bed but stopped when a knee drove hard into his solar plexus and a gun was jammed roughly against his upper lip, almost entering one of his nostrils.

There were two of them, big men, fairly young, wearing suits and bow ties like bouncers from a nightclub.

"I'm sorry about this," said one of the men kneeling on Haslitt's chest in a parody of politeness. "I do hope you'll understand. I'm only obeying orders."

He lifted Curly's coat and removed the gun from its shoulder holster.

"After all, you and me are mates, aren't we, Curly?"

He tossed the gun to his colleague who caught it and slipped it into his pocket.

"What do you want, Arkwright?" Haslitt squeezed the words out through compressed lips.

The man jerked his head towards Little Peeley who was still wailing as she lay sprawled amongst the broken dishes on the floor.

"Do something about her. Me and Curly's trying to have a conversation."

The other man walked over and knelt beside the hysterical girl. He bunched his hand into a fist and pointed at it with his other hand. She stared up at him with big, frightened eyes and the wailing petered out until she was silent. The man smiled and stood up.

Arkwright said, "You've taken a lot of finding old friend. My, my, you do move about a bit." He could see the question in the other man's eyes. "I reckon every pub and club in town has you as a customer. You're a big man, Curly. Everybody knows you. We kept getting sent on—he's not here they'd say. Try the Eight Bells pub or try the Blue Moon Club. It's been a bit like Monopoly. We've really seen London tonight." He waggled the end of the gun in Haslitt's nostril. "That mucky little cellar where your little scrubber works was the last place we looked." He settled down and sat his whole weight on Haslitt's chest.

"It's a relief to be sitting down at last, me feet are killing me."

Haslitt could scarcely breathe but he managed to ask again, "What d'you want Arkwright?"

Arkwright ignored the question. "Now then, Curly," he said. "Cos you and me are friends, are you goin' to be a gent and come with us all peaceful and quiet or are you going to make a fuss and get a bullet up your hooter?"

Haslitt's eyes squinted down the barrel of the gun, still pressed painfully against his top lip. It moved back a couple of inches so that he could speak.

"Where are we going?" Haslitt asked.

"Aha, now then, don't let us rush things. Let me just say there is a gentleman who wants to see if you can help with his enquiries."

"Frank Thomson!"

"No guessing games."

"I want the bastard too."

Arkwright climbed off Haslitt's chest and stood up, still keeping the gun trained on his face.

"Well, isn't that a fortunate coincidence." He gestured with his gun and Haslitt hauled himself unsteadily to his feet. He had sobered up rapidly but the room seemed to be tilted at an angle and it was hard to stand without tottering.

Arkwright said, "Come on Donald. Where's your manners? Help the gentleman."

The other man who had not uttered a word since entering the room moved forward obediently and took Haslitt's arm. The three of them walked slowly towards the door. Little Peeley, who had been holding her breath with fear, suddenly let out a choking sob. Arkwright turned and looked down at her.

Good 'eavens, Curly. Whatever next? Trying to leave without paying? Dearie me." He searched round Haslitt's body, extracted a thick bulging wallet and tossed it to the girl.

"Thank you darling," he said. "You were wonderful." He pushed Haslitt forward with the gun and they walked out of the room.

Little Peeley waited, not daring to move. Her face hurt badly from the impact of the door and she had cut her arm when falling into the crockery by the sink. She wanted to cry with fear and pain, but instead she sat motionless, holding her breath and staring at the shattered door. Only when she heard the car start and move away down the street did she allow herself to start sobbing and wailing, letting the tears and mascara trickle down her cheeks. She knelt amongst the broken dishes until the cold drove her to climb back into bed. Under the covers she found that she was cuddling Curly's wallet. Somehow, it seemed to comfort her.

CHAPTER 10

A Partnership

I walked out of the bank and joined the tide of pedestrians flowing down the Mile End Road. It seemed unusually busy for ten in the morning but then I remembered it was market day. The barrow boys would be out in force and the pubs would be full. They'd picked a nice day for it. The sun blazed from a cloudless blue sky and a light breeze ruffled the canvas awnings of the carts lined along the pavement's edge.

I glanced down at the slip of paper which the cashier had given me when I'd asked to see the state of my account. It was not good news. Sixty-three pounds and forty-nine pence was all that I owned. Somehow I was going to have to get some money. I smiled ruefully. Thirty million unspendable pounds were salted away in my front garden and only sixty-three pounds in the bank. There were a few hundred pounds in a savings account at the building society but it was in joint names and there was no use hoping that Miriam would help me to get at it.

I turned away from the crowded market street and walked slowly along the pavement fronting a parade of shops which, unable to compete with the street traders' prices, were almost deserted.

Hislop owes me money, I thought. *You can't give anybody the sack without a month's notice or at least the money in lieu.* I cursed softly. There was no way that I would go cap in hand to Hislop and ask for the wages due to me. I knew it and Hislop knew it too. Oh yes. He'd would just love that. Being able to demand a grovelling apology before he would condescend to hand over what was legally mine.

I stopped outside a jeweller's shop and stared down at the assorted trinkets laid out on velvet pads behind the crisscross mesh of a security screen. Maybe I could sell a few pieces of the jewellery that I'd taken along with the gold. Surely, necklaces, bracelets and rings would be fairly easy to sell? Some of the shops even had notices in their windows to that effect. My eyes wandered along the display of rings on the top shelf and sure enough there was a card propped up against one of the velvet pads:

D. HARRINGTON & CO
JEWELLERS
Gold bought and sold
Also high quality second-hand jewellery
Good prices given

I smiled and wondered what the man would do if I dumped thirty million pounds' worth of bullion on his counter. But the jewellery was worth thinking about. Just one or two pieces maybe and then another item at another shop on the far side of town. I gave this a moment or two's thought then turned briskly and walked away from the shop. Jesus! What was I thinking about? The jewellery that I had was the tops. It had been described in minute detail by the press after the robbery and would be recognised immediately by any specialist in gems who would have the police grabbing my collar before I could say "My auntie has left me these in her will; how much are they worth?"

I jumped on a bus and remained deep in thought all the way home. The phone was ringing as I unlocked the door. It was Miriam. She had her 'You've hurt me deeply and I'm willing to forgive' voice on.

"Hello Edward," she said. "Are you feeling all right now?"

"I'm fine thank you Miriam, just fine."

There was a pause, then "You don't deserve it, Eddie, but we're both willing to forgive and forget."

"Both?" I said. "Are you talking for both of us?"

"No," she said. "Daddy and me. He's taken quite a bit of persuading but I think I've won him round. You were influenced by others and not acting your usual self. Of course, an apology will be in order but you'll be able to have your job back and we'll say no more about it." I tried to interrupt her but she carried on. "Things will have to change though, Eddie. There must be no more of your midnight gallivanting and I think the less you see of your friend Mr Paterson the better for all concerned. Believe me, Eddie, he's a bad influence and you'll find it's all to the good."

She paused for breath and there was a long silence.

"Eddie, are you still there?"

"Yes."

"You can start back to work on Monday then. I think you've been very lucky. You don't deserve it."

There was another silence.

"Eddie?"

"I'm here."

"Well? Haven't you got anything to say?"

I sighed. Five minutes ago I'd been feeling relaxed. Now I could feel that old familiar tension clutching at my innards.

"Would you ask your father to send the wages he owes on to me, please."

There was a stunned silence for a second or two then she spluttered, "Didn't you hear what I just said? I've persuaded Daddy to let you have your job back."

"He knows the address. A cheque will do nicely."

"Eddie!" she almost screamed. "Will you listen. You're forgiven. Everything can go back to normal. It'll take a bit of time but—"

"Miriam," I said quietly, "You listen for a change. I don't want my job back and the last thing I want is for things to return to normal. Your father will never set foot in this house again. He can stuff his job. Just tell him I want my money."

I hung up. My heart was beating fast and I felt smothered. It was as though Miriam were in the room. Her voice lingered in the air and I felt unaccountably nervous, like a small boy caught stealing apples, knowing that I would soon have to face the consequences and get punished. I walked through the house and into the back garden.

The usually immaculate lawn was starting to look overgrown and the flower beds were filling with weeds. I slumped down on the garden roller and took a few deep breaths to calm myself.

The sun was at its hottest and it seemed all the energy I'd had earlier was seeping out of me. I dabbed at my forehead with a handkerchief feeling tired and confused. It would have been so much easier if I had someone to talk to. Someone to share the burden of having a wall full of gold bullion, a marriage on the rocks, sixty-three pounds in the bank and no job.

I yawned. The nightmare had returned last night. The same one that I'd had the last three nights: I am in a corridor, at the end of which is a door. The door opens and Baseball Cap, Smalley and Winston come in. They are dead, their faces white, dark, empty sockets where eyes should have been. They have their arms outstretched reaching for me and their hands clawing at the air, feeling for me as they stumble and shuffle slowly along the narrow corridor...

I turn to run and find that at my end of the corridor there is only a blank wall. There is no door and no way out. The three corpses get nearer and nearer.

Winston touches me first. His hand brushes across my chest, quickly the other hand comes up and goes for the face. The hands are wet and cold; the skin feels loose as though ready to peel off. Winston gives a howl of triumph. The other two have their hands on me now, gouging at my eyes, squeezing at my throat... I'd woken screaming and trembling, half in and half out of bed in my scramble to get away.

Sleep afterwards had been impossible and I had lain in bed with the light on, staring at the ceiling, unwilling to risk going back into that dream.

I sighed and tried to push all the worrying thoughts to the back of my mind. Perhaps the best therapy for my problems would be to straighten up the garden. A sudden movement caught my eye and looking up to the far end of the lawn I saw two magpies pecking at the grass. This cheered me up. It was a good omen. 'One for sorrow, two for joy'. Maybe my problems were about to be magically erased.

All at once there was a flurry of activity. One of the birds decided that the other's patch of grass was more interesting than his own and made a takeover bid. Its mate put up a brief show of resistance then with a noise like a stick dragged across a washboard, hopped up onto the edge of the incinerator.

I watched drowsily. It was a tranquil scene and one that shouldn't have sent a stab of alarm shooting through my body but there was something wrong. For a few seconds I couldn't think what it was and then I realised and was on my feet and running up the garden, sending the squawking birds flapping into the air, matching my panic: the incinerator was empty!

I stared frantically around the garden then dashed into the shed, scattering tools and throwing the lawn mower to the side, hoping idiotically that I had had a lapse of memory and the bloodstained coat would still be where I had left it for the first time. There was nothing. I walked back out into the garden, my mind in turmoil and my heart threatening to beat its way out of my chest. The police were on to me. I was sure of it. I'd slipped up, left a fingerprint or a hair. Those forensic boys were too clever. I'd been stupid to think that I'd get away with it. I walked across to the incinerator again and leaned heavily against it. The strength seemed to drain out of me and I felt weak and tired. For a long time I stayed in that position, desperately trying to sort out my thoughts and decide what to do. Then suddenly, without having to look, I became aware that there was someone else in the garden watching me. I lifted my head slowly and looked towards the house, expecting to see a policeman.

Mike Paterson was standing on the concrete path. He was wearing dungarees and wellingtons and looked slightly nervous. In his hand he carried his habitual walking stick. Not in the normal fashion. The stick was upside down and grasped tightly near the rubber ferule and held menacingly away from his body like a club. Draped over the other arm was my bloodstained coat.

We stood staring at one another for a few moments then Paterson walked slowly up the path until we were face to face. He held out the coat and I took it and clutched it to myself like a prized possession.

Paterson said, "I know about the robbery."

I didn't answer for a while then said, "Robbery?"

Paterson nodded. "I know about your part in the Fletton Stewart bullion robbery."

My mouth must have dropped open and I stared up at the older man, fear rushing through my body.

Paterson said, "Can we talk?"

*****

The short walk between the garden incinerator and the rear door of the house was like that between the condemned cell and the noose.

The path seemed to sway beneath my feet and my vision had become blurred. I wiped my face and saw that my hand was wet.

A cell. I could not face the thought of being confined to a cell. I had been in a cell all my life and had thought that I'd broken free. But an eternity of confinement in a small, drab room seemed to stretch before me. Three dead men and a fortune in stolen property would ensure that the remainder of my life would be spent rotting and alone. Unable to see the sun. The feeling inside me was not that of fear but of numbing acceptance. My fate seemed now to have been decided; there was nothing I could do; no alternatives and no fight left in my body.

At the kitchen door, I leaned dutifully against the wall at Paterson's order and felt the big man run his hands across my chest, sides and legs, then I was sitting at the kitchen table and the man who had been my friend yesterday was on the other side of the room, near the sink, frowning and clutching the walking stick menacingly in both hands and demanding that I should talk.

Strangely, there was no need for persuasion. It was a relief to let it all out. I put my head in my arms on the kitchen table and then, like a man at the confessional, I started my story, hesitatingly at first, making sure that I didn't miss anything out; I described in detail the events that had happened since I took that fateful late-night walk, an eternity ago.

When my story was finished, nearly two hours had ticked away on the dial of the clock on the wall. Paterson had put down his stick and had produced from somewhere a bottle of cooking sherry and two glasses.

It was as though a great burden had lifted from my shoulders and I no longer felt the numbing fear in my stomach, only relief and tiredness. I sat back in the chair and signalled the end of my tale with a sigh of relief.

There was a long silence between us before Paterson reached across the table and touched me gently on the arm.

"Here," he said. "Drink this," and pushed my untouched sherry glass towards me.

I sat up feeling completely wrung out and took a sip from the glass. "How did you find out?"

"I suppose it was because you're a rotten liar," Paterson said. "When you told me you were burning some old gardening clothes I got an inkling that you weren't telling the truth. I'd seen you wearing the fairly new coat only a few days previously. So when Sally was treating your face, I nipped over the fence and had a look."

He paused and refilled my glass. "I've seen bloodstains before, Eddie lad."

I hung my head and didn't say anything, so Paterson continued, "It was just a matter of putting two and two together. I remembered you telling me how you'd been mugged and had your wallet stolen, then seeing you get it out in the pub and pay for a round of drinks, and I happen to know that all mugging victims are given a thorough medical check. The police would never have let you go with your face in that condition. I remembered the night after the bullion robbery being woken up by you making that wall of yours outside. I couldn't believe what my suspicions were telling me, but I've just had a look under the earth in your wall."

I slumped further down into my chair.

"What are you going to do?" I whispered.

"I don't mind telling you now, Eddie, when I confronted you with the coat two hours ago, I was scared stiff. I thought if he's killed three men he could easily kill me. I thought maybe you were a cold-blooded killer..."

I put my head back into my folded arms.

"I am a killer," I said.

Paterson snorted and patted my arm.

"You're no killer. I think you're exceptionally brave... and bloody lucky, but you're no killer."

"What'll happen to me?"

There was no immediate reply, so I sat up again. I felt scared but resigned.

"What'll happen to me?" I said again.

Paterson leaned forward until his face was very close to mine. He spoke in a low whisper.

"Well you might buy a yacht and sail to the Caribbean, or you could go off on a world cruise, maybe buy yourself a Rolls Royce, invest in an oil well or two..." His voice trailed off.

I was perplexed.

"Aren't you going to tell the police?"

Paterson shook his head.

"After all you've been through? I'd never forgive myself. Listen, don't feel guilty about killing the scum who robbed the security firm. They deserved to die. The world's a better place now they're gone. They shot those security men and didn't care one jot that they were taking away human lives, innocent men with wives and children and years of living ahead of them. The bastards half-killed a policeman who tried to stop them getting away. The papers say he'll be confined to a wheelchair for the rest of his life. They would have killed you too without thinking twice about it." He paused then said, "I'm really glad they didn't. I'm starting to have a lot of respect for you, Eddie. I like you a lot."

I stared at him open-mouthed.

Paterson smiled and added, "You were bloody lucky though. My God, you were lucky."

My mouth must have opened even wider. Paterson laughed and slapped me on the shoulder. "Come on, Ed, laddie. You're not going to prison. I'm going to help you. This calls for a celebration. He picked up the sherry bottle and waggled it under my noise. "Haven't you got anything else in the house but this? It tastes like cough mixture."

I stood up.

"You're going to help me?"

"Yes."

"You're not going to tell the police?"

"No."

I took a huge breath.

"Oh, thank God!" The relief was overwhelming. "Oh God! Oh Jesus! You scared the shit out of me!"

He waggled the bottle again.

I shook my head in amazement and walked out of the kitchen into the hallway, reappearing a minute later with a half-bottle of single malt whisky.

"Ah. That looks more like it," said Mike. He emptied the dregs of the sherry into the sink, swished the glasses under the cold tap, refilled them with the whisky then clinked his glass against mine.

"To Eddie Wheatley. Millionaire," he said.

We both took a long swig.

"Lang may yer lum reek!" he added.

I had no idea what that meant so said, "How are you going to help me, why are you getting involved?"

"Well, now I know that you were not part of the original robbery, that you didn't kill any innocent security guards and that you got into the whole thing accidentally, I'd like to give you a hand."

"How?"

Mike took his time answering, knocking his pipe out on to a plate then, sucking on the empty stem, said, "Before I retired I had quite a few dealings with the criminal world. I think I know where I could get a good price for the jewels."

He hesitated then added, "The gold might take a bit more effort." He saw my face fall. "Don't worry though, I think I'll find a buyer for that too."

"Mike, you don't know what a relief it is to have somebody else who knows, somebody to speak to about it… and a partner who knows how to change all that yellow metal into stuff you can pay the grocery bills with."

He smiled. "Not exactly a partner, Ed. You've done all the work so far. I'll only want a small cut for my efforts."

"How do you propose to start?"

"With the jewels, I've got someone in mind to contact. The last time I saw him he was living over at Battersea."

I leaned forward eagerly. "When?"

"Tomorrow," Mike said and with a 'whoop' of excitement I filled our glasses again to the brim. He raised his in the air.

"To our partnership," he said.

Later when the bottle was empty and Paterson was leaving, I asked, "With all these contacts you had in the criminal world, Mike, what business were you in?"

My partner in crime stopped as he reached the door and turned to face me. He looked slightly embarrassed.

"I was a policeman," he said

*****

Meanwhile Miriam lay on a small single bed in her friend Carrie's spare room, staring up at the ceiling and wondering at how her life had been turned upside down in the space of two days. She didn't feel depressed, just amazed. Her timid, unassuming husband had suddenly turned into a different person, had become a modern-day Jekyll and Hyde, transforming himself into someone she didn't recognise. Forty-eight hours was all it took for him to find himself a man friend, get drunk as a skunk, insult her father, give up his job, resulting in her walking out and moving in with Carrie. It was probably just a blip, she thought, caused by the booze. Or maybe, she mused, because he'd discovered his true sexuality. She had always assumed that he was a teetotaller without any sexual urges.

Life had suddenly become full of surprises, the biggest of them being that she didn't feel the least unhappy about the new situation. At least something was happening. A large boulder had been thrown into the dull, unchanging, monotonous pond that was her life causing a tsunami of change.

The recent confrontation Eddie had had with her father had been the last straw, but even before that, before his dramatic change, what had they got? A tedious existence without an iota of excitement or even the prospect of having any. Every day was the same as the last. Eddie goes to work, Eddie returns from work. Eddie eats his supper, Eddie puts up a shelf or paints an already painted bit of furniture. They very rarely had a proper conversation, shared a joke or had a cuddle.

She shook her head and admitted to herself that it was her own fault. She had worried she'd be a spinster forever, left on the shelf and likely to end up living alone with just a cat for company. Eddie had seemed to be her last chance so she had pursued him relentlessly, even faking a pregnancy. Big mistake. She had tried to change the unchangeable but in vain, he had remained stuck in his ever-deepening rut determined not to budge.

She turned her head and looked around the small room. It was normally Carrie's office. The camp bed she lay on was wedged between an ornate Victorian desk and a filing cabinet. There were two shelves just above her head stacked with box files and at the foot of the bed was her hurriedly packed suitcase, bursting at the seams with stuff she thought she'd need when she left the house.

Her parents had begged her to come and live with them but she had refused, knowing full well that within a week she would be their chief cook and bottle washer. Much as she loved them, living with her mother and father was out of the question, so as soon as they'd gone, taking Rufus the dog with them, she had phoned her old friend, explained the situation and asked if she could stay for a few days until she had sorted things out. Carrie had agreed straight away, driven over, helped her pack a few essentials and moved her into her tiny flat. So far it had been fun. Carrie had done her best to stop her feeling morose, assuring her that she'd done the right thing. Miriam hadn't had time to dwell on her situation and in truth didn't want to. She felt that for the first time in ages that she was on a kind of holiday.

They'd been ten-pin bowling on the previous afternoon and afterwards dined at a *Pizza Express* just around the corner, after which they'd sat up till one thirty in the morning chatting and drinking copious glasses of wine. She smiled as she remembered. Oh my, it was so nice to have some company and intelligent conversation. The only argument they'd had was when she had insisted on phoning Eddie to say she'd persuaded her father to let him have his job back.

"For God's sake," Carrie had groaned. "Don't creep around the bastard. He doesn't deserve you or his job. Let him stew in his own goddammed juice!"

Just then her thoughts were disturbed by a knock on the door and Carrie popped her head through the gap.

"Hi there, sleepy head," she said. "I've brought you some tea. Can I come in?"

"Wow! What a treat," Miriam said. "Come on in."

"Sleep well?"

"Like a log."

Carrie handed her a steaming mug.

"Well, that surprises me. I could never get to sleep on that damn thing. I've tried a few times but it's as hard as hell."

Miriam laughed. "I think the wine helped," she said. Her friend sat on the floor beside the bed. She was still in her pyjamas. Blue silk with a Chinese dragon embroidered on the back. She hadn't yet put on any make-up and Miriam thought she looked younger without it.

"Got an idea," Carrie said.

"Go on."

"How's about we get in the car and drive over to Kensington? It's a great place for a walk. Lots of ducks we could feed. See the Lady Diana memorial, mingle with the crowd then have a coffee and chat. Ever been there?"

Miriam shook her head.

"No, never have. Always wanted to."

"Well then?"

"Carrie, you don't have to entertain me. I'll be okay. Honestly. And what about your work?"

The American leaned forward and brushed a lock of hair away from Miriam's face.

"Honey," she said. "I'm taking a few days off. C'mon. What d'you say? Let's have some fun!"

Miriam smiled.

"What a pal. You're an angel in disguise."

"Great," Carrie said. "But first there's about to be a plate of bacon and eggs with your name on it in the kitchen." She stood up and walked to the door. "See you in a min."

*****

The birthday cake had been a hard thing to hide, especially as the person it was being hidden from was fond of cooking and frequently used the utensils and cupboards of the kitchen. It had taken hours to make. A work of art made up with icing sugar, marzipan and love. It was large. Beautifully iced and carried sixty candles around its outside edge, surrounding an iced replica in pink of *The Financial Times*. The initials 'FT' were picked out in large black letters and cleverly written in icing sugar under the word 'Financial' was the name Frank, then under the word 'Times' was written 'Thomson'. A decorative frill encircled the sides of the cake, depicting in silver and gold paper the words 'Happy Birthday'.

Janet Thomson carried the cake down the stairs from the bedroom where it had been hidden and took it into the kitchen. She was wearing a black dress with the deep V-neck, which was her husband's favourite and the triple row of pearls with the sapphire cluster necklace, which had been a gift from him on her last birthday.

Sixty candles were difficult to light. It took a whole eight minutes and ten matches so by the time she reached the sixtieth candle, the first candles had burned almost halfway through. She stood back for a second or two to admire the effect, then picked up the tray and carried it as fast as was possible without the candles blowing out, through the hall and across to the large carved oak door of the dining room. Before opening the door, she breathed a silent prayer that the surprise of the cake would achieve what the new cufflinks, the antique Tantalus and the special meal she had cooked had not done. She had hoped all these gifts would lift the burden of gloom that had hung like a heavy black cloud around her husband's shoulders since the night that they had eaten dinner at the Freemans' house.

When asked, he had insisted that there was nothing at all to worry about, just a small business transaction that had gone slightly wrong, and everything would be all right in a day or two, and he didn't want her worrying her pretty head about it. She hated his male arrogance at times like these. Women were not supposed to have brains apart from those needed to arrange a dinner party, coffee morning or to choose a new dress. She longed to be more involved with his life away from the house, was keenly curious about how and where he earned his money so that she could share the worries when things went wrong and the euphoria when they went right. Sexual equality was not, however, even remotely considered by the keen business brain of her husband and as far as he was concerned, a woman's place was definitely and most emphatically in ignorance and at home.

She did not believe that his unusual bad temper, his pacing of the floor and his general worried demeanour could all be attributed to a small business transaction that had gone wrong. There was, she knew, much more to it than that. He slept fitfully, spent hours on the telephone in his study, raged furiously at the TV news bulletins and when she enquired why, he ignored her and seemed hardly to notice that she existed.

Tonight's intimate little birthday party, she hoped, would change all that. Deliberately she had not invited any guests, choosing instead to supply the ingredients for a romantic evening together alone, and hope that his mood would change as the evening progressed.

It seemed destined not to be. Twice that evening he had left the table to make phone calls. He had insisted on watching the television news and his presents had been received with distracted indifference.

Janet Thomson took a deep breath and pushed opened the dining room door.

The room that she had carefully left in semi-darkness to heighten the effect of the cake candles was now brilliantly lit. She tutted and turned the dimmer switch down on the wall beside the door then advanced into the room singing the first few bars of 'Happy Birthday to you ...'. She faltered to a stop. Her husband was on the telephone just inside the door.

He had been writing something on the telephone pad, but now he turned angrily, hand over the mouthpiece, and hissed, "For Christ's sake, Janet. I'm on the telephone."

He took a pace forward, pushed her roughly to one side and turned the dimmer switch back on to full power. "Now leave me alone please, this is private," he snapped.

She stood rooted to the spot, mouth gaping open, unable to comprehend this new, cruel facet of her husband's character that had not been revealed before.

"Out!" he shouted and when she still did not move he slammed the phone down on the sideboard and seizing her by the shoulder, pushed her violently through the doorway into the hall, slamming the door shut behind her with his foot.

She reeled across the hallway, tripped and fell heavily to the floor. The birthday cake flew from her grasp and smashed into a thousand pieces against the stone slabs.

For a minute she lay where she fell, the breath knocked from her body, then whimpering she crawled through the debris of the cake to the far wall, where she curled up like a frightened child, the high-roofed hallway echoing softly to her sobs and the flagstones beneath her body becoming wet with her tears.

A few minutes later, Frank Thomson emerged from the dining room into the hallway. His face was taut and angry. He seemed not to notice his wife's prostrate body on the floor, although he had to step over her to take his coat from the stand against the wall. He opened the front door and slammed it noisily behind him. In a few seconds she heard his car engine burst into life, a screech of tyres on the gravel driveway, and he was gone.

*****

Haslitt hated boats. The damned things never stayed still. There was no controlling them. Up and down, side to side. What a way to travel. Give him a car any day. He remembered a coach trip from the East End of London when he was just twelve years old and really enjoying being away from the big city for the very first time, and seeing the sea and playing on the machines on the Pier at Brighton, and his parents coming to get him from the amusement arcade for this extra special treat. A trip round the bay with forty adults full to their ears with beer and crisps on a boat that lurched and tossed and heaved its passengers like marbles in a tin until all of them, including himself, were leaning miserably over the sides, watching the waves discolour with their breakfasts, lunches and umpteen gallons of brown ale and best bitter.

He'd vowed then never to set foot on a boat again and for twenty-six years had managed to avoid doing so, but now, very much against his will, here he was in another fibreglass cocoon, rolling and pitching and bumping into the walls. Only this time he couldn't hold on, couldn't fend off the sharp bits and pieces of the vessel that cracked against his head and dug painfully into his ribs. This time his hands were tied firmly behind his back, his feet roped together and linked to his wrists at the back with his own tie.

They hadn't allowed him to lie on the floor safe from the sharp table edges and other protuberances that some sadist of a marine architect had designed. A short piece of rope leading from the binding around his waist was tied to a beam in the roof of the cabin which kept him suspended in a horizontal position, which meant that when each really large wave rocked the boat, he was swung like a pendulum across the cabin.

Earlier, when Arkwright and his silent partner had hauled him up on to the deck and allowed him to unload the contents of his stomach overboard, he had seen a cargo ship steam past. The deck was lit by a spotlight ready for unloading and he could see a stack of wooden crates with the words 'Wivenhoe Port' printed on the sides. He had guessed they were somewhere off the coast of Essex.

The boat swayed violently and he tried desperately to cling with the back of his knees to the wooden bunk above which he was perched, but for the umpteenth time he lurched forward on his tether and cracked the side of his head against a storage locker on the other side of the cabin. The boat righted itself and he swung back, the corner of the galley door cutting neatly between his shoulder blades and causing him to cry out in pain and rage. He kicked against the galley wall and tried to wedge himself between the bunk and a wooden table. At last he had something to hold on to. By drawing his legs up as high as he could he managed to grip the edge of the table between his stomach and his knees. This meant that his face was pressed hard against the table top and the rope from the bulkhead was pulled hard making the binding around his wrists cut deep into the skin.

He lay there ignoring the pain. Grateful that at last he wasn't swinging around the cabin beating his brains out. But cursing softly under his breath and making promises to himself about what he would do to Arkwright if he ever got out of this mess. There had been no need for the rope to the bulkhead. Tying his hands and feet would have been enough. But Arkwright was a sadistic bastard and this had been his revenge. He was a small-time crook and nightclub bouncer. Haslitt had got to know him when he had started using his club, 'The Parrot Perch' on his nights off or when he was out of work. Arkwright was a man who spent quite a lot of his time staring at himself in mirrors or adjusting his immaculate designer hairstyle in shop windows. He felt that somehow he had missed his vocation and that sooner or later someone in the film industry would spot his good looks and plead with him to do a screen test. Undoubtedly the ladies did find him attractive, admired his handsome face and big muscular body but unfortunately so did he and enjoyed nothing better than luring a woman to his bedroom where he would strip off and entertain the poor creature with body building poses and romantic conversations about male posing pouches and dynamic tension exercises. Invariably he would finish the evening off by beating his guest up. Either because she had objected to his behaviour or because perversely it increased his feelings of masculinity.

One of Haslitt's girls at the club had turned up for work with a severely beaten face and when Arkwright had strolled in two nights later, Haslitt demonstrated what it was like to be on the receiving end, damaging Arkwright's screen test chances for several months. Afterwards he had thrown Arkwright out into the litter-strewn alley at the back of the club and suggested that he should take his custom elsewhere.

He heard the approach of a dinghy a full minute before it came alongside. The whine of its tiny engine reverberated through the water into the hull and up the leg of the table to the surface where his ear was pressed. Frank Thomson! A red wave of fury welled up within his body causing him to release his hold on the table. He heard the sound of the dinghy come alongside and the murmur of voices outside as he swung across towards the storage locker. He managed to avoid smashing his face against the wooden door by turning his head and taking the full impact against his shoulder and neck but on the return journey once more the galley door caught him neatly between the shoulder blades and he grunted with pain. Before he could swing again and further damage himself, however, Frank Thomson had him by the lapels and was screaming and spitting into his face, his own face contorted with such fury that Haslitt was sure the man would explode.

The locker, the shelf, the galley door, the table edge all took their turns to bite into Haslitt's flesh as Thomson swung him around the cabin from his tether, flailing at him with slaps and punches and gouging at him like a woman scorned. He wondered where Arkwright and the other man had gone. It wasn't like Arkwright to miss any of the action, especially of the violent kind.

At last Thomson's fury calmed slightly and he left Haslitt to swing from his rope, his face bruised and bloodied, while he stood with his arms hanging loose and exhausted by his sides, breathing heavily, the blood-red colour of his face subsiding slowly to that of nearly normal.

Haslitt said through his swollen lips, "I thought you were the man who didn't believe in violence."

"Shut up," Thomson hissed. "I am against violence to human beings, not to two-timing scum like you." He pulled Haslitt towards him so that their faces were almost touching. "Where have you put the gold? You'd better tell me now or I promise I'll kill you."

The boat lurched again and the big man swung away. He shouted angrily, "If you want to talk, Thomson, for Christ's sake undo that bloody rope."

Thomson hesitated for a moment or two staring up at the rope, then he turned and walked into the galley. He reappeared a few seconds later with a long thin, black-handled knife and cut the big man down, allowing him to fall unceremoniously and painfully onto the table then the deck. He leaned forward and cut through the tie linking the man's wrists and feet, then putting the knife on one side, he grasped Haslitt's lapels and hauled him up till he was sitting on the bunk.

The two men sat facing each other across the small table, each with an expression of intense loathing on his face. Thomson was the first to speak.

"I'm waiting."

"You put on a very good act, Thomson," Haslitt said through clenched teeth. "I don't know what your game is."

"Act?"

"Yes. I don't know what you're up to. There were five people who knew about the robbery. Three of them are dead.

That just leaves you and me and I'm damned sure it isn't me who's the two-timing bastard who wants the lot for himself."

Thomson stared at him for a few seconds then said, "I don't believe you Haslitt. I think you're a stinking liar. Why didn't you go back to the safe house? How come you were so conveniently out of the way when the other three got killed? If you are innocent why did it take Arkwright and Solomon so long to find you? What were you running away from, Haslitt?" The other man made to speak but Thomson cut in.

"I don't believe all this crap that the papers are putting out about a rival gang. I think that's what you would like me to believe. You were the only man in the team with brains enough to work out a double-cross and you very nearly succeeded. I would've found you Haslitt even if you'd holed up in a cave in Outer Mongolia."

Again, Haslitt tried to get a word in but Thomson continued.

"You have a choice, my friend. Either you tell me where you've hidden the bullion and jewellery or perhaps you'd rather divulge that information to Mr Arkwright and Mr Solomon."

A look of sudden enlightenment spread across Haslitt's bruised face.

"I've just sussed it out, Thomson. I know what you're up to. You're going to get that over-muscled poof to beat me half to death knowing full well that I 'aven't nicked anything, then you'll drop me over the side. Very clever. Nobody will know a thing about it apart from Arkwright and his mate and I bet they don't even know what they've brought me here for. A thousand quid each for their trouble and good old Frank Thomson has got thirty million quid all to his greedy little self."

Thomson stood up. "What's it going to be?"

"Please yourself."

"You're a fool," shouted Thomson and hit Haslitt hard on the side of his head with his clenched fist. The big man saw it coming and rode the blow, falling sideways on to the bunk. As he did so Thomson followed up and he expected another punch, but instead Thomson reached down and took something from Haslitt's inside pocket. It was the envelope that had been exchanged an eternity ago in the lay-by near Colchester containing the advance of four thousand pounds. He opened the envelope and looked down at the contents, which were still intact, then stared down at Haslitt with an expression of puzzlement on his face. After a moment he turned and climbed up the steps leading out of the cabin and disappeared through the louvered door at the top.

Haslitt braced himself for the arrival of Arkwright and Solomon and strained to hear the voices from above. He could imagine the delighted anticipation on Arkwright's face as he had waited for the summons by Frank Thomson. It must be like Christmas.

Five minutes ticked by. He tried to position himself on the bunk so that he could get one good kick at the man before he started work. If only the damned boat would stay still.

The door opened and a pair of legs appeared in the hatchway. By the time the man had reached the foot of the steps a cold sweat had broken out all over Haslitt's body, but then he let the air rush from his lungs in a gasp of relief as he saw it was Frank Thomson and he was alone. Thomson stood in front of the swinging lamp on the ceiling, his silver hair, dishevelled by the wind outside, forming a halo around his head. He stared down at the trussed figure on the bunk. Haslitt didn't speak but stared up at the man puzzled.

After a few moments, Thomson turned and picked up the knife that he had used earlier. He moved towards the bunk, the knife held in front of his body. Haslitt squirmed away terrified and tried to flatten himself against the wall of the boat but Thomson leaned down and sliced the rope that bound his ankles. He gestured to Haslitt to turn over and when the big man responded, he cut through the ropes around his wrists. Haslitt sat up on the bunk astonished, rubbing his wrists, waiting for the blood to flow freely into his hands and feet again. Thomson still held the knife in front of him, inches away from Haslitt's throat.

"I believe you," he said.

Haslitt swallowed, unable to speak for a long time, then said huskily, "I believe you too, Frank."

Thomson threw the knife into the corner of the cabin and stretched out his hand towards the man on the bunk. They clasped hands firmly.

"Arkwright and Solomon?" queried Haslitt. "What about them?"

"I sent them back with the dinghy. They're on land," said Thomson, "waiting for my signal. I don't want them to know that this is anything to do with the Fletton Stewart thing."

"How come you suddenly trust me?"

"Because you chose to face Arkwright and because you still had my four thousand intact on you."

Haslitt stood up, staggered and then stretched his aching limbs.

"But what happened? I still don't understand."

"I don't either. We're going to have to work together on this, Haslitt." He frowned and pushed back the silver mane with his long bony fingers. He looked spruce and smart. Haslitt ached all over and felt a wreck.

"Before we do," he said, "and just so that you'll know what the last few hours have been like…" He swung one massive fist and struck the older man on the side of the jaw.

Thomson's feet left the ground and he crashed through the galley door, scattering crockery and pans in his wake. He pulled himself up onto his knees, eyes glazed over and a small rivulet of blood running down his cheek. The big man picked him up easily with one hand and dusted him down with the other.

"You do understand, don't you?"

Thomson dabbed at his cheek with his handkerchief.

"I take your point," he said.

The boat lurched and Haslitt grabbed the table. "Another thing," he said, "if you don't mind I'd like to do any talking we're going to do on terra firma."

Thomson nodded and then climbed the stairs to the deck. It was pitch-black and the sea was being agitated by a strong wind. A few lights glimmered about fifty yards away on the starboard side. They seemed to rise and fall but it was the motion of the boat. Haslitt once again felt that familiar queasiness deep down in his stomach as he watched Thomson make signals with a torch in the direction of the land. He was looking forward to being back on shore again, but most of all, he wanted to see the look of disappointment on Arkwright's face.

*****

Twelve o'clock midday. Battersea and already the pubs were beginning to fill. The secretaries and the office workers would come later. The unemployed, drifters and builders who were working on the old Battersea Power Station, converting it into another small city, filled the bar. Outside the Plume of Feathers, a table meant for those customers wanting to drink in the fresh air was stacked high with overalls and dungarees placed there by manual workers obeying the handwritten notice on the door: 'Sorry, no soiled working clothes allowed'. Underneath the table were various pairs of wellingtons and metal-toed shoes. It mattered not that the people propping up the bar inside stood in stockinged feet, singlets, old jeans or even some who were bare from the waist up. The management was being obeyed and no soiled working clothes were offending the eye or sullying the interior of the drinking area.

Mike Paterson ordered a pint of bitter and while it was being pulled, gave a cursory glance at the pub's clients. The man he sought was not in the room. Disappointed, he carried his drink to a vacant table facing the doorway. He was wearing his customary flat cap and fawn mackintosh. In his hands he held a square, black leather briefcase, which he gripped tightly, placing it on his lap when he sat down and resting both arms upon it as though at any moment it might try to escape. Under his arm was the walking stick he always carried but never used for its true purpose. He sipped at his beer and watched the door, trying hard to stop the trembling in his hands.

The situation he was in reminded him of a day twenty years ago when, as a desk sergeant almost due for retirement from the police force, he had chased a young thief who had just cleaned out the window of a jeweller's shop near Covent Garden. He had been on his way in to do a turn of duty when the thief had charged out of the shop and almost knocked him over. The man had been young and fit and there was no way Paterson could have caught him in the chase had the idiot not looked round and run straight into a hole that had been dug in the pavement by workmen digging up the drains. When Paterson had arrived, breathless and red-faced on the scene, the thief was sleeping peacefully five feet down on top of a broken drainpipe with a large gash over his head and two rather surprised-looking road workers staring down at him.

Later he had marched the young man handcuffed to his left wrist into the police station, carrying in his other hand the bag containing the proceeds from the robbery.

He remembered well how proud he had been at the time. Quite a coup to retire on. Nice way to go out. The papers had covered the story and he'd been a bit of a hero for a couple of days. Fifteen thousand pounds' worth of jewellery had been in the bag. A hell of a lot of money in those days. It had made him feel quite shaky handling that amount.

He looked down at the briefcase on his lap and the butterflies in his stomach started a war dance. Nearly two million pounds' worth of gems balanced on his knees and this time he wasn't on the side of the law. This time he was taking the chance of wrecking the clean sheet that had been his career and the untroubled, uncluttered, law-abiding retirement that he had enjoyed for the last eighteen years. Oh God! What would his old colleagues in the force think if they could see him now? Mike Paterson. Good old reliable Sergeant Paterson. Father figure to the young aspiring coppers just starting and needing a guiding hand. Giver of advice. Decision-maker in times of crisis. Epitome of solid, clean living British justice—now sitting in a grotty pub with a fortune of stolen jewels hoping to do business with an East End crook.

The plain truth was that good old Sergeant Paterson, having scented the possibility of a little nest-egg, had fallen prey to that very human emotion: greed. This much he admitted to himself. Pensions do tend to erode after eighteen years, what with inflation, rent increases and the like. He wanted so badly to spend a little money on Sally. Buy her a few gifts, take her on a nice holiday. It could work wonders for their relationship. Women liked a few treats, liked to be wined and dined. Impossible on his meagre savings though. He shuddered to think what Sally's reaction would be if she knew what he was up to. Cathy, bless her heart, had she been spared, would never have believed it.

He found it all a bit hard to believe himself. Not too many people have neighbours whose garden walls are filled with gold bullion. Not too many people had neighbours like Eddie Wheatley come to that. The man's calmness was incredible. That morning he'd dug into his wall with a trowel and fished out this fortune in jewels wrapped in a plastic bag and handed them proudly to Paterson as though he were passing on his prize spring onions. He had been as excited as a child looking forward to a treat.

"Hope you get lots of money for this, Mike," he'd said and patted him on the back. Waving at him from the garden gate as he went off down the street, the gems transferred safely into his briefcase. A child waving to its daddy who was off to work in the big city. Not sure how he gets them, but he brings back the pennies at the end of the day. He was probably still there sitting in the window waiting. Tense with excitement and eager anticipation.

Paterson finished his beer and took it to the bar for a refill. The barman was fat and tired looking. Stretched across his belly was a white tee shirt, bearing the words 'The end of the world is nigh and it's your round'.

Paterson said, "Does Charlie Webster still come in here? I'm an old friend of his."

The man tossed his change down on to the counter and turned to his next customer.

"I wouldn't know, mate."

Back at his seat Paterson cursed softly. There was no way that he could disguise his appearance. Once a bobby, always a bobby. Straight back, ruddy face, big feet. He should have known from past experience that you don't just walk into a Battersea pub and start asking questions. Especially if the questions concern the whereabouts of someone with a record.

He was halfway down his second pint and wondering what to do when Charlie Webster walked in. Heavens, how the man had aged. He was still thin and smartly dressed with the gold cufflinks and rings adorning each finger just as Paterson remembered him from years ago. But his body had become more stooped, the scraped-back hair no longer black but silver grey, the face pale and lined.

Webster walked up to the bar. The barman dropped the customer he was serving and instantly started a whispered conversation with him, nodding occasionally in Paterson's direction. Webster didn't look over at him straight away but stood back from the bar and went through the elaborate business of dropping his newspaper on the floor so that he had to turn round to pick it up and take the opportunity to glance in Paterson's direction. He stopped in mid-crouch, a look of disbelief spreading across his face, which changed in to a tight smile as he stood up and walked over to his old adversary.

"My goodness gracious me!" he said, holding out his hand. "I didn't think I'd ever see you again, Sergeant Paterson. Well, well, well, who would have thought it!"

"Hello, Charlie." Paterson grasped his outstretched hand and shook it. "Mr Paterson now."

"Course," said Charlie. "You must have retired some time now. How's things going?"

"Just fine; can I get you a drink?"

"I've ordered one. I take it this is a social call then now that you're plain Mister."

Webster went back to the bar and picked up his drink. When he returned to the table he said, "Now look, Mr Paterson, I've been a good boy for a long time now…"

"Don't worry, Charlie. It's nothing like that."

"What then?"

Paterson looked around the bar. The office workers had started to come in and it was becoming fairly crowded.

"Can we talk someplace else?" he asked.

Webster looked puzzled. He stared down at Paterson for a moment or two, then said, "Yeah, okay. It's a nice day for a walk."

They left the pub and Webster took Paterson through several narrow streets and alleyways until at last they came to Battersea Park. Neither of the men spoke from the time they left the pub until they were sitting on a park bench surrounded by disillusioned pigeons under the impression that anyone sitting on a park bench must automatically have food.

It was a warm day and Paterson had taken his raincoat off. Webster had carefully pulled his trousers up near the knee so as not to spoil the creases and leaned down to flick a minute speck of mud from his shiny, black shoes. Afterwards he leaned back against the bench and said, "What's all this about, Mr P?"

Now that the moment had come, Paterson found himself even more nervous than before. Not looking at the other man he said, "Are you still in the business, Charlie?"

The little man sat upright.

"Leave it out. I told you back in the pub..."

"I know you did and I told you I was plain Mister."

"You're trying to set me up!"

Paterson turned to face the man.

"I swear I'm not, Charlie. I want to do business with you."

Webster looked at him with incredulity. Then he laughed.

"Don't tell me... no, I can't believe it. You *are* setting me up. Sergeant Mike Paterson, upholder of the law. The man who kept London safe whilst citizens slept safe in their beds, going bent?"

Paterson's face had gone red. The little man stood up. "Nice to see you again Mr P. My love to the wife." He turned away and started to walk back up the path to the park gates.

Paterson called after him. "The Fletton Stewart bullion raid, Charlie..."

Webster carried on for a few more paces then stopped. He stood with his back to Paterson for a long time then turned slowly and walked back to the bench, pulling the trousers up at the knee again before he sat down.

"Go on, I'm listening," he said.

"I have to know Charlie. Are you still in business?"

"Look, Mr P, you're an ex-copper. Do you really expect me to say 'Oh yes, I'm in the business. I buy stolen goods'. You're losing your touch. You're getting rusty."

Paterson knew then that he had to take a chance. The man was right, he was getting rusty. How could an ex-policeman expect a fence to confess all after a few minutes together, just so that he could feel reassurance?

He tapped the briefcase. "Inside here Charlie, are the gems from the Fletton Stewart job."

Webster stared at the case. "But how...?"

"Never mind how. Just believe me. Now, do you want to do business?"

Webster continued to stare, fascinated with the briefcase. He licked his lips nervously then stood up again.

"Why are you doing this?"

"Because I'm broke. Because of the measly pension I'm existing on."

Webster got up and walked towards the path again.

"Come on," he said.

*****

They took a cab. It crawled laboriously through the thick London traffic, edging its way to the east side of the city, only gaining speed as it went through Clapham, slowing down to a snail's pace again when they plunged into the porridge which was the traffic of Brixton, then half an hour later they had picked up speed once more and were heading towards Lewisham. Again, neither of them spoke throughout the journey save for the occasional muttered curse about the traffic jams.

Webster chose instead to whistle tunelessly and stare out of the window, although once or twice Paterson saw the little man give a surreptitious glance towards the briefcase, then quickly look away.

Eventually the taxi drew up outside a pleasant little semi-detached Victorian house somewhere in Eltham. He paid the taxi driver and then led the way into the front garden. The lawn was neatly trimmed and the borders were chock-full of flowers and nicely tended shrubs. Webster broke the silence between the two men. He waved his arm at the garden.

"Pretty eh, Mr Paterson?"

"Very nice," said Paterson enthusiastically.

"My pride and joy, this garden."

Paterson said, "I always thought you lived in Battersea."

"I work in Battersea. I'm a bit of a commuter."

"Then why…?"

Webster anticipated the question. "I've got a little office quite near the Plume of Feathers. Even got a bed there in case I have to work late. But there's another bloke uses the facilities. Kind of a partner you might say. If you're selling what you say you're selling I didn't want him to know about it. Not just yet anyway."

The front door to the house opened and a jolly little ball of a lady stood on the threshold. She was probably in her sixties but her grey hair was frizzed out like a dandelion around her head and she wore large, circular-framed glasses. Around her ample frame was tied a white pinafore and below that was a shocking pink track suit. She looked surprised to see Webster standing in the garden and when she saw Paterson he thought her expression changed slightly to one of anxiety.

"Hello love," she said. "Is everything all right?"

Webster smiled. "Don't look so worried, Doreen. This is an old, er, acquaintance of mine from way back. Business acquaintance."

She stood to one side so that they could enter the house.

"It's not like you to come home in the middle of the day."

"Nice to meet you, Mrs Webster," Paterson said, holding out his hand.

She shook it, still with that worried look on her face, and hurried after her husband.

"It's just not like you," she said.

Webster kissed her affectionately on the cheek. "Everything's fine, silly girl. Mr Paterson and I are going to go upstairs to talk about business and what would go down really well is a nice cup of tea." He opened a cupboard in the kitchen wall and took out a bottle of whisky and two glasses. "But we'll have a tot of this just to be going on with." He took Paterson by the arm and led him to the staircase.

She seemed to brighten somewhat and turned to put the kettle on.

"Tea would do you much more good on its own," she called over her shoulder.

Up on the landing Webster fished around in his pocket and produced a key. He unlocked the door of a room at the end of the landing and stood aside for Paterson to enter. There was a desk under the window, a chair and an old, scratched filing cabinet. A few pieces of paper lay on the desk together with a carton of Silk Cut cigarettes, an ashtray, which was brim-full, and an old brass reading lamp with an ornate glass shade. The floor was covered by a yellow carpet which was dotted by burn marks and had a large blue stain, which looked like the contents from a bottle of ink. On the wall was a peg board to which were fastened several pieces of paper covered in figures, a pin-up photograph and a child's drawing in crayon of a house with a lollipop tree. Over everything was an all-pervading smell of stale tobacco.

Webster motioned for Paterson to sit down then brought a stool from another room for himself. He closed the door and poured two generous helpings of whisky.

"Right then, Mr P," he said. "Are we allowed to have a look?"

Paterson opened the case and took out the plastic bag. This would be his first good look at the gems, so when he tipped them out on to the desk there was a gasp of admiration from both men.

Webster leaned forward and delicately picked up a diamond ring encircled by a cluster of rubies.

"You know, Mr Paterson, I didn't believe you," he breathed. "And I still find it hard. How the hell did you get hold of these?"

He opened a drawer in the desk and took out a jeweller's eyepiece, screwing it into his eye and staring intently at the diamond.

The others were given the same scrutiny. Paterson felt like a boy showing his school report to a parent. Each item was closely examined and put aside then picked up again and later re-examined. Webster was whistling that tuneless whistle one more.

There came a gentle rap on the door and Doreen's voice called out that their tea was ready. Paterson sat, still unwilling to leave the jewellery, aware that he hadn't counted the pieces. So easy for Charlie to slip one in his pocket. He heard the sound of a tray being put down outside the door and then the muffled thump of Doreen's slippered feet going off down the stairs. Webster shouted, "Thanks, Doreen," and went back to studying the glittering array spread out before him. After what seemed an age, he slowly got to his feet, walked across the room and opened the door. Paterson scooped the jewellery into the plastic bag and replaced it in his briefcase.

Webster walked back into the room with a plastic tray. There were two mugs of rather milky tea and a plateful of chocolate digestive biscuits. He put the tray on the desk and pushed one mug towards Paterson, gesturing with his other hand for him to help himself to the biscuits.

"Well?" said Paterson.

"They're very, very hot, Mr P."

"I know."

"Photos of these have been in all the papers."

"I know."

"Men have been killed."

"Yes, I know."

Webster lit a cigarette.

"Did you…?"

"I don't think you need to know about the killings, Charlie."

"I think I do, Mr P. If these are traced back to me I'd be involved wouldn't I? Might even get put up on a murder charge." He blew smoke towards the ceiling.

"I'm not going to talk about the murders, Charlie. Are you interested or not?"

"Well, you see, Mr P. My problem is going to be getting rid of the stuff. These aren't any ordinary jewels. These are top notch. High class. I've a few contacts of course, but it would be very, very dodgy. I'd be putting my head right on the line." He paused and took another long pull on his cigarette. "How much are you asking?"

"Make an offer."

"I won't get much for them myself, Mr P. I might even get stuck with them. Can't say a lot... twenty grand?"

Paterson leaned forward and poured himself another whisky. "Let's be serious, Charlie. You've just been looking at two million quids' worth. Don't mess me about."

"Fifty. Take it or leave it."

Paterson stood up. "Sorry I wasted your time. I thought perhaps we were at the beginning of a nice little earner for each of us." He turned to the door. "Don't forget Charlie, these gems weren't the only items to go missing from the Fletton Stewart job."

There was a moment's hesitation before Webster grabbed his arm and pulled him back to his seat.

"How much will you take for the jewels?"

Paterson drummed his fingers on the briefcase.

"Three hundred thousand pounds," he said.

"And you'll come to me regarding the other stuff?"

Paterson nodded.

"Okay," Webster hesitated then looked Paterson full in the eyes. "You'd better be on the level, Paterson. I've got a lot of friends."

"I've got the message."

"When do you want the money?"

"Now would be nice."

Webster laughed.

"Oh yes! I keep that kind of money in me piggy bank downstairs."

Paterson stood up again.

"Well, you tell me when and I'll meet you at your office in Battersea."

Webster stayed put, stroking his chin with his forefinger.

"Tell you what I'll do," he said after a while. "Park your rear end again. Charlie's got to make a phone call."

CHAPTER 11

Sophia Loren

Hardly able to believe my luck I had sat at my bay window for a long time after Paterson had left. It seemed that the fates were combining to help me to shuffle the untidy pack that was my life into some semblance of order.

The great burden of decision had been lifted from my shoulders by a wise new friend. Someone I could rely on and who knew about and could deal with matters which were beyond my comprehension. My biggest worry over the last few days had been that of turning the contents of the garden wall into usable currency. I had no idea how to start. Now this guardian angel, this Fairy Godfather, had materialised, not from out of the blue, but from only next door. The possibility that Paterson might fail never entered my head. My trust in the big, genial ex-policeman was total and so far as I was concerned, my worries were over.

So while Paterson was going through the fairly stressful business of flying off at an abrupt tangent from his up till then honest and incorruptible path through life, I spent the same period of time tidying up the garden and doing a little shopping.

I had suggested that we should go to meet Charlie Webster together but this had been declined by Paterson who considered that he was more likely to win the man's trust on his own.

I set about mowing the lawn and weeding the borders in the garden. I clipped, trimmed, hoed and raked throughout the morning, humming and whistling, enjoying the warm sun with the feeling of well-being which I hadn't felt for a long time.

At lunchtime I decided to clean myself up, get changed and treat myself to a bite to eat away from the house. I had a shower, washed my hair and put on a smart pair of trousers and a check sports jacket. When I looked in the mirror I was reasonably pleased with my appearance. Sally Russell seemed to have worked wonders on my face. The bruises were still there but they had mellowed and I no longer looked as if I'd been made up to star in a horror movie. So feeling that I had shed ten years and that a great burden had been lifted from my shoulders, I walked jauntily down the street – my hair still wet and flattened – with more confidence than I could remember feeling for a very long time.

In only a few minutes I was browsing around the shops, enjoying being part of a crowd, eavesdropping happily to the conversations taking place around me, breathing deeply of the intriguing variety of succulent smells which reached my nostrils from the restaurants and cafés and baker shops and telling myself for the umpteenth time how lucky I was to be alive.

I bought a newspaper and took it into a place called Franco's Pizzeria, standing patiently beside a neat little sign respectfully asking diners to wait until shown a table by their friendly waiter, until a waiter with a frown on his face at having to make a table for two into a table for one, ushered me into the far corner of the room. But nothing was going to spoil my mood and I ordered from the gigantic placard sized menu a pizza Sophia Loren (hot and spicy) and a half-bottle of red wine. Judging by the age of most of the customers seated around me, I guessed that I and the proprietor were probably alone in knowing who Sophia Loren was.

The wine tasted slightly vinegary but the pizza was excellent. I scanned the newspaper. It seemed that Fleet Street had lost interest in the bullion robbery. A member of the Cabinet had confessed to visiting vice-girls in Bayswater. The story took up four pages. Would he resign? Would the government fall? I didn't care. I felt elated. I picked up the bill and squeezed between the tiny tables to the till which was situated near the exit.

The meal was surprisingly cheap so I left a decent tip. Outside the throng of shoppers had almost completely vanished but I could hear in the distance the sound of a couple of buskers playing saxophones to a fast disappearing audience. I wandered off in the direction of the supermarket, mentally compiling a list of things to buy and I'd just added marmalade and cornflakes when I heard somebody shout my name.

"Eddie."

I turned but couldn't see who'd called.

"Eddie, over here."

I looked across the street and saw Sally Russell weaving her way between two parked cars and waving her arm. She waited for a bus to pass then came over.

She was dressed in blue jeans tucked into knee-length brown boots and under a fur-collared leather jerkin wore a black roll-neck sweater. She was smiling and I noticed her spiky hair now had been tinted purple at the tips. I thought she looked stunning.

"Hello," she said. "Remember me?"

I nodded, suddenly at a loss for words.

"Nice to see you again. Isn't it a beautiful day?" She stopped right in front of me.

"You do remember me, don't you?"

I smiled down at her. I'd forgotten how small she was.

"How could I forget?" I said. "Florence Nightingale. Nice to see you too."

She looked me up and down. "You're looking very smart. Are you off somewhere nice?"

"Well, I did plan to go to Tesco's."

She laughed. That lovely, gurgling, breathy sound that I remembered hearing the last time we met.

"I'm having a late lunch," she said. "I had to take two or three learner drivers out myself this morning. Our usual man is off sick. So I thought I'd treat myself to a pizza. Great place I know up the street called Franco's. Have you been there?"

"Well, I…"

"Have you eaten? It would be lovely to have some company."

I chose the pizza Sophia Loren and Sally the pizza calabrese. The waiter's eyebrows shot up when he saw me back again but to my relief all he said was, "Hello again, sir," before escorting us to a table in the window. He pulled out Sally's chair, dusted it with a cloth and sat us down as though we were celebrities dining at the Savoy.

"Gosh," Sally said. "You're obviously a regular customer. Have you been in recently?"

"Fairly recently," I said. "Would you like some wine?"

"Better not. I've got another lesson later on."

Relieved, I ordered soft drinks for us both.

Sally said, "So it is true. You have lost your job."

"Yes, I'm a man of leisure. Not a care in the world."

She smiled. "I don't believe you. I bet you do care. Will you be able to get another one?"

"After a while maybe. I'm not in too great a rush."

She pulled a face. "Well lucky you."

Her skin had a healthy glow, a tan as though she was permanently out in the open air or had recently returned from a foreign holiday. Apart from lipstick, she wore very little make-up. That sweet fragrance which was uniquely hers had drifted over the small space dividing us, causing that weird buzzing sensation at the base of my neck to start up again.

She said, "Your face looks better."

"Yes, thanks to you."

She shrugged modestly and I said, "Have you just been on holiday?"
She looked surprised.

"Holiday? No, why?"

"Well, you look so tanned."

She shook her head and laughed. "I'll let you into a secret," she said. "Unlike you, I'm not a person of leisure. I can't afford a holiday."

"But how…?"

"Purely cosmetic," she said.

I was silent for a while, then said, "I thought company directors were always whizzing off around the world. So you haven't you got a private yacht then?"

"I'm afraid not."

"Not even a jet plane?"

She leaned back in her chair, smiling. "Not even a bike! Do you mind slumming it with such a down and out?"

"Well, it's not quite what I'm used to."

The waiter arrived with the food and drinks. Sally sipped at her glass and said, "When I bought the driving school I had a three-year plan. Two years of solid hard work building up the business then in the third year, a little bit of relaxation. That meant holidays and pampering myself a bit."

"And how's the plan going?" I asked.

"This is year four. Still no holiday. Still no pampering, I'm afraid."

I forced a chunk of Sophia Loren down. "What went wrong?" I asked.

Again that little shrug of the shoulders before she answered. "Three months after I started the business, the British School of Motoring opened up just across the street. Huge plush office. Big advertisements in the press. We couldn't compete. They even managed to lure away two of my instructors."

"Wow, Sally," I groaned. "That's terrible. How are you managing?"

"Oh, don't worry. We're struggling along. We're not folding up or starving. It's just not as lucrative as I'd hoped." She shrugged. "Oh gosh. This isn't a sob story. Everything's perfectly all right, honestly."

"I hope so," I said and held up my glass. "To the Sally Russell School of Motoring. May they fend off all comers."

She raised her glass. "To the High Street Job Centre. May they come up with the goods for you."

For a while we concentrated on the food. My second Sophia Loren (hot and spicy) seemed even more voluptuous than the first but I chewed manfully on feeling at any moment soon I would burst at the seams. For a small women Sally had a healthy appetite. She was well into her pizza while I had only managed a couple of slices. She dug in enthusiastically, looking up at me occasionally with that warm smile of hers.

Eventually she put down her knife and fork, dabbed her mouth with a serviette and said, "Do you mind if I ask you a question?"

I wondered what was coming. "No, not at all," I said. "Fire away."

"Why did you dash off the other day?"

"Dash off?"

She nodded, once again attacking her pizza. "It was a most peculiar day to say the least. Mike invited me round for tea, which was lovely. I met you, lovely again. Then suddenly you gulp down a boiling hot cup of tea and rush off as though we both had the plague. But it wasn't only you. After you'd gone, Mike was in a very agitated state, pacing up and down, not talking, absolutely preoccupied by something that was on his mind. Seemed like he couldn't wait to get rid of me, so I went home." She looked up at me and shrugged. "Maybe I was just imagining things, but I must admit I have been puzzled about it ever since."

I knew exactly why Paterson had been pacing up and down. He'd just found out that his meek little next-door neighbour was a triple murderer and thief. I decided to give excuses for my own bad behaviour first. I told her how I had felt in the way, felt conspicuous by my battered appearance, thought that she and Mike would have wanted to be alone.

Sally laughed. "So that was it. Well, you daft bat. You needn't have scooted off like that. Mike and I are only friends. He's a client. A really nice man but there's nothing more than that, honestly. No hearts and flowers or violins playing." She flashed that wonderful shy smile again. "Thanks though, it was sweet of you."

There may not have been any violins playing in Sally Russell's life at that moment but a full orchestra was suddenly creating the most wonderful sounds in mine. The news that Sally was not attached emotionally to Mike Paterson had magically lit the room. The pizzeria had vanished. We *were* in the Savoy and an orchestra of violins was in full swing. Feelings of disloyalty to my friend clamoured for attention along with those of euphoria but after all, it wasn't my fault that Mike's romantic feelings for Sally were not reciprocated.

"Why was Mike behaving in that peculiar fashion though? The pacing up and down, I mean."

I tried hard to think of a believable explanation. Then said, "I got the feeling that perhaps he was a little jealous of all the attention you were giving me and my bruises."

Her face suddenly fell. "Oh dear, I hope not." Then after a moment, "I'd hate to think I'd been leading him on, giving him false hopes. I don't want to hurt him."

I said, "Well, I don't think I'd be giving away any secrets if I was to say he is fairly keen."

She slumped suddenly, her chin in her hands, staring dismally down at her plate.

"Oh shit!" she moaned. This was the first time I had heard her swear and it came as such a surprise that it made me laugh.

"It's not funny, Eddie. I hate the thought of Mike being hurt."

"Me too," I said. "I wasn't laughing at that. I'm sorry."

She looked up at me. "Oh hell. Why can't people be content to be just good friends. I like Mike. He's warm and

161

friendly, but he was lonely and I responded to that. That's why we meet, because of his loneliness." She shook her head with a sudden frown of annoyance on her face. "Oh, who am I kidding? I suppose I was lonely too."

As I watched her, it seemed to me that her features were constantly changing. One second her face would be that of a shy, young woman and then, in the next, a maturity would emerge, the vague suggestion of a line around the mouth, a crinkle near the corners of her eyes. There seemed to be an amazing mobility about her that came from within. An animation behind the eyes as though all kinds of turbulent emotions were flying around inside her head and yet on the outside, she was still and serene. She caught me staring at her and I looked quickly down at my meal.

After another minute or two had been given over to eating, she leaned forward and said, "Talking about hurting people, would your wife be cross if she saw you with me now?"

I thought about this for a moment, then said, "Well, at least she'd think it normal. I think she'd be angry on the outside, relieved on the inside."

"You've lost me there."

"She's got it into her head that Mike and I are having an affair!"

"Mike and you? Whatever made her think that?" She giggled into her serviette. "Have you two been caught cuddling in the kitchen?"

"No, but she says Mike's moustache tickles her ear when I bring him to bed with us!"

Sally threw back her head and laughed. It was a lovely sound, not raucous, but gurgly and terribly feminine. She leaned forward wiping her eyes and then her face took on the serious mature woman look again.

"I'm sorry you've got problems. I mean between you and your wife."

"It takes two. I have a feeling that I'm not very easy to live with."

She squinted through narrowed eyes, giving me a long sustained scrutiny, then said, "There can't be anything gay about a man who orders a Sophia Loren pizza."

Or two I thought, but said, "I'll drink to that," and raised my glass again.

The meal progressed pleasantly for another half an hour. I managed with great effort to see off Sophia Loren number two, while Sally told me about her husband Malcolm, who had died of cancer a few years ago, and about her two children, Nicholas and Katie, both of whom had chosen to live abroad. They wrote regularly but for financial reasons couldn't visit very often. She had not seen either of them for over a year. It was obvious by the way she spoke that she missed them a lot.

They had moved from Reading to London six months after her husband had died and for a short while she had taken up secretarial work for an accountancy firm in Charing Cross Road, an old established firm run by old established accountants, which soon established old established boredom. When the children left she decided she had to make some changes and invested the small amount of money she had accrued from her husband's insurance into the driving school.

She was now decorating the flat that she rented up near the park and although not making as much money as she had with the accountancy firm, was a good deal happier.

Soon, if the pressure of work allowed, she hoped to join the local Amateur Dramatic Society and perhaps start playing tennis again. She looked slightly embarrassed as she told me this.

"It'll be a way of getting to know people," she said. "Crazy, isn't it? I've been here four years and hardly know a soul."

Not just crazy, I thought. Astounding was the word to describe such an attractive woman having so few friends.

What I can't understand is if the driving school business is doing badly, how come you've got this pressure of work?"

She laughed and wagged a finger at me.

"Ah, a neat bit of detective work there, Holmes. As a matter of fact I do a bit of freelance typing." I must have looked puzzled so she explained. "You know, computer work, emails, self-employed people need that kind of work done from time to time and they come to me. It's very handy. I couldn't get by without it."

I was about to ask why she didn't just sell up the driving school when she looked at her watch, slapped her forehead with the palm of her hand and cried, "Good grief! Look at the time. I've got a client in three minutes."

"Ooops. That's my fault for nattering too much," I said. "I didn't even get you a coffee." She stood up. "I'm sorry Eddie." She started to fumble in her purse. "I'll have to run. Don't think me rude."

"Of course not." I put my hand over her purse and said, "Don't worry about that. It's been my pleasure."

She leaned over and kissed my cheek. "Bless you, thanks. Sorry about this," she said over her shoulder and then was gone.

I watched her go, my cheek still tingling from the unexpected kiss which was at that moment a pleasure equal to having thirty million pounds' worth of gold hidden in my garden wall.

The waiter appeared at my side. "Would you like some coffee, sir?"

I shook my head. "No thanks."

"Perhaps another pizza Sophia Loren?"

We both laughed and I followed the man over to the till where I paid the bill.

Afterwards as I pushed my wire trolley and bloated stomach around Tesco's supermarket and tried to recall what had been said during the period we'd spent together. I started to worry that, in my enthusiasm to get to know Sally better, my part of the conversation had been all questions. A bit like the third degree. She probably thought I was too nosey. Maybe there hadn't really been a client and she hadn't really had to rush off but wanted to get away. Just like the old me. By the time I reached home with my groceries, my lunchtime euphoria had changed to a feeling of inadequacy and depression.

I opened the front door and carried the bags into the house. Miriam had been there in my absence and had cleared out all her things plus a sizeable amount of furniture and knick-knacks. Somehow, this seemed to cheer me up considerably.

*****

Paterson did not return home until nearly midnight. I had been waiting in the bay window, growing increasingly worried as the time went by. But at last, the big man had appeared in the light cast by the lamp to the side of my front door. I hurried to the door like a mother waiting for her daughter's return after a first date. We spoke in whispers until the door was closed and Paterson was safely in the house.

"Thank heavens. I thought something had happened to you," I said. "Come on in. Would you like a coffee or something?" Mike walked into the kitchen and threw himself down on a chair. "To hell with coffee," he said. "Haven't you any Champagne?"

"Come on," I said eagerly. "Out with it. Have we got something to celebrate?"

"I'm not speaking till something in a glass suitable for the occasion is put in my hand."

"It'll have to be cooking sherry or whisky."

He didn't say anything, just looked at me with one eye closed. I brought two glasses and a bottle of whisky I'd bought that afternoon.

"Come on," I said, "don't keep me waiting any longer. What happened?"

"Guess how much?" Mike said gleefully.

"Thirty?"

"Nope."

"Fifty?"

"Try again."

"Oh, for God's sake, Mike!"

"Three hundred thousand pounds," Paterson said dramatically.

I sat down with a thump on the chair. I couldn't speak. My jaw had dropped and become temporarily out of order. I watched Mike put the leather briefcase on the table, open it, and take out the largest amount of twenty pound notes I'd ever seen in my life. They were in wads of five hundred pounds each, tied by an elastic band. Paterson, with a huge grin on his face, started tossing them one by one on to the table in front of me. The pile grew and as it did, so did my eyes. Eventually I found my voice again.

"Now that somehow looks better than jewellery to me."

Paterson tipped the case up and emptied the remaining bundles onto the pile. A few slipped off and landed on the floor.

"This is only the beginning," he said.

I picked up a bundle of notes and flicked through them. "Are you sure they're real?"

"Don't worry. I was in the Force long enough to know how to check for dud notes. These are the genuine articles all right."

"Tell me what happened. Tell me everything."

Mike told me about the evening with Charlie Webster, the trip across to his home in Eltham, and the haggling he'd done in the tiny bedroom-cum-office. The calls that Webster had made from the telephone that was kept in the drawer. How Webster told him that there would be a bit of a wait.

The bit of a wait had turned out to be almost seven and a half hours, during which time they had left the small office and gone downstairs. It was almost as though he'd been a distant relation or friend who'd popped in. Doreen had lost her worried expression and had become quite animated and chatty. She had cooked them all a meal of steak and kidney pie and chips and a very tasty apple tart with custard. Paterson said he felt like he'd somehow slipped into the cast of a comedy play.

During the telling of his story, Paterson mimicked the voices of Doreen and Charlie. Putting on their facial expressions to suit and also his own when the situation had seemed to border on farce, making me almost fall off my chair with laughter. I dabbed my eyes with a handkerchief.

"What happened after the apple pie?"

"We all sat and watched television."

"Television? I don't believe it."

"It's true," Paterson said. "A terrible quiz programme then an old John Wayne film."

"Go on." I settled my arms on top of the pile of money, my chin cupped in my hands. I felt like a child hearing a bedtime story.

"Well, John Wayne had just shot the man in the black hat when the front doorbell rang. Charlie Webster's front door I mean. Charlie went to the door and I could hear a muffled conversation going on by the front doorstep then the door closed and I heard footsteps going up the stairs. I suspect whomever it was had been taken into Charlie's office. Well, as you can imagine, my attention was no longer with John Wayne. I was in a terrible state of nerves. Doreen's eyes hardly left the screen. Maybe it's the kind of thing that happens most nights at her house. Anyway I sat there for a full hour. It seemed like ten. Then I heard footsteps come back down the stairs, the front door open, a few snatches of conversation, a car go off down the road, then Charlie's head popped around the door, asked me if I'd care to pop up to his office again. It was a kind of 'the dentist will see you now' situation. When I walked into his room again, Webster was transferring all this money from an old plastic dustbin liner into my briefcase." Paterson shrugged. "And in a nutshell, that's it."

"Didn't you see the other man at all?" I asked.

"Nope. But bless his little cotton socks. Look what he brought us."

Mike scooped up a fistful of notes and kissed them happily.

"And what about the gold?"

"Ah, the gold." Mike poured a generous helping of whisky into both glasses. "Well Charlie knows that I'm going to negotiate for a very, very big sum of money for the gold and it's not the kind of sum that he can get hold of quickly by just making a few phone calls. So he has to go through whatever his usual procedure is. Making contacts with buyers, etc. I've given him a week, then I'm going to contact him at his Battersea pub."

"Mike, you've done a fantastic job."

He looked suitably modest, then said, "You do realise we've just let three quarters of a million pounds' worth of stones go for a third of their value."

I nodded. "As far as I'm concerned, this morning I was all but broke, tonight I'm godawful rich. I don't care if somebody else I don't know is even richer." To emphasise the point, I scooped an armful of notes from the table and threw them into the air with a loud "Yee hooooow!" then clutched at Mike's arm. "How shall we celebrate? We ought to have a huge party. A colossal binge."

He shook his head. "Steady now, Ed. That would be the worst thing we could do. We've got to carry on almost as normal. There should be no rushing out and splashing money about. That would only draw attention to ourselves." He thought for a moment then, "I suggest a fairly fantastic dinner for three at the Savoy Grill at the end of the week, Friday perhaps."

"Three?"

"Yes. I'd like to invite Sally."

I thought this was a wonderful idea but I resisted saying so. Instead I asked, "How are we going to explain to her about our new-found wealth?"

"I've already thought of that. It's a lottery win. We needn't say how much, but we'll tell her that I've won a bit of money on the lottery."

I smiled, satisfied. "Terrific. What a brain I'm working with."

We fell silent for a while, then Paterson, looking slightly embarrassed said, "Look Eddie, this is a bit difficult for me but… well, to tell you the truth, I'm not absolutely sure how rich I am."

"Eh?" I was puzzled. "What do you mean?"

"Well the money's yours. You did all the hard work."

I caught his drift. "Don't be daft. You get half. For God's sake, Mike, we're partners."

"But…"

I leaned forward and poked him in the chest with my finger. "No buts. Just remember you're sitting here with a mighty dangerous criminal, so don't argue. You get half. Half of everything."

"Och, you're scaring me to death," he smiled

I started sorting the money into two equal piles. When I had finished I stuffed one of the piles into Mike's briefcase and pushed it across the table.

"Don't spend it all at once."

Mike yawned and rubbed his eyes. "I think I'll go and get some shuteye," he said. "It's been a long day." He watched me, his new partner in crime, shovelling the rest of the loot into a plastic bag.

"What d'ye plan to do with yours?"

"I've given that a bit of thought. I've got an idea in my head but I'm not sure how to set about it."

"Go on."

"I can't forget that I've killed three men. Okay, they were killers themselves but they probably had wives and families. Also there's the guard that got shot in the raid and the policeman. They've got or had families. Well, I want to send them some cash. Anonymously, of course. Just an envelope with a little note in it. Something that can't be traced. They can keep it or hand it to the police. Up to them really. It would... oh, I dunno, just salve my conscience I suppose. Make me feel better."

Mike patted me on the shoulder. "You're a good man, Eddie Wheatley. I hadn't thought about that side of things." He stood deep in thought for a moment or two. "Could be risky. Let's leave it for a couple of days. I'll try to think out some way of getting their addresses."

"Nothing can compensate for the lives lost but it'll be a small gesture."

"Right." Paterson picked up his case. "I'll give you a knock in the morning. I'm bushed."

I saw him to the door. We grinned conspiratorially at each other and then he disappeared into the darkness.

Before going to bed myself, I took two hundred pounds from the plastic bag and put it into my wallet. I then sealed the top of the bag with a thick elastic band, took it to the fireplace in the dining room and pushed the whole bundle up the chimney. I smiled to himself. Miriam had often complained about the draught from that chimney and how it needed blocking up to keep the central heating from being wasted. Well, she'd be pleased now. Another little job around the home had been successfully completed.

*****

We decided not to tell Sally where we were going or why. It would be a surprise. The only information she was given was that it was a very special evening and she had to dress up. Mike and I had been out and treated ourselves to new suits, shirts, ties and shoes. A taxi had been booked to arrive at Mike's house at seven o'clock and by seven fifteen we were parked outside Sally's flat. She must have been ready and waiting for no sooner had the taxi drawn to a halt than she appeared. My heart gave a little lurch when I saw her. She had put on a bright red dress showing off to full advantage her long and slender neck. Around it was fastened a fine gold chain with a jade pendant which lay just above the scalloped neckline of her dress—a shimmering, silk creation which glinted as she moved and showed off her slender figure. There was a silver bracelet around her wrist set with green opal stones and across her shoulders was a white fur jacket worn like a cape. At that moment, I realised that I was in love with her. It had taken thirty-nine years but at last I knew what that emotion felt like.

Mike climbed out of the cab to open the door and she climbed in and sat next to me, pushing up tightly so that Paterson could squeeze his large frame in on her other side.

"Wow!" she exclaimed. "This is the life. Two gorgeous men for escorts. Eddie, you look super and so do you, Mike."

I said, "And you look terrific too, Sally."

"Thank you," she said, obviously delighted.

Mike gave a little cough and said, "Not just terrific. Absolutely stunning."

The taxi moved off and headed in the direction of the West End. I could feel the warmth of her thigh against mine, her soft upper arm pressed against my shoulder. Her hands, clasped loosely on her knees, were tantalisingly close to mine and I longed to take hold of one of them and intertwine her fingers with mine or to stroke her slender wrist. She was fairly bubbling with excitement.

"Where are we going? Please tell me or I'll burst."

"Sorry," Mike laughed. "It wouldn't be a surprise then would it?"

She turned to me. "Come on, you'll tell me, won't you? I promise not to tell mean old Mike Paterson."

"My lips are sealed."

"Well, will either of you give me a clue?"

Two voices in unison said, "No!"

The taxi wound its way through the evening traffic, passing along the Embankment, up past floodlit St Paul's Cathedral standing imposing and proud amidst the modern shopping precincts and offices which huddled too closely to its walls, then down the hill into Fleet Street and up towards the Strand.

At last we turned left into Savoy Court. A uniformed doorman was opening the door of the cab and we were all stumbling out onto the pavement, Sally making little exclamations of delight and me feeling disappointed that I was no longer squeezed up against her. We watched a play at the Savoy Theatre. A comedy about a woman caught in the eternal triangle of having both husband and lover. There was much to-ing and fro-ing, doors opening and closing, beds being bounced upon and hidden under. Each man trying, but never quite succeeding, to catch the woman in the act of betrayal. The cast worked hard to an appreciative audience, but the eternal triangle theme made me feel a shade uncomfortable, sitting as I was, in the best seats of the stalls beside a woman who I'd fallen in love with and knowing that on the other side of her sat another man who felt the same way.

Afterwards we dined at the Savoy Grill. All three of us intimidated by the amazing opulence and the over-attentive waiters. There seemed to be more waiters than diners. I counted six at our table alone. So it was a relief when, at last the meal was ordered, and we were left to get on with it.

Champagne was ordered and Mike proposed a toast to the most beautiful woman in London, wishing secretly to himself that he was alone with Sally.

"Hear, hear," I said, sharing the same wish.

Sally laughed. "Flattery will get you everywhere."

She clinked glasses with us both then asked, "Now, are you two going to tell me what this is all about?"

Mike said, "Well, you've heard of the lottery...?"

CHAPTER 12

Betrayal

At exactly the same moment that Mike was lying about his lottery win, Doreen Webster was sitting at the table in her kitchen in Eltham filling new numbers onto a lottery form. A born opportunist, she had carried on buying tickets each week for at least ten years, even though she had only won once and that was a measly twenty quid.

This week she had decided that putting down birth dates and ages on the coupon was a waste of time. A change was needed. She had decided to concentrate on the house numbers of friends.

When she was a child, a regular Thursday evening event was the filling in of the football pools coupon. As soon as the tea things had been cleared away her father would sit engrossed with the forecasts produced in his daily paper, studying form, comparing this year's results with last year's and making all manner of checks and calculations before putting pen to paper. Only once did he vary his procedure and that was after he'd had a few drinks, given the pen to Doreen and asked her to put eight crosses in a line. She had only been six years old at the time and her crosses were large and scrawling in the tiny boxes. It was the only time in his whole life that her father had won anything on the pools. Not a large amount but enough to make him feel that his previous efforts had been a total waste of time. From then on it had been little Doreen who had filled in the weekly coupon. Now it was the lottery.

The concentration was interrupted as the door opened and her husband came into the kitchen. He picked up the kettle and filled it at the sink. He was whistling absently and when the kettle was plugged in he stood staring out of the window, whistling and drumming his fingers on the metal draining board. Doreen tried to get back to the lottery but it was no use. Her peace had been shattered. Concentration was impossible. She put down her pen and turned to face her husband.

"What's the problem Charlie?" she said in a resigned, 'come on let's sort it out' kind of voice.

"I've come down to make a cup of tea."

"Twenty-nine years we've been married, Charlie Webster, and throughout that time I've learned if you start that terrible whistle of yours, there's a problem. If you drum your fingers at the same time, that means an even bigger problem. Now tell Doreen what's the matter and we'll try to sort it out."

Webster brought two cups of tea to the table and sat down. The whistling and drumming of the fingers had been Doreen's only clue that her husband was worried. His dark, red-rimmed eyes and anxious expression had not helped a bit because that was how he always looked. He lit a cigarette before speaking.

"Doreen, I've got a problem," he said.

"We've already got that far Charlie. Spit it out."

He took a sip of tea and sucked at his cigarette.

"Remember that bloke who came the other night? Big bloke, stayed for supper and watched telly with us."

"The policeman?"

He looked surprised. "Yeah, that's the bloke. Well he's been retired for years. Not a copper now. Strayed from the straight and narrow he has. That's why he came to see me." He stared down at his cup, nervously flicking the ash from his cigarette into the saucer.

"Well? Go on."

Webster said, "Doreen love, because of a little transaction him and me did that night, you and me have come into quite a bit of money. I mean real money."

"So, what're you worrying about? It sounds smashing."

Webster spread his hands flat on the table and started drumming with his fingers again. She put her hands over his.

"Come on Charlie."

"Have you heard of the Fletton Stewart bullion job?"

She stared at him. A feeling of apprehension creeping up her spine. "How deep are you into that?"

He looked into her eyes. "Oh, don't worry. I wasn't in on the job. I don't know the first thing about it. Only what I read in the papers or picked up in the Plume of Feathers in Battersea."

"Well?"

"Well, I've just done a deal, a very nice little deal with the stones from that job. I got them fairly cheap and I've sold them for double what I paid. That's fine. All hunky-dory. I'm not worried about that side of things. Nobody can trace the deal back to me. It's the other stuff I'm bothered about. The gold bullion."

"Charlie, you're not going to touch that stuff," she said, a note of panic in her voice. "There's already been all that killing. You'll get yourself hurt."

"Well, I've half promised I would shift it."

"Don't be so bloody daft!"

He squeezed her hand. "Don't worry, Doreen. I've changed my mind. I'm not going to touch the gold. It's too big for me. I can see that now. But what do I do? I mean now that I know?"

"How do you mean?"

"Well, do I just forget thirty million pounds' worth of business or do I try to get a little reward for my bit of information?"

She looked at him incredulously. "You mean the police?"

"No. Don't be so stupid. If I put it about that I know something, whoever nicked the stuff in the first place might want to pay quite a bit of money to get his hands back on it. Stands to reason, doesn't it?"

Doreen looked thoughtful. "But what if they find out you've made a lot of money out of their stolen jewels?"

"I told you, nobody will be able to trace them back to me. All they need to know is I've picked up a bit of information about the gold bullion and I'm willing to sell it for a certain price."

"Hmm, what about your ex-policeman friend?"

"That Doreen, my love, is what you might call my moral dilemma."

A look of intense annoyance appeared on her face. She leaned forward and helped herself to one of his cigarettes.

"I'll tell you something, Charlie Webster. If I'd know what he'd been up to when he came here I wouldn't have let him into the house."

"Er, why not?"

"Two innocent blokes killed at Fletton Stewarts and you ask why not? That man's a bloody murderer. I hope the original thieves do catch him and give him what for."

Webster laughed. "Aren't you forgetting something? Three of those thieves 'ave been found dead."

"Well," she said huffily. "Whoever did that is just as bad. I haven't got time for any of their kind."

Her husband gazed out of the window for a time taking little, short puffs at his cigarette and whistling quietly his little tune.

Doreen broke his thoughts. "Will it be worth your while?"

"I wouldn't give that kind of information away for nothing. Not by a long chalk."

"Well, I don't see as how you've got a problem."

The conversation was over as far as she was concerned. She started work again on her lottery numbers. Webster stood up and kissed his wife on the forehead.

"What would I do without you to help me sort things out, Doreen?"

She patted his hand and he walked from the room. Upstairs in his little office, Webster took a battered old London telephone directory off the windowsill and carried it to his desk. He skimmed through the pages until he found what he was looking for. There were a lot of Patersons but only three prefixed by the letter 'M'. One of them lived in Mayfair, another in Knightsbridge and the other in the East End. The last one had to be it. He jotted the address down on a pad of paper, then reaching into one of the drawers in the desk he took out a well-thumbed red notebook. He skimmed through the list of names and telephone numbers until he found the number he wanted.

Lastly, he took a mobile phone from the bottom drawer in the desk and with his hand trembling, nervously dialled the number.

After a few seconds, the phone at the other end was picked up and a voice said, "Smart Removals. How can I help?"

*****

"Try to look as though you're enjoying it. Smile for heaven's sake." Carrie Donaghue pointed her mobile and took a couple of shots, then said, "You look terrified."

"I *am* terrified, that's why." Miriam was standing rigidly with both arms outstretched, three bright green parakeets on one arm, four on the other and one on her head. She was trying hard to smile but it was more like a grimace, an 'Oh my God, I'm about to be pooped on!' kind of smile. In her part of London there were not many birds apart from a few drab grey pigeons and certainly no parakeets. This spot by the Serpentine was particularly popular for visitors walking in Kensington Gardens where these colourful and comparatively recent immigrants to the UK congregated in their hundreds, lured by bread, nuts and other tasty morsels offered by tourists as payment for the many photographs they were happy to pose for. Carrie put the phone in her pocket and shooed the birds off.

"Were you scared they might poop on your coat or whisk you off to Africa?" she asked.

"Both," Miriam replied with a sigh of relief. "They're beautiful… but best from a distance. I know where I am with a good old British pigeon."

It was another hot day with not a cloud in the sky. The park was bustling with activity. Walkers, cyclists, skate boarders, joggers, all doing their own thing amongst multitudes of ducks, swans, moorhens and geese doing theirs.

The two friends carrying their coats over their arms weaved a path through all the scrounging birds towards a café beside the water. They bought coffees and parked themselves on a bench which was shaded by a massive willow tree.

"This is great," Miriam sighed. "Why haven't I done this before?" She stretched her arms along the back of the bench and murmured dreamily, "I think I'll move to Kensington."

"In your dreams!" Carrie snorted. "Go look in any estate agent's window around here and see what they're asking for a one-bedroomed flat."

"Aw, don't spoil it. I can fantasise if I like."

"Okay, but make sure to hire a butler."

"Mmm," Miriam said. "Brad Pitt will do."

Carrie was wearing a pair of large round-lensed sunglasses. She took them off and perched them on Miriam's nose. "Here," she said, squinting into the sunlight. "They'll stop you hurting your eyes." Miriam turned to look at her. "But what about you?"

"Hey. They really suit you. You look great."

"What about y…"

"Aw heck. Don't worry about me. I've got this hat." She pulled the brim of her bright yellow sunhat down over her eyes.

They sat for a while not speaking and just soaking up the sun, then Miriam said, "Y'know something, Carrie Donaghue?"

"Uh huh?"

"I feel like Lazarus… just come back from the dead."

"How come?"

Miriam said nothing for a few seconds then, "It's like I've just been released from prison. As if some great weight has been lifted from my shoulders. What have I been doing with myself? All those wasted years hoping things would get better." She waved her arm at the scene in front of them. "Look at where we are. Look at what we're doing. This is fun. Why haven't I done this before? Till a couple of days ago the only activity I did was walk to the shops. Oh God. I've been such a fool."

Carrie smiled sympathetically, reached across and squeezed her hand. Miriam turned to look at her again. "You've opened a window for me Carrie, and let the sunshine in. You're a true pal. It's a bit late now but I've come to realise that Eddie hasn't been a husband to me, more of a millstone around my neck." She gave a little laugh, then added "… and I dare say I've probably been an even heavier one around his."

A grey squirrel scampered across the path in front of them and climbed up a tree on the other side of the path. Another one appeared from the branches just above and they chased each other around the trunk.

Miriam said, "Boredom and monotony can be habit-forming I guess and after a while acceptance creeps in. I should've walked out a long time ago or maybe, even better, wrung his neck."

"Well at least he wasn't a drunk," Carrie said.

"Ha. There's always a first time." Miriam told her about Eddie's drunken outburst when her parents had come for Sunday lunch then stopped abruptly when she noticed her friend was trying not to giggle.

"What's so funny?" she said.

"I'm sorry honey," Carrie said trying to pull a straight face but not succeeding. "It's like a scene from a sitcom. Posh lunch, everybody on their best behaviour, pinkies raised, Sinatra crooning quietly in the background, polite, terribly English conversation going on then, Pow! In comes the villain puking over everybody before deciding to have a nap in the ruins of your best Sunday tea service."

Miriam tried to suppress a smile but couldn't and said, "Well it wasn't funny at the time."

"Just shows we have a lot in common. You had a harmless drunk and I had a violent one."

"Yes, but then mine turned out to be gay."

"You really do have a thing about homosexuals, don't you?" Carrie said.

"I suppose I do. Especially men. I think what they do is disgusting."

Carrie sighed and said, "Miriam, honey. You really ought to loosen up a bit. This is the twenty-first century, for God's sake. We're all different. Live and let live." She stood up. "C'mon," she said. "This is getting too heavy. We're gonna cheer ourselves up with a spot of lunch. Just down the road I know of a great pub. What d'ya say?"

"But—"

"No buts. If Doctor Donaghue prescribes something that's good for you, don't argue. Right now she's prescribing a pub lunch. Now get your ass off that bench. If we're lucky we'll get a table outside."

It took them twenty minutes to get to the pub which was in one of the quieter streets just behind the Royal Albert Hall and sure enough, they were lucky. An outside table was vacated just as they arrived. Here they spent a very pleasant two hours during which Carrie managed to steer her friend away from her marital problems and told her about an article she'd been commissioned to write for one of the Sunday supplements and how she had considered getting herself a cat for some company. They both chose a ploughman's lunch which was washed down by a fairly decent Chardonnay.

Miriam was in a state of euphoria. This was the new Miriam. A happy, vibrant Miriam who had shed the dry husk of the cocoon she'd been trapped in for so long and was at last spreading her wings. They drove back to East London singing along to pop songs on the radio.

That evening they sat on the settee back at the flat nibbling crisps and watching a film they'd chosen together on Netflix. Miriam felt she was glowing. A warm feeling of contentment flowed through her veins accompanied by quite a lot of alcohol. Carrie had opened a bottle of full-bodied claret but who cared? Marlon Brando was in front of her doing his stuff in *The Godfather*, which was one of her all-time favourite films, so what more could she want? All was well with the world. Life was good.

There is a scene in the movie where the young Michael Corleone has to shoot a rival Mafiosi boss and a corrupt cop which, no matter how many times she had seen it, always made her heart thump. She found herself clutching Carrie's hand and found it comforting to hold on to it until the film ended.

Carrie picked up the remote and switched the TV off. "What a film," she sighed. "It gets better every time I see it."

"Me too. Heck. I must've seen it at least three times." Miriam gave another long sigh of contentment and glanced around the room. "It's been great staying here for the last couple of days," she said. "But I don't want to outstay my welcome. I'll sort something out tomorrow." Carrie had her arm resting on the back of the settee and was twirling a lock of Miriam's hair between her fingers. She gave the hair a gentle tug and said, "Sweetheart, I've loved having you here. You've been great company. There's no rush. It's been fun hasn't it?"

"Not just fun, it's been magic. A real tonic." Miriam glanced at her watch. "Good grief," she exclaimed. "Look at the time. It's nearly one thirty." She turned to face her friend.

"Thanks, Carrie. You made today very special. I'll never forget your kindness. You've been wonderful."

Carrie leaned closer and whispered in Miriam's ear. "I think you're pretty wonderful too."

For a long moment Miriam stared into Carrie's eyes. Their noses were almost touching. An unaccustomed tingling was welling up in her stomach. It had been a long time since she'd had physical contact with another human being but she recognised the feeling. It was desire. She glanced down at the full lips so close to her own, wanted to pull away but found that she couldn't and instead moved hesitantly forward and pressed her lips to Carrie's. It was meant to be just a peck but then Carrie's arms were wrapped around her and she felt their tongues collide and something akin to an electric shock charged along the length of her spine. Suddenly she wanted more and she grasped her friend's face in her hands and crushed her lips against Carrie's with an almost desperate urgency, then pulled away again gasping, "Oh God, I'm sorry. I'm sorry. This is wrong, what am I doing?"

Carrie said, "If it's wrong, Miriam honey, it's a very nice wrong."

She pulled Miriam closer and they kissed again, this time a softer, more prolonged kiss. For a while they sat, foreheads touching, Miriam staring, with a mixture of astonishment and longing, into Carrie's eyes. She opened her mouth to speak but Carrie put a finger softly against her lips. "You just asked what you were doing," she whispered. "Well I'll tell you what you're not doing... you're not sleeping on that crappy camp bed tonight."

*****

Three o'clock in the morning. It had started to rain and the windows of the house had steamed up. The place was in darkness but from a lamppost further down the street enough light penetrated the windows of the uncurtained room to pick out the silhouette of a man standing staring out into the darkness. He stood completely still, only standing back when he imagined he'd seen some movement or the lights of a car way up the street. There was another man in the room. He sat in a big soft armchair beside the fireplace, his feet resting on the seat of a similar chair opposite. He too was still. The only movement was that of his eyes, which moved from time to time towards the window where his companion stood.

An old Victorian school clock ticked comfortably on the wall beside the fireplace, a slight smell of pipe tobacco tainted the air and there was about the room an air of cosiness and tranquillity, which was to last but briefly.

The man at the window moved further back into the room. A vehicle was moving slowly up the street towards the house.

"This could be it," Haslitt said in a low voice. Frank Thomson got out of the chair and joined the big man beside the curtains. They watched a taxi pull up directly outside and two men climb out on to the pavement.

A mumble of voices, the chink of coins. The taxi moved off and the two men stood laughing and talking in whispers to each other. At last they split up and the smaller of the two walked away into the darkness.

The other man opened the gate and walked slightly unsteadily up the path towards the front door.

Haslitt moved quickly into the hallway. Thomson following standing behind the big man, pressing himself to the wall beside a heavy, mahogany coat stand. The door opened and Paterson stumbled into the hallway, burping and giggling to himself, fumbling for the light switch, muttering under his breath when it didn't work, turning and bolting the door, humming a little tune—and then retching and gasping for air as Haslitt's enormous fist slammed into his stomach.

They dragged him into the tiny sitting room and threw him into one of the armchairs. Thomson drew the curtains and switched on the overhead light, then casually walked back across the room and sat on the other chair. Haslitt remained standing behind Paterson. They waited patiently for the late-night reveller to get his breath back, the brick-red face to return to normal and the bulging, astonished eyes to regain their focus. It took a full three minutes, by which time the face colour had changed to ashen white. Paterson wanted badly to be sick but the nausea had subsided just in time. Slowly his blurred vision righted itself and the room came back into focus. He stared bewildered at the elegant-looking man with the silver hair sitting comfortably in the armchair opposite him. Suddenly annoyed, he tried to get up but a strong hand from behind grabbed him by the hair and wrenched him painfully back into his seat. A cold tinge of fear crept swiftly up his spinal column.

What are you doing in my house?" he gasped. "What do ye want?"

Thomson spoke slowly and matter-of-factly, like a headmaster addressing a wayward schoolboy.

"Mr Paterson. I want you to listen very carefully. You've put me and a number of colleagues to a great deal of inconvenience. The fact is you have stolen an enormous amount of gold bullion and jewellery which belonged once to the Fletton Stewart Security Company and now belongs to me. You have killed three men who were in my employment and you have caused the gentleman behind you considerable pain and discomfort. We now know where you disposed of the jewellery, and that matter is being dealt with. I want to know where you have hidden the gold. Before you start your denials, Mr Paterson, I must tell you that delaying telling us will be extremely painful for you. My colleague, who is standing behind you, will hit you and continue to hit you until you divulge the necessary information. It would be so much more convenient for us and for your good health if you were sensible, don't you think?"

Paterson turned his head, caught a glimpse of the big man with his tight curly hair standing menacingly behind him and spluttered, "I don't know what you—" His voice was cut off in mid-sentence by Haslitt's fist crashing down between his neck and shoulder making him gasp in agony and sink further down in the chair, a hot searing pain stabbing across his shoulder blades and down his back.

The other two men again waited patiently for him to recover after which Thomson leaned down beside the armchair and picked up Paterson's leather briefcase. He laid it on his knee and patted it.

"We found this upstairs, Mr Paterson, in your wardrobe. One hundred and fifty thousand pounds. My, my, is that all Charlie Webster would give you? I think you could've done better than that. How much were you going to ask for the bullion? Not much of a businessman are you, Mr Paterson."

He smiled at Paterson's defeated expression.

"You see, we know everything, Mr Paterson. Everything that is apart from where you have put the gold. Now, perhaps you would oblige by telling me."

Paterson closed his eyes and thought about Charlie Webster. Charlie Webster, the Judas. Nice, friendly Charlie Webster with all that warm hospitality. His cosy little wife, steak and kidney pie and television set, Charlie Webster who had feathered his nest to the tune of thousands of pounds then turned round and stabbed its provider in the back.

At that point he wanted to tell them. Wanted to get them off his back. After all, it was Eddie Wheatley who had stolen the stuff, not him. Eddie who had killed the three men. He felt tired and extremely scared. His heart was hammering and his shoulder felt numb from Haslitt's heavy fist. If he told them they would surely leave him alone. Why should be he the one to put up with the pain? Mentally he put Eddie into his own position. How long would he be able to endure this treatment? Not long he guessed. The man had already has his fair share of punishment at the beginning of this whole sorry mess. He surely would not be able to take any more. A picture of Eddie's battered face came into his mind. Friendly, trusting Eddie Wheatley who had insisted on giving him half the money. Eddie, who had endured so much. How could be betray him at the first obstacle?

Thomson was starting to look impatient. Paterson held up his head.

"Please," he said, playing for time. "Don't hit me again. I'll tell you. I'll tell you." He turned his head and looked up imploringly at Haslitt. Twisting slowly back to face Frank Thomson, taking in as he did so the fact that his heavy walking stick was propped in its usual place beside the fireplace where he had left it before going to the Savoy.

"We're waiting, Mr Paterson."

"Well, you see…" Paterson threw himself out of the chair, driving his fist hard at Thomson's face. Too slow, too damned slow. Age had slowed him down. Thomson was too quick, ducking to one side, letting Paterson's punch ram harmlessly into the armchair.

He grabbed Paterson's lapel but the old man had the walking stick in his hand by now and brought it down with a crack against his wrist. Paterson turned, swinging the stick in despair at where he thought Haslitt would be, catching the big man a heavy blow on his upper arm, who came like a bull from behind the chair. Haslitt grunted in pain and ducked as the stick swung again, missing the top of his head by a fraction. The next swing caught Thomson on the hip, making him cry out with pain and then Paterson was making for the door, his breath coming out in great rasping sobs, his face contorted by fear and desperation.

He reached the door, opened it and would have escaped but suddenly he stumbled and fell to his knees. Again his face had changed to a deep red colour and his eyes were bulging as though from a restriction of the throat. The walking stick clattered on to the polished wooden floor of the hallway, while the two other men recovering from the surprise of Paterson's attack, had scrambled across the room, fists raised, ready to resume the fight. Paterson merely coughed and slid forward on his face.

"Get up," snarled Haslitt enraged by the pain in his shoulder. "Get up you old bastard."

The old man lay, unmoving, eyes staring blindly at the carpet.

For a few moments, the three men were still, then Thomson reached down and grasped Paterson's shoulder, pulling him over till he lay on his back. He pressed his ear to Paterson's chest, a look of horror spreading across his face. Abruptly he straightened up and stared pummelling the rib cage of the prostrate form, screaming in a panic stricken voice, "For God's sake. Help me, quickly. He's had a heart attack."

Haslitt took over, squeezing hard down on Paterson's chest, then released the pressure, squeezing down again, releasing the pressure. There was no response.

"Come on, you stupid old sod! Live!" Thomson hissed through his teeth.

He tilted Paterson's head back, pinching the nostrils shut with his fingers, blowing into the still lungs. They persevered for another five minutes but Paterson was dead.

Haslitt lifted the body up by the lapel and spat angrily at the face. "Damn you. Why didn't you wait five more minutes and then die?" He slammed Paterson's body back on to the floor and said, "Christ. Now what are we going to do?"

Thomson got off his knees and walked slowly back to the armchair. He sat down and put his head in his hands. After a while he said, "There's got to be a clue somewhere. Surely he couldn't have been working on his own. He must have had accomplices."

"We searched the house before he got home. There's no gold and no clues." Haslitt was still prowling angrily around the room.

Thomson turned his head and stared gloomily at the body. "Have a look and see if there's anything in his pockets."

Haslitt knelt and went carefully through Paterson's clothing. There was a handful of coins, pipe-cleaners, a pen-knife, a bill from the Savoy, a wallet containing eighty-five pounds, a provisional driving licence and a photograph of a dark-haired woman. They were tossed in disgust on to the floor. Then from the inside pocket of the jacket Haslitt produced a small red book. He flipped through it and looked up with a smile at Frank Thomson.

"We just might have hit the jackpot; it's his diary."

The diary was snatched from his hand. Thomson was leafing anxiously through the pages, his face falling when he saw that a lot of the book was empty with only a few notes scattered throughout the pages, mostly reminders to keep dental appointments, times of driving lessons and other personal trivia, but here and there were snippets of information written in bold, clear handwriting which was more interesting to the two readers. There was nothing written on the date of the killings of Smalley, Winston and Munroe. But on the following day there was a reference to somebody with the initials E.W. It said *'saw E.W. today. Says he's been mugged, probably that wife of his. Poor chap's face a bit of a mess.'*

Later there was another reference to E.W.

"Something funny about what E.W. says. Doesn't ring true. Might have a word."

On another page:

'I was right, confronted E.W. and he's admitted it. Good grief, who would have thought it.'

The last entry was that of three days previously.

'Went to see C.W. Very successful day. E.W. was over the moon. Hope this will be the beginning for Sally and me.'

"C.W. must be Charlie Webster," Haslitt said. "But who the hell is E.W.? Some relation?"

"I doubt it. Charlie wouldn't have shopped a relative of his." He put the diary into his pocket. "I wonder who the little man was. The man who got out of the taxi with Paterson? Did you see where he went?"

"No, I was only watching Paterson. He probably went off again in the taxi."

Haslitt turned and looked through the curtains as though the smaller man they sought might still be out there.

"Might've been E.W. Could've been anybody."

Thomson looked at his watch. He seemed to make up his mind about something, turning quickly and going over to where Paterson lay, "Come on," he said. "Help me get him to bed."

Haslitt stared. "Bed? What are you talking about? He's dead!"

"Precisely. It's important that whoever finds our dear departed Paterson here assumes that all is perfectly normal and the poor old boy died in his sleep. If we leave him as he is, there will be police enquiries, post-mortems and all manner of time-consuming delays before the burial."

"He pointed towards the briefcase. "And that must go back in the wardrobe," he said.

"Have you gone crazy?" Haslitt spluttered.

"Do it. I told you. Everything must stay as it was."

Haslitt did as he was bidden, hoisting the body up underneath the arms whilst Thomson lifted the feet. They carried him towards the stairs.

"A hundred and fifty thousand quid," Haslitt groaned. "I still don't understand. Who cares if the burial is delayed."

"We do Haslitt. Think who might just turn up for the funeral."

"E.W.?"

"Exactly."

*****

It was seven thirty when the alarm clock on the bedside table started its tinny bleeping sounds and almost seven thirty-two before a hand emerged from under the duvet to switch it off. Five minutes later a head emerged. Sally Russell squinted sleepily at the clock and groaned. How could it be time to get up? She disappeared back under the duvet and tried to get back into that nice, warm dream she had been enjoying but whatever the theme had been, it eluded her now and all that she could think of was that if she didn't get up, Mrs K. Robinson of Forest Hill would be late for her driving test.

She climbed out of bed and made her way towards the kitchen. A cup of boiling water with an infusion of lemon was the most important start to any day for Sally Russell and doubly so this morning. Was that tight feeling across her temples the beginnings of a hangover? How much did she drink last night? She tried to remember. Not really very much. The men had consumed most, both in tremendous high spirits. Couldn't blame Mike. Not every day you win the lottery! And Eddie, you'd think that he'd won as well the way he was splashing out on Champagne. She put the kettle on and sliced up a lemon. It had been a really wonderful celebration evening together. Nice of Mike to include her. On reflection it might have been more sensible to break up the party a little earlier. Must have been gone... two thirty before they left. Only intended to have them in for coffee after the trip from the Savoy but inevitably the drinks had come out.

She smiled to herself, thinking how tired and probably hungover they would be. Although what did it matter? Neither of them had work to go to. Not at all bad for Mike Paterson with his pension and his lottery win, but what about Eddie? Strange how he didn't seem to mind being out of work. Maybe he had money saved up. Didn't seem at all bothered that his wife had walked out on him either. She pondered that for a while. What happened there? Mike had told her that Eddie's wife was a very overbearing type of woman but if that was the case, why didn't he leave her, rather than the other way around? It all seemed a bit odd. If they were so incompatible, why did they get together in the first place?

Hard to imagine why any woman would want to leave Eddie. Maybe there was something in his character that she didn't know about. He seemed such a nice man. Quiet, but at the same time good company. He looked so serious and yet suddenly could be so funny. There was no pressure from him, no flirtatiousness, no innuendo, no guile. He was just simply himself. Perhaps a little over-anxious to please, as though he was not used to friendship and was frightened that it would go away, but he was open and honest and behind these qualities she sensed that there was about the man a resoluteness and firmness as though once started on a certain path, nothing would be allowed to get in his way.

She was attracted to him, no doubt about it. She liked his smell. There was definitely some kind of chemistry the man exuded that was compatible with hers. She enjoyed sitting close to him in the taxi. Had felt an almost irresistible urge to kiss his bemused face on that first meeting, when she had played the part of nurse in Paterson's kitchen.

Odd really, how she was always attracted to smaller men. Her first husband, Malcolm, had been on the small side.

Sally took her hot lemon water into the sitting room, wincing at the sight of empty glasses and dirty cups on the coffee table, the smell of Paterson's pipe hung in the air and all the unsightly reminders of a good night cluttered the room. She opened a window and decided to breakfast in the kitchen.

After a shower and a cup of coffee, work in the outside world didn't seem such a bad prospect after all. It was a nice, sunny day and she enjoyed the short walk to work, stopping on the way to pick up tea and biscuits from the shop on the corner and to have her usual chat with the pleasant Pakistani owner.

The instructor, who had been off work sick earlier in the week, had recovered and had turned up for work, so Sally was able to get on with some much neglected bookwork, managing to work without interruption until midday, when the phone rang. She was pleasantly surprised to hear Eddie Wheatley's voice.

"Hi Sally. It's me, Eddie."

"I know. What a surprise. How are you feeling?"

"I'm fine. Listen Sally, I'm afraid I've got bad news…"

*****

At first I had thought that Mike was having a lie-in after our late night out. I'd knocked earlier and then gone away but at eleven fifty-five when hammering on the door and ringing the bell had still not roused a response, I'd become quite anxious. I put my mouth to the opening of the letter box and hollered Mike's name then, when the door moved slightly, I realised it wasn't locked but just wedged shut. I went into the hallway, called his name again, searched the downstairs room then climbed the stairs.

Mike was propped up in bed. Cold and stiff, legs straight, arms under the covers. He looked like a dummy from a tailor's window. Not a man who had died peacefully in his sleep. His head was pressed against the headboard of the bed and his calves and feet spread wide at the foot were the only parts of the body that were touching the bed. It was as though he had had a spasm or heart attack, had raised the centre of his body upwards in pain and rigor mortis had immediately set the body in that position, freezing the open mouth and staring eyes into a look of shock and surprise.

He must have died in great pain. I sat on the bed and looked at the dead stranger who had once been my friend.

"Aw, Mike, Mike, Mike," I said sadly, touching his cold white hand. "Just when things were going to be so good."

I knelt beside the bed and stared at his face, feeling empty and lost. It was hard to associate the grotesque husk before me with the laughing, joking person I'd been with last night. He'd looked so well, he certainly hadn't looked ill. Was it the booze that had seen him off? I tried to remember how much he'd put away but couldn't. Maybe it was the excitement of last night coupled with the tension he must have been under when he went off on his own to sell the jewels.

I patted his hand again. "I'm so sorry, old friend. Why did I let you get mixed up with this? You would be still here if it weren't for me."

I turned away and walked over to the window. Down below was my front garden with its new wall. A feeling of futility and sadness filled my whole being. I felt tears pricking my eyes. "What now, Mike?" I said. "What now?" After a while I left the bedroom, not looking at his body again, preferring to remember him as he was when he was alive. I took out my mobile phone and rang the police, telling them what had happened, explaining that he had been a good friend and neighbour. Yes, I'd be next door if the police needed me and no, I didn't know the whereabouts of any next of kin. Next I rang Sally. She broke down and cried and I cursed myself for not going round to tell her personally.

When we finished talking it occurred to me that the police might arrive at any moment and somewhere in the house was a briefcase containing one hundred and fifty thousand pounds. An amount that would be sure to cause suspicion and lots of awkward questions to answer.

I started on the ground floor and worked my way through all the cupboards and possible hiding places, even checking the chimneys in case Mike had had the same idea as me.

Eventually I found the briefcase in a wardrobe upstairs. The money was still intact and I carried the case with me to my house, transferring the money into another plastic bag and then returning the case back into Mike's wardrobe. The new, full plastic bag was then used as yet another draft preventer. This time in the chimney of the sitting room.

Half an hour later there was a knock on the door and two policemen were standing on the step. They were polite and courteous, asked a few questions about the deceased, told me not to worry, everything would be taken care of, these things did happen. Told me that an ambulance would be calling sometime during the day, thanked me for being a good neighbour and then departed. All so matter-of-fact, all in the line of duty. I felt as though I'd just arranged the collection of some unwanted object that I wanted rid of.

At eight o'clock that evening it struck me that I'd been sitting on the settee for most of the day in a kind of stunned stupor, that I hadn't eaten since early morning and was starving. The contents of the usually well-stocked pantry had been reduced to a few unappetising looking tins and the fridge was keeping perfectly chilled one small piece of cheese and a half-pint of milk. I decided to eat out.

I washed, put on a tie and a jacket and was just going out of the front door when the telephone rang. It was Sally. She was feeling low and just wanted someone to talk to. I told her how I'd spent most of the day sitting staring at the wall.

"Me too. After you telephoned I couldn't carry on working. I took the afternoon off." Her voice faltered. "And last night, I can't believe… it's so awful."

"I wish I'd called round to tell you. I'm sorry."

"Crazy, isn't it?" she said. "You're feeling sad and depressed at your house and me feeling the same way in mine. It's so nice to be talking to you, Eddie. It's better being able to share it all somehow."

"You're right. It is. I should have rung you."

"What are you doing now?"

"Well, the cupboard is bare. I was just on my way out to find something to eat."

"Oh, I see."

I tried to keep the eagerness from my voice and said, "Would you like to join me or have you eaten?"

"As a matter of fact," she said. "I'm busy making myself a curry right now. I know you like spicy foods so if you're hungry, why don't you save yourself some money and share it with me? I owe you a meal."

I pondered the question for at least half a second, thanked her then raced upstairs and got changed again, this time taking extra care, combing my hair, patting aftershave on my cheeks and squinting at my remaining bruises. Ten minutes later I was in a cab heading towards Sally's flat, stopping on the way to buy two bottles of wine.

Her place seemed different to how I remembered it from the previous night. Perhaps I had had too much to drink at the Savoy or maybe it was because the three of us had been so engrossed in conversation that I hadn't taken notice of my surroundings.

There was a bowl of flowers and comfortable soft print armchairs. An oriental rug hung on one wall and another was completely covered by a display of paintings and photographs. There were lots of paperback books stacked on shelves and in an old pine bookcase. A collection of tiny china boxes was laid out on the top of an ancient sewing machine stand and a huge stuffed toy panda sat on a marble pedestal in one corner of the room.

Sally was wearing jeans and a check shirt. Her hair, although short, was dishevelled and I thought she looked pale. Her eyes were tired and I could tell that she had been crying. Still, she gave me a bright smile when I arrived and I followed her into the kitchen which was full of the delicious smells of curry and rice.

"Thanks for coming," she said, pouring me a glass of white wine from a bottle already opened on the work surface.

She nodded at the bottle and smiled. "Cook's perks." I raised my glass. Another reason for the flat seeming different had dawned on me. Last night there had been three people here together, this time only two.

"To absent friends," I said. She nodded solemnly and touched my glass.

"Have you sorted everything out?"

"The police are seeing to it."

"Poor you. It must have been a terrible shock."

I nodded. "Crazy really. We were neighbours for a year and hardly ever spoke apart from saying good morning or nice weather, then in the last couple of weeks I felt that we had become good friends."

"He was very fond of you."

I smiled. "Even fonder of you."

She turned away from me and stirred the contents of a saucepan on the stove. "Are you hungry?"

"If you've cooked a horse, I'll eat it."

We ate in the kitchen at a small round table with a green gingham cloth. The curry was excellent and the wine that I had brought with me complemented the food well.

At first the mood and conversation were solemn, Mike Paterson being at the forefront of our thoughts, but as the evening progressed and the second bottle of wine was all but consumed, the talk veered off in many other directions.

Sally was a good listener as well as an interesting talker. She laughed easily and infectiously and had a way about her that made me feel completely relaxed.

When she got up to make coffee, she asked, "What kind of music do you like Eddie?"

"Oh, Neil Diamond, The Beatles… I quite like jazz."

She took me by the elbow and walked me into the sitting room. In the corner was a slightly battered-looking record player. I was pleased to see she had good old-fashioned vinyl. Underneath the turntable were shelves stacked with long playing records and a few CDs.

"I don't play a lot of CDs," she said. "You're looking at the musical tastes of my youth and middle age, some of which were my dad's. I'd hate not to be able to play them.

I pulled a record from the middle shelf, put *Stan Getz plays Jazz Samba* on to the deck and swung the needle arm round.

The breathy sound of a saxophone filled the room. I turned the sound down slightly as Sally called from the kitchen, "That's one of my favourites." She appeared carrying two cups. "You like jazz then?"

"I like most music apart from opera," I said. That familiar perfume floated with Stan Getz around my head and sent my pulse rate up several notches.

"It's a good job you do," she said. "Practically all of them are jazz." She leaned forward and pulled out half a dozen or so records. "... apart from a bit of Beethoven, Elgar and Beyoncé."

"At least I've heard of Elgar and Beethoven," I said.

"Oh stop. You sound like my dad!" she tutted. "Ever been to the Proms?"

"Nope."

"That's one hell of an experience. You should go."

"Maybe one day I will."

"... and try a Beyoncé concert. You'll be blown away."

I picked up an old and well-thumbed Louis Armstrong LP. Inside the sleeve were lots of photographs of the trumpeter with his band. Some of the man blowing, cheeks like a replete hamster. Some with Bing Crosby and Ella Fitzgerald and others just grinning that famous grin at the camera. There were a few sleeve notes. Sally moved closer to read one of the captions: "Louis Armstrong had a bellyful of music..." she read.

"And a mouthful of pearly white teeth," I said, putting on a gravelly voice. "Why honey lamb, I sometimes blow so hard I'm scared they're all gonna come whistlin' out the end of mah trumpet an kill somebody in the audience."

I turned my head and grinned what I hoped would look like a Louis Armstrong grin. My face was very close to hers. She was giggling at my little joke and as our eyes met I badly wanted to kiss her.

She looked away and said, "Hey, Louis. You're letting your coffee go cold."

I rolled over on my stomach and pulled the cup towards me.

"Y'know something, Sally?"

"Mmmm?"

"Well this might seem strange, I dunno, heartless even. I don't mean it that way. I'm really upset about Mike dying like he did and tonight I know I should feel terrible about it…" I paused, groping for the words, then blurted, "Well it shouldn't be but tonight's one of the nicest nights I can remember."

Sally sitting cross-legged on the floor beside me put her cup down slowly and said, "Y'know something, Eddie?"

"Mmmm?"

"Me too."

I pulled myself up and moved closer to her. I felt like a child on Christmas Day. My stomach was fluttering and I had a strange tingling sensation in the back of my neck. I said, "Would it spoil things if I kissed you?"

She shrugged and smiled. "I won't really know till you give it a try."

Stretching forward I put my mouth against hers. A light peck at first, lips barely touching. Her mouth was cool and moist and her warm breath and sweet fragrance made my head spin. I felt as though I'd suddenly become a character in a Barbara Cartland novel, but believe me that lady knew what she was writing about because that's how it was.

I reached up and put my hand under the thick black hair at the back of Sally's neck and pulled her gently towards me. Our lips touched again, this time with more intensity. Now we were both kneeling and I felt her arms go around me. We were locked together and my heart soared with the closeness of her body and her soft sweet-tasting lips pressed against mine.

I moved my head away, cupped her small face in my hands and kissed her eyes and nose then back to her mouth, feeling her tongue against mine and her fingernails against my neck.

Gently I pushed her down until she was lying on the carpet. She pulled my face down to hers and kissed me fiercely again, filling my whole being with sensations that I had never experienced before. She must have felt my arousal. Something I couldn't hide and Barbara Cartland never wrote about.

"I've loved you, Sally," I said. "Ever since that first day. Don't ask me to go home tonight."

She pulled way and looked me in the eyes. "Just you try getting away," she said.

*****

The police had managed to trace Mike Paterson's only remaining relative. A sister of about sixty-five years. Tall, like her brother, but thin and angular with a very modern medium cut hairdo that swept across her forehead like a dove's wing. She spoke without a trace of a Scottish accent. Her name was Moira Fanshaw and she lived somewhere in Kent. She turned up one morning with her husband, Trevor, a retired draughtsman with a florid face, a goatee beard and a very pronounced pot belly. They were here, they said, to sort out her late brother's affairs.

They knocked at my door and thanked me for everything that I'd done after finding Mike's body and I invited them in for a cup of tea. The old lady was visibly distressed by her brother's death although she said that they had not seen each other for many years. Her brother, she told me, would be cremated on the following Thursday and she would be pleased if I came along.

Trevor seemed only to have two words in his vocabulary which he used over and over again. "Terrible business," he'd say, shaking his head. "Terrible business."

After they'd gone I was washing the cups in the kitchen when I heard someone enter the house by the front door. I thought, *Who's got a key? Who the hell is this?*

I walked into the hall. Miriam was hanging her coat on the hall stand. I stood there for a moment, dumbfounded. I didn't know what to say. She seemed a stranger in the house.

This was my wife. The person whom I'd shared so many years with turning up like some remote and distant acquaintance. I realised with a twinge of shame that I'd not given her a thought since our telephone conversation a few days ago.

"Ah," she said. "You're in at last."

"Hello Miriam. Would you like some tea?"

"I've been trying to contact you," she said coldly. "Don't you answer the phone?"

I turned and walked back into the kitchen. "I've been out quite a lot. Would you like some tea?"

"Yes. I think we'd better," she said. "There's a lot to talk about."

She followed me into the kitchen, rubbing a forefinger along the top of the work surface as she did so, disappointed perhaps that not too much dust was evident. For a few seconds she wandered around the room touching cupboards, peering out of the window, then settled herself at the kitchen table and waited while I brought her a cup of tea. I sat down opposite her and put on a smile.

"And how are you, Miriam?"

"I'm fine." She was fiddling with her teaspoon in the sugar bowl and I was surprised to realise that she was nervous. I waited patiently. Eventually she said, "Eddie, I'm afraid this will come as a bit of a shock to you but I want a divorce." She was right—it was a shock. I sat speechless, trying to keep the pleased look off my face.

"A divorce?" I said.

She nodded. "Let's be honest Eddie. We're not suited. Things have never been completely right between us." She looked up at me. "I need someone that I can talk to, someone who's not all the time trying to escape." She hesitated, then said, "I think you know what I'm saying is true."

I nodded. "What are you going to do?"

There was a long pause. "Promise not to get annoyed, Eddie, but I'm going to do your old job. You must know you've burnt your boats with Daddy. Well, I'm going to fill the gap you've left at Hislop's. A woman is quite capable of doing the job you know."

"Easily," I said.

Miriam started fiddling with her teaspoon again. "And there's somebody else," she said.

"Somebody else?"

"Yes. I'd rather not talk about it at the moment Eddie, but there is somebody else in my life. We only get one life Eddie, and it's not right that I should spend time with someone who makes me unhappy."

I was astonished. "That was quick," I said.

She shrugged. "These things happen."

A picture of Sally sprang into my mind, lying sleeping, her hair black upon the white pillow.

"I suppose they do," I said.

I found I was filled with genuine happiness for Miriam. Everything she said was true. We certainly were not suited, never had been, but somehow I had always imagined that this conversation would be the other way around and that it would be me asking for the divorce. That I had found someone else. It came as a considerable shock to find the boot on the other foot and I was suddenly consumed with curiosity.

"Miriam. I'm genuinely very pleased for you. I mean it. We weren't right. May I ask who the new man is?"

She looked uncomfortable and started fiddling with her spoon again. Her cheeks had taken on a different hue and I saw that she was blushing.

"One day," she said. "Not just now."

I wondered if this new man knew what he was letting himself in for.

"What do you want me to do?" I asked.

She stared down at her hands. "Just make things as easy as possible, please."

"What about money… the house?"

She stopped fiddling with her teaspoon and opened her handbag, then took out a brown envelope and pushed it across the table towards me.

"Daddy has sent you this. It's two weeks' money and he asked me to say that you don't deserve a penny of it."

I picked up the envelope. "I didn't mean this money. I meant, well, everything." I raised my hand and pointed at our surroundings.

"The house is yours."

"I know it's in my name, but..."

"I'm trying to be fair, Eddie. You inherited this place from your mother. It's only right that you should have it. I've already taken most of my things away plus a few bits of furniture. I shall be staying with... with a friend until my circumstances change. I just hope you'll find yourself a job soon so that you can look after yourself. I know Daddy's fairly comfortable but—"

"Oh, don't worry," I butted in. "I wouldn't dream of coming to your father. I'll manage, I promise."

She was being quite human. Suddenly I was seeing my wife in a new light. With one visit she had solved a problem that had been weighing heavily at the back of my mind for ages. I had no need now to go cap in hand to her and ask for a divorce. She had pre-empted me but it had surprised me, shocked me even. Miriam had always stood like some gigantic obstacle between myself and freedom. Now here she was opening the door and being almost apologetic about it.

She stood up and held out her hand.

"Thank you for being so understanding Eddie. I hope you'll be very happy. Perhaps you might even find someone yourself... a nice girl," she said pointedly. "I expect you'll be hearing from my solicitor. I don't know when."

I shook her hand. The whole situation seemed utterly bizarre. I wanted to laugh. I followed her out to the front door.

"By the way," I said. "A terrible thing happened. Mike Paterson, next door, passed away in his sleep." Miriam turned to face me on the garden path. She looked surprised and after a moment's thought said, "It's probably for the best. You'll see." Then she turned again and walked away through the gate along the pavement and out of my life.

*****

Maria Pryke slumped down into a chair and gave a sigh of relief. Lunchtime at last. The morning had seemed to be endless. No sooner had she got rid of one customer than in walked another. At one point she'd had six customers in the shop at once. A fine time for the boss to go away and leave her to cope on her own. It had been worse than Mother's Day. She decided to lock the door for an hour.

Strewn across the floor of the tiny room in which she was sitting were pieces of coloured tissue paper, bits of string, stalks from various varieties of flowers and little pieces of bright, shiny ribbon. Behind her head were cardboard reels holding ribbons of different widths and colours and beside her chair was a bench with half completed bouquets of flowers, a pile of order books and a pad for customers wishing to send flowers by Interflora.

She picked up a string bag from the floor and withdrew a large red Thermos flask, some sandwiches wrapped in silver foil and the *Sun* newspaper. Then, opening the lowest drawer of the bench, she rested her feet on it and settled back to what she considered was the best part of the day,

The newspaper carried a photograph on its front page of the remains of two houses which had been gutted by fire in Eltham, under the headline:

MURDER INFERNO

The houses were semi-detached and inside one of them, the burned bodies of a married couple had been found. The police had said they were treating it as a murder enquiry. Before the fire, the bodies had been mutilated. Both people had had fingers removed and had died from gunshot wounds to the head.

The elderly couple who lived in the other house had managed to escape when the fire spread to their property. They said their neighbours, Mr and Mrs Webster, had been a lovely couple, devoted to their house and garden. It was hard to believe anyone could wish them any harm.

"What a cruel world we live in," Maria thought to herself. "Nothing but murder and mayhem." On another page was a report of another gang murder. A man called Arkwright, well known to the police and who had done time in prison for assault, had been found dead at his home. He had been castrated and hung naked from a tree in his own back garden.

The shop bell rang. Dammit, there was always someone! Opening hours were nine o'clock until one o'clock and from two until five thirty. Enough time one would think for anyone to purchase what they wanted without having to disturb the poor old staff during the lunch break. She decided to ignore whoever it was and went back to her newspaper.

The bell rang again. A prolonged, impatient ring, this time accompanied by the sound of the door being rattled violently. Maria swore softly under her breath, got up and walked into the shop, weaving a small zigzag path between the potted shrubs and vases of flowers on display. A face was peering at her through the glass door.

She shouted, "We're closed. Open again at two," and was almost back into the little office when the bell started ringing again furiously, the door almost being shaken off its hinges. She turned angrily and went to the door, opened it and scowled up at the huge man standing on the step.

"What's the matter with you? Can't you hear? We're closed."

"I'm sorry love, really I am," the man wheedled. "It's a funeral you see. I came in and ordered a wreath the other day and I've come to pick it up. The funeral's at two. You wouldn't want me to be late, would you?"

She recognised him then. He'd been very polite when he'd ordered the wreath. Nice smile, she remembered, good teeth. A bit on the flirty side. About half his size and she would have been more interested.

"Oh, come on then," she grumbled. He waited in the shop while she fetched the wreath. The card had been written on the day of the order. It said, *'Mike Paterson, a really good man. We'll miss you. Ron and Sam.'*

She put the wreath in a box and took it to him in the shop, smiling sweetly, no sign of the scowl as she felt the crisp ten-pound note pressed into her hand.

The big man put the box on to the passenger seat of a black sports car, then miraculously folded his enormous bulk behind the steering wheel. He blew her a kiss as he roared away from the kerb and she responded with a smile and a wave of the ten-pound note, watching the car until it was out of sight before returning to her newspaper.

Twenty minutes later, Haslitt eased the car into a space a few hundred yards from the cemetery. From the glove box he extracted a brown paper bag. It contained a black tie that he had purchased that morning. He exchanged it for the one he was wearing, eased himself out of the car, fed the meter and walked towards the cemetery gates, wondering as he did so whether a hearse had to pay to park. Was it ever wheel clamped? Towed away before they got the coffin out?

In the doorway of the small chapel, a man with a mournful expression bowed gently at the waist as Haslitt approached and whispered that the wreath should be left with the others outside on the lawn. He pointed and Haslitt saw a row of wreaths and bunches of flowers laid neatly on the ground near the chapel entrance. He laid his wreath at the end of the row and took time to read the cards on the other floral offerings. Most of them confined their inscriptions to first names. There was no E.W. but there were three male Christian names beginning with E. There was a Ewan, an Eric and an Edward.

"At least it's a start," he muttered then turned away and went in to pay his last respects.

The small chapel had a congregation of about a dozen people. Haslitt took a seat in an empty pew at the back. An elderly lady turned and smiled at him as he sat down. A thank-you-for-coming smile. He wondered who she was. He smiled back. Looked a bit like Paterson, he thought. Bet she wouldn't be smiling if she knew who had beaten and frightened her dear departed relative into that box.

A piece of white card was thrust into his hand with the order of service written on it and a young man, barely old enough to have left his mother, mounted the steps of the pulpit, his face pre-set in to an expression of awful sadness for someone he didn't know.

The service began. Haslitt knelt, sat and stood when everyone else knelt, sat or stood but he did not join in the singing, neither did his lips move during the prayers. The white card of service hung limply in one hand as he studied the rest of the congregation.

Occupying the front row were four people. The old lady who had smiled at him and a man of about the same age with a red face and a bored expression. Next to him, another couple. The woman dark and fairly attractive, the man small, broad-shouldered but inoffensive looking. Obviously married and devoted to one another. Possibly nephew or niece of the deceased with spouse? Relatives anyway. They and the old lady in the front pew were grieving more genuinely than anyone else.

On the other side of the aisle dressed in a green duffel coat and carrying a small child sat a young woman. She seemed not too perturbed by the sad proceedings, more anxious that the child should not disturb them. She rocked the youngster in her arms, glancing at her watch from time to time as though anxious to leave. Definitely not a relative, Haslitt considered. Probably a casual acquaintance. Immediately behind mother and child was a row of seven men. All fairly tall with short haircuts and straight backs. Possibly work mates? A lot younger than Paterson though. Maybe friends from a pub? They puzzled Haslitt.

Something military about them. Had Paterson been a soldier at one time?

His attention was distracted by a high-pitched whining sound which came from an area behind the coffin. Two tiny curtains parted and Paterson, inside his wooden container, slid slowly through an aperture at the back and disappeared. The curtains fell back into place. It was so much like a final curtain at the theatre that Haslitt wanted to clap. Perhaps if they all clapped the curtains would part again and Paterson would appear at the opening bowing and smiling at his appreciative audience.

Instead, the young vicar started to intone a prayer and someone at the front started to sob loudly. Haslitt yawned and waited through one more interminably long hymn and yet another prayer until at last, merciful release, they were out in the weak sunshine, forming into little groups, talking in muted voices with solemn faces. Haslitt was anxious that everyone might disperse before he could find out their names. He approached the old lady who had nodded at him earlier on. She was standing with the group of men who had been at the back of the chapel and the bored little man with the red face. She held out her hand to him and said, "Hello. We haven't met. It's so good of you to come. I'm Michael's sister... Moira Fanshaw."

Haslitt squeezed her hand. "Nice to meet you," he said. "I'm an old friend from way back. It was an awful shock."

The old lady waved her hand at the red-faced man.

"This is my husband, Trevor."

"Terrible business, terrible," Trevor said.

"And these gentlemen have come along from Michael's old station. Isn't that kind of them to remember?"

"Station?" Haslitt asked.

"Yes. His old police station. I don't know who's looking after the city with so many policemen here at Michael's funeral."

Haslitt was stunned but managed to force a smile and shake the proffered hands. He wondered if they had noticed the colour draining from his cheeks and the tremble in his hand.

What a fool he had been not recognising a copper. Of course, they were all policemen. It was obvious. They stood like policemen, moved like policemen, even smelt like bloody policemen. Christ! One of them was even wearing a uniform under his raincoat. What the hell was the matter with him? Normally he could sense a copper's presence within a mile's radius. Something badly wrong with his radar equipment.

The oldest of the bunch was smiling politely at him, shaking the hand that had helped kill an old colleague.

Suddenly tension was gripping at his innards. Why did the stupid old bastard have to have been a copper? Thank God for cremations. Probably cinders by now. No chance of any evidence turning up. What were the police here for? Did they know about Paterson's connection with the gold bullion? Don't be stupid! The station would be bound to send a representative or two to a retired colleague's funeral.

In turn each man grasped his hand and as they did so managed to help Haslitt's cause by introducing themselves. The second man was Norman Belton and the fourth a Neil Hulme. E.W., it seemed, was not a policeman.

Haslitt was relieved when after the polite handshakes the men turned away from him and made their apologies to Paterson's sister, saying that they had to get back on duty. There had been no sign of recognition and he certainly did not know any of their faces. Relieved, he watched them hurry off down the gravel driveway.

Moira Fanshaw stared after them and said, "What nice young men." She turned to Haslitt. "We're having a few people back to the house. Would you like to come? It's only for a sandwich and a drink if you'd fancy."

"I'm afraid I don't know anybody," Haslitt said.

"Oh, it's no great crowd. There's just myself and Trevor and Michael's neighbours."

She pointed to a group of people standing a few yards away.

"Trudy will be there, she's the one with the baby. Lives a mile or so from Michael's house. Then there'll be Edward and Sally and..." She took hold of his arm.

"How silly of me. Why not meet them now. Oh, by the way, what is your name?"

Haslitt hesitated then said, "Gregson, Pete Gregson."

She led him over. The little circle parted as they approached and they filled the gap.

"Excuse me interrupting," Mrs Fanshaw said. "I'd like to introduce an old friend of Michael's. This is Mr Gregson. Mr Gregson, this is Trudy Jackson, Mike's old friend and her little boy Timothy; Sally Russell, and Edward, Mike's next-door neighbour." There was a discreet cough from behind her and she said, "Oops! I nearly forgot the Reverend Seagrove who gave us such a lovely service."

*****

We had spent at least ten minutes cooing over the baby and saying how good he was during the service. I was eager to get away and be alone with Sally but it seemed bad manners to rush off without the expected handshake and polite chat. Then just as I thought the time had come when it would be okay to leave, Mike's sister approached with a man the size of a brick outhouse, a granite-like face topped with a mop of curly blond hair. He looked like an all-in wrestler poured into a too-tight suit which strained at the seams to contain the muscle beneath.

Mrs Fanshaw introduced him as an old friend of Mike's and he pumped my hand in one of his gigantic paws.

"Nice to meet you, Edward," he said. "But surely we've met before?"

I felt sure I'd never seen him in my life but said, "Oh, have we? I'm sorry I don't remember."

"Yes," he said, releasing my hand. "Where was it now?"

"Maybe Hislop's, the ironmongers? I used to work there."

The big man snapped his fingers.

"That's it," he said. "You're Mr Wilson aren't you?"

"Wheatley. Eddie Wheatley," I said. "Sorry but we had so many customers. Was it long ago?"

The man called Gregson shook his head. "Maybe I was mistaken."

The child chose that moment to wake up and start to cry. Trudy Jackson said, "If you'll excuse me I'll have to take Tim home. I think he's telling me it's grub time."

"We'll see you later I hope," Mrs Fanshaw said.

"Of course."

"I think we'd better get back too, Trevor," the old lady said. "Will you join us, Mr Gregson, in about half an hour?"

Gregson said, "I'm sorry, I've just remembered. I'll have to go back to my office. I have to see someone before he goes home. Thanks for the offer."

"Oh well, it's been nice to meet you. Thanks once again for taking the trouble to come. See you later you two."

She and her husband moved away towards their car followed by the young vicar who seemed determined to console the bereaved until they were off the property.

Sally said, "Had you known Mike long, Mr Gregson?"

"We hadn't seen each other for a long time but we were pals way back. Used to play snooker together."

"He was a really nice bloke," I said.

Gregson nodded but said nothing. He was staring down at me with a quizzical expression on his face, looking me up and down as a tailor might when measuring someone up for a suit.

Sally said, "I think it must have been the excitement that killed him off. Ironic isn't it? Being lucky made him unlucky."

I tried to stop her going further.

"No Sally," I said. "That was a mistake."

"I don't understand," Gregson said.

She shrugged. "Well it was a rotten bit of timing. Just before he died, Mike won the lottery."

I had to shut her up. This man was a stranger and Sally was giving out too much information.

"It was a mistake," I repeated. "He checked and found he'd got the numbers mixed up."

Sally laughed. "Eddie, what are you talking about? He was throwing money around like confetti at the Savoy. So were you come to that. How could it be a mistake?"

"I forgot to tell you."

"But darling. You didn't see Mike again until he was dead. How could he have checked?"

"Look, I don't think Mr Gregson wants to hear all this. I'll explain later."

"Oh, don't mind me," Gregson said. He had a huge grin on his face. "I've got to dash anyway. I was right y'know. I have seen you before. It's been great meeting you, Edward. You just don't know what a pleasure it's been." He hesitated then said, "I'll see you real soon."

He turned abruptly and strode off down the driveway. We watched him until he was out of sight.

Sally took my arm. "I'm surprised you don't remember meeting him," she said. "He made me feel like a dwarf."

"I don't think I've ever met him," I said.

"Well, he seems to remember you."

I had an uneasy feeling welling up in my stomach. There was something about Gregson's manner I didn't like and I couldn't figure it out.

"Ed?" Sally said. "Is something wrong?"

"I didn't like him," I muttered more to myself than to her. "Something odd about him."

"He seemed quite pleasant to me. Was it something he said?" I shook my head. "No, nothing like that. I'm just being silly I suppose. Let's forget it."

We walked through the cemetery in silence for a while then Sally said, "Eddie. What was all that about Mike not winning the lottery?"

We had reached the gate. I held it open for her and we walked to Sally's car before I answered.

"We found out that there had been a mistake on the Saturday. He only had four numbers, not five."

"You mean before we went out to the Savoy?"

"Yes."

"Well, why didn't you tell me? What about all that money you both spent?"

I turned to look at her. I hated having to tell her lies but couldn't think of a way to avoid it.

"Everything had been arranged. We both agreed that we didn't want to spoil your fun, or ours come to that. We decided to go ahead and have a slap up, no expenses spared evening, even though Mike hadn't won very much."

She looked horrified. "But it must have cost you a fortune."

"Mike was going to tell you the next day. He just didn't want to cancel and disappoint you.

Sally went round to the driver's side of the car. She leaned her elbows on the roof and stared across at me. "I feel awful… I know neither of you could really afford it."

I took a deep breath and waded further into the quicksand of lies.

"Stop worrying. Mike had a bit put by and I had some spare cash. Honestly, Mike was happy treating you to a night on the town and so was I. We're not broke you know. It didn't bankrupt either of us."

"But I…" she began and then stopped when I put my finger to my lips.

"No more, Sally, or you'll spoil what was a lovely evening." I waited until she climbed into the car and unlocked my door from the inside, then said, "Right, my good woman, you may drive me home now."

She smiled and leaned over to kiss my cheek.

"Chauvinist pig," she said and pulled the car away from the kerb into the traffic.

*****

Mrs Fanshaw and her husband had prepared a small buffet and a few bottles of wine in the sitting room of the house. It was a rather gloomy assembly.

Trevor Fanshaw had obviously started on the wine earlier and after a few more renderings of 'terrible business, really terrible,' fell asleep in an armchair and lay undisturbed throughout the proceedings, oblivious even to the unrelenting wails of the child which Trudy had brought along with her again and had, it seemed, not managed to coax into good humour with food.

We all tried to quieten the child without success until at last the young mother, flushed with embarrassment, apologised and left. I watched her pass the window on her way home and thought she looked relieved. I wondered if she had been secretly pinching the baby's bottom to make it cry so that she could leave early. Certainly the child was quiet now.

I turned and looked over to where Sally sat on the settee chatting to Mrs Fanshaw. She caught my eye and smiled before returning to the conversation. I longed to be alone with her and wished that I too had an excuse to leave. I felt guilty about wanting to leave a good friend's funeral so early. The good friend's sister, such a nice old lady, doing her best in the company of complete strangers.

I walked over to the settee. "Would you mind if I helped myself to another glass of wine?"

"Oh please do," Mrs Fanshaw said. "It's got to be used up."

"Can I fill your glasses again?"

They nodded and I brought the bottle to where they sat. The old lady was talking about her childhood, recollecting escapades that she had shared with her brother Michael. Sally listened attentively, asking questions, laughing. I ached with love for her. The aura of easy-going warmth and kindness that she exuded was almost tangible. It seemed to disturb the air like a heat haze, mesmerising and captivating whoever was in the vicinity. I sat cross-legged on the floor and listened to Moira Fanshaw's memories. Intimacies that would have deeply embarrassed Mike had he been there, but were a fascinating insight into the man that he had been.

At six o'clock, Trevor woke with a start and announced that he hated to break things up but he had an appointment in Sevenoaks which was urgent and would they all excuse him if he dashed off. It seemed an appropriate time to depart and with a profound sense of relief we bade the Fanshaws goodbye and walked round to my house.

In the darkness of the hallway I closed the door and leaned back on it, letting out a long sigh of relief. She turned to face me, her face a pale glow in the dim light from the street.

After a while she reached out and took my hand in hers and we stood silently for a moment or two before I spoke.

"Y'know something? I've missed you," I said.

"Me too," she whispered.

"All that time in your company and I wasn't able to touch you."

She came closer and placed her lips gently against mine and we stood for several seconds that way, unmoving. Each content with the touch of the other's lips. Eventually she pulled back and looked up at me.

"I think I love you, Eddie," she said. "In fact I know I love you very much."

I cupped her face in his hands and stared into her dark eyes. I felt as though this could only be a dream. This was something that happened to other people, not to the Eddie Wheatleys of the world. I knew that never before in my life had I experienced such complete happiness. Hearing her say those simple words sent a flood of emotion surging through my body, constricting my throat and making the tears prick at the back of my eyes.

"I love you too," I said.

She reached up and wiped my eyes with her thumb. "Sorry," I said. "My cup runneth over."

She smiled, pulled my head towards her and placed her warm lips softly against mine. Then she put her arms around my waist encircling me, pulling herself against my body. I felt the incredible, nerve-tingling sensations that her proximity provoked explode through my entire frame and then I was kissing her eyes, ears and neck. Fumbling with the buttons on her blouse, exposing her warm, white shoulders and pressing my mouth to the soft flesh above her breasts. We undressed quickly, almost desperately, then lay amongst our discarded garments in the darkened hallway and made love.

Later when the hall had started to get chilly I led her upstairs and while she lay under the warm duvet in the big double bed I went downstairs and made steaming mugs of tea and huge chunks of cheese and toast and we sat up in bed feeding each other the pieces of hot stringy cheese and spilling tea over the bed clothes.

Afterwards, when we had finished the food and were lying clasped in each other's arms, Sally said, "Eddie, do you think we've been disrespectful?"

"How do you mean?"

"Well, it was a funeral we've just been to and Mike was a really dear friend..."

I tilted her chin up to look into her eyes. "Are you feeling guilty about being happy?"

"Yes, I suppose I am in a way."

I thought for a moment then said, "Mike Paterson was very fond of you, Sally, and I think he liked me too. I reckon if he's looking down on us now he'll be happy for us."

She laughed suddenly and I could feel her body shaking against my side.

"What's the matter? What did I say?" I asked.

"Well, I was just thinking," she said, pushing her face into the pillow. "I hope he wasn't looking down on us when we were in the hall."

I laughed. "That's a thought. Angelic voyeurs. There might've been hundreds of them up there watching us." I pulled the duvet over our heads and wriggled further down into the bed. "Now that's got you all," I called. "Can't see us now." We clung on to each other laughing.

"Hey, what did you think of Mike's sister?"

"She was lovely, wasn't she?"

"Trevor was the life and soul of the party, wasn't he?"

"The Dormouse in the teapot," Sally said. "Do you know what his farewell remark to me was? It's been very interesting to have had such a nice chat with you."

"Terrible business, terrible," I said. We lay snuggled under the duvet for a while and then Sally said, "Oh my goodness, what time is it?"

"Bottom biting time."

"No seriously. What's the time?"

"I don't know. It's a bit dark down here."

She scrambled from under the duvet and squinted at her watch, then gave a little yelp. I sat up beside her. "What's the matter?"

"Do you know who's at my flat at this precise moment?"

I must have looked bewildered. "Who?"

"The fire brigade?" She flopped down on the pillow. "I made us a casserole," she wailed.

"So? What's that to do with the fire brigade?"

"I didn't know we'd be going next door for drinks. I made us a casserole and set the timer of the oven to switch on at three o'clock. It's now nine fifteen!"

"Charcoal is good for you," I said, kissing her neck. She hit me with a pillow and climbed off the bed. "Whatever happened to sympathy and compassion? My poor old casserole!

Eddie, I'll have to go and check if it's okay." She went downstairs to retrieve her clothes.

"That's right," I called after her. "Leave me now you've had your evil way."

She reappeared a moment later, her clothes bundled under her arm. I watched her dress appreciatively. "I've got an idea," I said. "If your casserole is ruined what about coming out with me for a bite to eat somewhere?"

"Isn't it a bit late?"

"There's a nice Indian restaurant near the market square. They're always open late."

She sat on the bed and put on her shoes. She leaned down and kissed me. "That sounds lovely, though I reckon I might just save the casserole. See me in half an hour?"

"I'll just sort out a few things here and I'll be straight over."

She smiled, patted my cheek and hurried out of the room. I heard the front door close behind her and lay for a while with my hands clasped behind my head, enjoying the feeling of blissful euphoria which seemed to radiate from my body like heat waves to fill the room. Turning over I smelt her perfume on the pillow and clutched it to me, remembering the feel of her soft body against mine and the sweet warmth of her breath on my cheek.

"Wheatley, you lucky bastard!" I whispered into the pillow. "You lucky, lucky bastard!"

The doorbell rang.

CHAPTER 13

Ultimatum

On most nights it was easy to find a parking space outside the flat. Tonight both sides of the street were jammed with cars, some even parked across driveways, hemming the occupants of the houses in should they wish to venture out.

Sally decided to drive around the block again. On the corner of Hazeloak Road a pub was ablaze with lights and the throb of heavy rock music pumped out into the dark street. A fluorescent sign outside the door announced that 'Manic Fit' were performing inside and she thought that the title aptly described the group's music. It also explained the shortage of parking in the area.

She passed the flat for the third time, expecting on each circuit to see flames shooting from the windows, almost sure that she could smell the burning casserole a hundred yards from her front door.

At last she saw the winking yellow light of a car leaving the kerb and with a sigh of relief, she parked her car in the empty space.

A delicious aroma assailed her nostrils as soon as she opened the door, but there were no sign of flames or the fire brigade and when she pulled the hot, bubbling dish from the oven it was a pleasant surprise to find that the food, although a trifle overcooked, was not burnt. She pushed the dish back on to the wire rack and turned the oven off, pulled out the vegetable drawer and started preparing potatoes and broccoli to accompany the meal.

While the potatoes were cooking she undressed and had a hot shower. She put on a clean blouse and skirt, freshened up her lipstick and changed the silver pendant and pearl earrings she had been wearing for a black choker necklace and long amber droplet earrings.

After plumping up the pillows on the bed she put a bottle of wine in the refrigerator then laid the table with great care, placing two silver candlesticks ready to be lit as soon as Eddie arrived.

She glanced at her watch. An hour had passed since leaving Eddie's house. He was late. Maybe it had been a mistake to leave him in bed. Probably, he'd fallen asleep. She took her mobile phone from her bag and dialled his number. The phone rang for what seemed ages then went on to 'Leave a message' mode. Maybe he was in the shower or had already left and was on his way round. She dialled again, waited and then just as she was about to cancel the call there was a click and Eddie's voice, strangely quiet, came on the line. He said, "Hello," and waited for her to speak.

Sally said, "Come on dozy, you're supposed to be here eating my burnt offering. What happened? Did you fall asleep?"

There was a pause then I said, "Oh Sally... hello... I'm sorry—"

"Whatever is the matter with you?" she said, feeling strangely concerned. "You sound like an answering device. Are you all right?"

Another long pause, then "Sally, look, I'm sorry. Something's come up... I won't be able to come round after all. See you tomorrow maybe, eh?"

"Eddie, what are you talking about? I've got the meal all ready. You sound so strange. Are you sure you're all right?"

"I'm fine... see you tomorrow then."

She was stunned.

"Eddie, for God's sake. I don't understand. Why?"

There was no immediate reply so she stammered, "Shall I come back to your house?"

"No!" he shouted. She thought she detected a tinge of panic in his voice. "I've told you. I'll see you tomorrow."

There was a click and the line went dead. She stared at the phone in disbelief. After a while she put it down on the table then walked back into the sitting room. She sat down on a chair at the dining table, unable to grasp what had happened. Only a few minutes ago she had felt buoyant and alive. Now all those good feelings had drained away, leaving her feeling empty and desolate. Her mind in such a turmoil of confusion that she couldn't even cry.

An hour went by before she got up from the table and made her way slowly into the kitchen, turned off all the switches on the oven and walked from there into the bedroom. Not bothering to undress, she climbed on to the bed and lay shivering under the duvet, unable to sleep, staring into the darkness.

*****

Moira Fanshaw closed the front door to her brother's old home and carried her bulging suitcase down the path towards the car. At the gate she stopped and gazed for a moment or two at the darkened house, remembering as she did so the last time she had paused at that gate. Michael alive, standing on that doorstep, his big ruddy face wreathed in smiles, waving her off, telling her not to make it such a long time before her next visit, she swearing to keep in touch more regularly. Trevor tooting his horn impatiently, wanting to get on the road. Driving off, waving at the tall figure in the doorway until they had turned the corner and pointed themselves in the direction of Kent.

On her own now, no parents, no more brothers and sisters, she had run right out of relatives. All dead, except Trevor and with him it was impossible to tell.

As if to prove a point he chose to press the horn at that moment, snapping her out of her reverie. She turned sadly, opened the boot of the car and heaved the heavy suitcase inside.

"I must say goodbye to Mr Wheatley before we go," she said, stooping down and peering through the driver's window.

"Very well, but be quick, Moira," Trevor answered, drumming his fingers impatiently on the steering wheel.

"Don't you want to say goodbye?"

"You say it for me. We'll only get chatting otherwise."

He wound up the window cutting off any further conversation.

She walked up Wheatley's path and knocked on the door, turning her back and facing the street while she waited, admiring the newly dug garden, the brick wall with its fresh earth and planted shrubs which were illuminated by the lamp inside the porch.

From the dark street Trevor gave another sharp toot on the horn. She glared in his direction and gave the door another knock. Why did he always have to be so impatient? There was no rush to get back to Kent. The urgent appointment he had spoken of had all been a sham, a lie, just to break up the small gathering. She glanced at her watch. Ten o'clock. Huh! Some urgency. She hoped Eddie had not been aware of her husband's obvious lie. She heard footsteps from the hallway. The door opened a few inches and Eddie's face appeared in the crack. Moira thought he looked pale and tired.

"I came to say goodbye," she said.

"Oh, you're off then?" The words came out in sharp bursts as though he was out of breath.

"It's been nice meeting you. I'm only sorry it was in such sad circumstances." She paused and then said, "Is Sally still here?"

"No, no she's not I'm afraid."

"Ah, well," the old lady smiled and held out her hand. "Say goodbye to her from me... and from Trevor too. Oh, and we're taking Mike's cat home with us."

He moved the door a little wider and shook her hand. As he did so he seemed to catch his breath and his face contorted suddenly as though he was in pain.

"Are you all right Eddie?" she asked, looking at him anxiously. He withdrew his hand and the door swung back again until she could only see his face.

"Don't worry. It's just an old back injury... I got knocked down when I was a child... always playing me up... nothing to worry about."

"Look after yourself, won't you. I do hope we'll meet again."

"So do I."

Moira nodded, aware that he wanted her to go. "Well, goodbye then." She smiled and moved off the porch on to the path. "Hope you feel better soon."

"Goodbye," I said and closed the door. The knife which had been sticking painfully into my side just below the rib cage was withdrawn and Gregson, who now I knew was really called Haslitt, patted me roughly on the shoulder.

"Well done Eddie. I reckon you missed your vocation. What an actor. Twice in one night too."

"Can I put the rest of my clothes on?"

The big man looked down at the scattered clothes on the floor of the hall and pretended to think about it, then looked down again at me. I was only wearing my shirt.

"Untidy little bugger aren't you? I usually keep my clothes in a drawer." He looped his toe into the belt of the discarded trousers then kicked upwards with his leg so that the trousers flew up in the air.

"Go on then. I'm sick of looking at your scrawny knees." He stood back folding the blade of the knife into its handle as I regained the dignity of my clothes. Then he gestured with his head towards the sitting room and I followed him reluctantly through the door.

Another man whom I hadn't clapped eyes on until that day was standing warming his backside at the gas fire on the far side of the room. He looked comfortable and at ease, as though this were his own home and I was just a guest. He had told me earlier that his name was Frank Thomson.

"What a popular man you are with the ladies, Mr Wheatley," he said. "And how nice you look in your clothes. I'll bet you looked delightful for the funeral. I was so sorry I had to miss it."

Haslitt pushed me down on to one of the two armchairs, squeezed himself into the other one and lit a cigarette. Thomson walked over and perched himself on the arm of my chair. He sat for a moment or two without saying anything then turned his head and looked down into my face.

"Y'know, Mr Wheatley," he said. "For a long time I really hated you. I vowed to myself that if I ever found you I'd tear the skin from your body." He waited for a response and when none came continued, "But now that I have found you, I must say that I do find myself harbouring a sneaking admiration for you. You don't look like a man who could kill three men. Or was it your friend Paterson who did the killing? Was it Paterson who lifted all that heavy gold? Maybe you are just the brains of the outfit. I have to admit it was very clever of you. Clever but rather naughty. There should be, after all, a little honour amongst thieves, don't you think?"

I didn't answer so Thomson prodded me with his finger. "Also there is the little matter of the cash you got for the jewellery. Your half and Mr Paterson's. I assume you had the sense to retrieve his suitcase?"

I shook my head and mumbled, "I've told you. I don't know what you're talking about."

"I'm talking about reasonableness and honour, Mr Wheatley. What I'm trying to do is to save you from a lot of unnecessary pain. I've told you, I admire you, I—"

He was interrupted by an impatient grunt from Haslitt. "For Christ's sake, Frank! This is like *Listen with Mother*. Take off his fingers till he talks."

Thomson waved his hand at him and turned back to me. "You see? That's exactly the point I was about to make. I want to be reasonable with you and hope that you will divulge the whereabouts of my property without bloodshed but Mr Haslitt here wants to get information from you by other methods." He leaned over me like an insurance salesman selling a policy and asked "Now, which way would you prefer?"

I didn't answer.

Haslitt pulled himself out of his chair and towered over us.

He pulled a large pair of industrial bolt cutters from a haversack he'd brought with him.

"Right you little shit," he roared. "We've tried the reasonable approach. I'm going to take your fucking fingers off one by one until you talk!" He grabbed one of my arms. Thomson pushed himself between us.

"Don't screw this one up," he ordered. "Remember what happened to Paterson."

Haslitt stepped back a pace or two glaring down at me.

"It worked with Webster. He soon blabbed when he lost a digit or two."

I pushed myself forward in my chair.

"Paterson?" I said. "What d'you mean? What happened to Paterson?"

Thomson patted Haslitt on the shoulder.

"There now, see what you've done, Haslitt. You've upset our little friend," he said, then turned to me.

"We questioned Mr Paterson in much the same way as we are doing with you. We allowed him to keep his fingers but alas, poor Mr Paterson was very uncooperative and… well… that's why he is where he is now." He smiled and shrugged. "One of those unfortunate things, I'm afraid."

I stared horrified at my two tormentors as the truth about my friend's death dawned on my befuddled brain. I remembered the stricken expression on Mike's face and the grotesque position of the body when I found him. They had probably beaten him, smashed his body in their frenzy to get the gold and dear, brave Mike Paterson had not talked, had not told them that it was I, Eddie Wheatley, was the person who had stolen their gold and killed three of their gang. He'd died keeping that secret. A terrible anger filled my brain and I sprang out of my chair with a roar of rage and swung a fist at Haslitt's face. The big man moved his head easily to one side letting the punch pass harmlessly over his shoulder and at the same time bringing the palm of his hand up under my chin which sent me flying back into the chair like a burst pillow. Frank Thomson watched this interchange with a half-smile on his face, as though he was watching a good match at Wimbledon. Twice more I struggled out of my chair to pummel ineffectively at Haslitt's enormous bulk, only to be thrown back down again until at last Thomson placed a restraining arm against my chest and said soothingly, "Come now, Mr Wheatley. This is not getting us anywhere. Calm yourself. There's nothing you can do to help Paterson now is there? These things happen when people meddle where they shouldn't."

He patted my hand and leaned back comfortably in his chair.

"Well now, regrettable as it is, we have to face the facts. Your friend Mr Paterson died because he wouldn't tell me where my property could be located. Now you know and I know that we don't want you to die before we get that information. That is why Mr Haslitt here has been so restrained with you. But don't feel complacent; I was rather hoping that you'd co-operate because I do sincerely hate physical violence…" He hesitated then added, "Especially against women."

I turned in the chair and looked up at Thomson anxiously. "Women? What have women to do with it?"

"Well, Mr Wheatley, as we don't want to lose you just yet and have to be so maddeningly restrained, I thought that perhaps if Mr Haslitt were to pay a friendly call on your charming lady, Mrs Russell…" He clapped his hands together and laughed as he saw the horror on my face. "I do believe we've hit the jackpot Haslitt. Just look at Mr Wheatley's expression."

I clutched at his arm.

"Don't, please! You're making a mistake. I don't know about your gold."

The smile disappeared abruptly from Thomson's face. He stood up.

"You stupid little shit! You've had your chance." He pulled a set of car keys from his pocket and tossed them to Haslitt.

"Get her," he snarled.

"Now you're talking."

"No!" I wailed. I tried to get up but Thomson slapped me hard across the face sending me reeling back into the chair. Suddenly a gun was jammed against my throat and he was leaning over me spitting hatred into my face.

"I told you, Wheatley. I can't kill you yet but by God I want to. I want to very much. You will talk, I promise you or your girl's going to look like an abattoir floor. Then my patience will be exhausted and to hell with the gold. I'll tear your guts out too!"

I heard the engine of Thomson's car burst into life outside and the squeal of tyres as it pulled away from the pavement. I found I couldn't breathe. I was paralysed with fear and my body numb with terror.

"Not Sally. Please not Sally. Don't touch Sally," I screamed.

"I won't touch her, Wheatley," he snarled. "I'll leave that to Haslitt. He has much more imagination when violence is needed."

"You don't know where she is!"

"Don't be so stupid."

"All right. I'll tell you," I yelled. "Only, call him back. Don't let him touch Sally!"

Thomson straightened up and stepped away from me.

"It's a bit late to call him back," he said. "But I promise he won't harm her until they're back here."

He picked up the bolt cutters and waggled them in front of my nose.

"Now, where is it?"

I stood up and walked slowly towards the door.

"Where are you going?" Thomson asked.

"Outside."

I switched the light in the porch off and walked into the darkness of my small front garden. Thomson rammed the gun painfully into my back.

"What are you up to, Wheatley? Why switch off the light?"

I turned and stared at him.

"Do you want every Tom, Dick or Harry to see your precious gold? … any passer-by? Do you want anyone to see you pointing that gun at my back?"

Thomson looked bewildered. He glanced quickly around the garden, then said, "All right, but no tricks. I can see you very clearly. The street light gives enough light for me to watch your every move."

I walked forward and stood beside the wall and looked from right to left along the street. It appeared to be deserted. I pointed. "It's in there."

There was a gasp from behind my back. "In the wall?"

"Yes."

"Show me."

227

I grasped one of the small shrubs that I'd planted in the top of the wall and pulled it from the earth, tossed it onto the path then scooped a few handful of earth from the hole until the dull yellow of the hidden gold gleamed up at me from the darkness. Leaning forward I squeezed my fingers beneath one of the ingots and heaved it out of the hole, then turning, held it out like a sacrificial offering to Thomson.

Thomson's mouth had dropped open in surprise. He watched speechless as I stooped and placed the shining ingot at his feet then turn to delve into the wall again and place another ingot beside the first. For him it must have been scarcely believable, ludicrous. Thirty million pounds' worth of gold sitting under a few inches of dirt in the garden wall of a grubby East End house within a couple of feet of the pavement.

I went back to the wall and dug my arms deep into the dark earth. Then turned to face Thomson, holding out another object. Not a gold ingot this time but something wrapped in shiny plastic. He stared at it with a puzzled expression, not knowing what I was holding until it kicked in my outstretched hand spitting out a flash of bright light and a bullet which entered the open mouth, shattering his spinal column on its way out at the back of his neck and sending his lifeless body crashing backwards against the brick wall beneath the bay window.

I let the gun drop down by my side and walked towards the body. A car came down the road and as it passed the house its light for a fleeting second picked out the sprawled figure under the window, eyes fixed and staring with astonishment, mouth still open, a river of blood flowing down the chin and a bright red stain spreading slowly across the immaculate, monogrammed white shirt.

The car, finding it was a cul-de-sac, did a U-turn and headed back the way it had come. I leaned over Thomson's body, cleared my throat and spat on him, then looking up at the black starless sky I whispered, "That one's for you Mike. Thank God the gun still worked, eh?"

I looked down at the weapon in my hand, still wrapped in the plastic bag I had placed it in on the night I had stolen the bullion. When I'd pulled the trigger I didn't even know if there was a bullet left in it to fire or if the gun would operate after such a long time being buried in the wall. My luck was in. I prayed it would last a little longer.

I walked over to the wall and peered both ways down the street. It was still deserted. At the far end on one side I could see the lighted windows of a few houses near the corner of the market square, where people were probably sitting watching TV or eating a meal, completely unaware of the murder and mayhem that was taking place a few hundred yards away.

I grasped Thomson under the arms and dragged him roughly to the wall, rolling the body tight against the brickwork in the black shadow cast by the street light, then I stood back and squinted into the darkness. Thomson's silver hair shone like a beacon from its muddy resting place. I walked forward and tugged the tail of the dead man's dark blue suit up until it covered his head, then stood back again and had another look. Satisfied, I picked up the two gold ingots, moved them into the shadow and replaced the discarded shrub into the hole in the wall. Then moving across to the bay window, I searched the spot where Thomson had fallen, feeling with my hands until I located his gun. It seemed heavier than the other weapon but was similar in that it had the same long, black silencer tube fitted to the barrel.

I carried the guns to the fence that separated my house from Mike Paterson's and climbing over the wooden railing, squatted down between two large flowering shrubs and waited in the scented darkness, my whole body consumed by a cold hatred for the man who had gone to tear Sally from her home and bring her to this place. Sweet, innocent Sally, whose emotions had already been crushed that evening, dragged from her clean, secure, untainted world into this grubby place of violence and murder. I would never forgive myself if she'd been badly hurt.

In the distance I could hear a group of young men noisily weaving their home from the pub. Minutes passed by. An ambulance wailed in the distance and the cold from the soft earth started to creep into my limbs. I was starting to wonder if Haslitt had got lost when a car screeched to a halt outside my house.

I raised myself up on knees and peered over the top of the fence. It was a gleaming blue Jaguar, sleek and ostentatious; a rich man's car—the kind of vehicle that one would expect a person such as the crumpled pile of dead flesh and bones lying in the mud a few yards away to have owned.

The lights were flicked off and the driver's door opened. Haslitt climbed out and walked around to the passenger side. He took some time checking that the street was clear then he opened the passenger door and leaned his huge bulk into the car, reappearing seconds later carrying a bundle in his arms. My heart lurched. It was Sally. She was wrapped in a tartan car rug. The only part of her showing was her head. It lolled sideways, black dishevelled hair hanging beneath Haslitt's arm, eyes closed and a dark smudge of blood showing high up on her cheek. I wanted to cry out, to run to her. To kill Haslitt for what he'd done, but I waited. I saw that a wide strand of sticking plaster covered her mouth which was also stained with blood.

Oh God, I thought. *Please Sally. Stay alive!*

The gate was pushed open with a kick and Haslitt hurried up the path to the front door. He waited for a second as though expecting it to be opened for him then bumped the door open with his behind and backed into the house.

I climbed silently over the fence and followed through the front door. In the hallway I heard Haslitt's bewildered voice in the front room call out.

"Thomson, where are you for Christ's sake?" A moment later he reappeared, this time without Sally, his huge frame filling the doorway. He turned his back towards me and walked in the direction of the kitchen door at the other end of the passage.

I said, "This way, Haslitt." The big man whirled round and stared like a perplexed bull at the gun in my hand. His mouth opened and shut and he seemed to have difficulty getting any words out. Before he could, I said, "Don't try anything or I'll kill you."

What's going on?" Haslitt spluttered at last.

"Put your hands behind your head."

"What's happened?"

"Now!" I snarled, raising the gun and pointing it at his head.

Haslitt clasped his hands behind his head.

I walked forward and patted his chest until I found the shoulder holster. I took his gun, threw it along the hallway and heard it clatter across the kitchen floor, then I dipped into the man's pockets and pulled out the folding knife. Thrusting it into my pocket, I stepped back, gesturing as I did so for him to walk to the front room.

"Where's Thomson?" Haslitt asked in a choking voice.

"He's dead! Now move!"

Warily I followed the huge figure into the room where Sally lay. She was piled in a heap on the sofa. The tartan car rug had partly fallen to one side showing lines of coarse yellow string bound tightly around her body, cutting into the flesh of her arms and the tender skin above her dress. Her face was deathly white and the blood on her cheek that I'd seen earlier was congealed in a rivulet that ran down her face and stopped at the edge of the sticking plaster on her mouth.

"You bastard!" I screamed at him. "I ought to kill you now." I pulled the knife from my pocket and sliced carefully through several strands of the string. Sally's limbs slumped and one arm flopped out of its binding, hanging loosely across the settee.

"Where is Thomson?" Haslitt said moving a step closer. I swung my arm round so that the gun was inches from the other man's face.

"Get back, you scum," I hissed through clenched teeth. "I've killed four men so far and making you the fifth will be the biggest pleasure of all. Now sit down and don't speak until I tell you to."

Haslitt's face was red with pent-up anger but the expression of utter hatred on my face must have convinced him that I was deadly serious. He took a step back and sat down in the armchair.

"Keep your hands behind your head." I leaned over Sally's body and gently pulled the sticking plaster off her mouth. It was a relief to see that she was still breathing and for a brief moment her eyes flickered and I thought she was about to wake up. I pulled the car rug around her body again then straightened up to face Haslitt.

"Get up."

"Where are we going?"

"Do you want to see your gold bullion?"

Haslitt got to his feet with a wary look on his face.

"That would be nice," he grunted.

I nodded towards the door and he walked obediently into the hall. When he reached the front door, I said, "Right, that's far enough. Turn around."

He turned and I could see the fear in his eyes. I knew he was thinking that this would be the place that I'd shoot him. Not outside where we might be seen and not in front of Sally. Now would be the time. I kept well back in case he tried to rush me or make a lunge for the gun. My mind was racing fast. I had to get him away from here and as far from Sally as possible. I wanted rid of him, rid of the gold and rid of the guilt that lay like a ten-ton weight on my shoulders. Most of all I wanted my life back without the constant fear of being found out. At that moment I didn't really know what to do. The priority was to get him away. But where? I had no idea so I said as convincingly as I could, "I'm going to take you to where the gold is hidden, Haslitt. We're going to leave this house and we are going to drive to the place. You can have it, all of it. Too many people have died and I don't want any more blood on my conscience. But I never want to see you again, Haslitt. If you come back here looking for revenge, I'll kill you. Do we have an agreement?"

He looked stunned, barely able to believe his ears. He let the pent-up air in his lungs escape in a gasp of relief.

"What's the catch?" he said.

"There's no catch. Do you agree?"

Haslitt nodded. "Need you ask? Now where's Thomson?"

"You're just about to be reunited."

We walked out into the darkness. I stayed beside the door. My arm was beginning to tire with the weight of the gun. "Okay," I said. "Move forward till you're about a yard from the left of the gate."

He ambled forward and stopped.

"By your feet."

Haslitt looked down, gasped, stooped down and picked up one of the gold bars. He stared at it for a moment or two, his mouth open in astonishment. Then he picked up the other ingot, stood up and turned to face me.

"I don't believe this," he murmured. "Don't tell me they're just scattered around the garden."

"Only those two."

He shook his head then looked at me with an incredulous expression. Then laughed. "Up to this minute I've never really believed that a little squirt like you could've pulled off something like this."

"Well, now you know," I said. I pointed the gun at Thomson's Jaguar. "Put them in the car."

"Where's the rest of it?"

"Just a short drive away. Now put them in the car on the floor, passenger side."

He obeyed, moved over to the car with me trailing a couple of yards behind, placed the gold on the floor as he'd been told and said, "Okay, now what?"

I said, "I'm going back into the house, Haslitt. I'm going to check that Sally is okay. You beat her up, you mindless bastard. How brave you were. How proud you must be smashing your fists into a woman a quarter of your size."

"She was fucking screaming. What else was I supposed to do?"

"Shut up!" I hissed. "Now listen. You might choose to climb into the car and drive away from here or you might have some idea in your head about attacking me and getting the upper hand again, but if you do either of these things, all you'll get is the gold that you just saw. If you behave yourself you'll get the lot. Think about it."

I turned my back on him and walked towards the house. When I got to the doorway I turned and looked back. Haslitt had not moved. He stood huge and bulky by the car door like a gigantic waxwork chauffeur. I walked back to the gate.

"Oh, by the way. You asked where your friend Thomson was. He's lying behind the wall near to where you picked up the gold. While you're waiting for me, would you put him in the car please? Back seat. He's cluttering up my garden." I turned again and walked into the house.

Sally was sitting up on the settee when I entered the room. The car rug had slipped from her shoulders and lay in rucks at her waist with strands of cut string poking out all around. She reminded me of a beautiful butterfly emerging from its chrysalis. She was holding her forehead with one hand and gently exploring the bruise on her cheek with the other. Placing the gun out of sight on the floor beside the chair, I knelt down beside her. She jumped in terror and cowered back on the settee, then when she saw who it was the expression on her face changed to one of immense relief and she held out her arms to me, bursting into tears as my arms went around her.

"Eddie, Oh thank God!" she whimpered.

"You're all right now Sally darling."

"Eddie, that man… where is he? What's happening?"

"He won't give you any more trouble, I promise."

She clung tightly to my neck and I could feel her whole body trembling. Little choking sobs burst uncontrollably from her lips and her tears flowed warmly against my cheek. After a while she pulled away from me and looked into my face with red-rimmed eyes.

"Tell me what's happening, Eddie. I don't understand."

"Listen Sally, the man is in the car outside. I have to go with him. I want you to be brave and wait here until I get back. It's something I have no choice about. I have to go. But when I come back I will explain everything." I kissed her on the forehead. "Will you do this for me?"

"Eddie, don't go with that man. He's a savage. Please don't go. I don't know what he wants but he might kill you." She clung tightly to me again and sobbed into my ear. "He just walked in… and hit me… and he kept hitting me. He didn't say anything. Wouldn't tell me what he wanted. He was enjoying it. Smiling all the time he was hitting… it was horrible."

I hugged her tightly.

"Shush now. It's all over. It's all finished."

I waited until her sobbing had subsided then held her away from me and dabbed at her swollen eyes with my handkerchief.

"Please Sally, will you do as I ask? Will you wait for me? I'll come to no harm, I promise. Just wait one hour and I'll be back with you and I'll explain everything."

She looked up at my face, her eyes searching mine then after a moment or two she nodded slowly and stared down at her lap. I wanted more than anything in the world the stay with her. To comfort her, bathe her bruised face and ask her forgiveness but right then it was not possible. I kissed her cheek and stood up. "Thanks Sally. I'll be back in an hour. Trust me please." I picked up the gun from the floor, concealed it behind my back until I was in the hallway and said, "I love you, Sally Russell. Remember that, won't you." She didn't reply so I walked down the hall and out into the garden.

Haslitt was sitting behind the wheel as I approached the car. He didn't look round but just grunted. "You took your time."

I ignored him.

"Move over," I said. "I'm driving."

Haslitt moved across to the passenger seat and I turned to face him. "Try anything stupid and you'll never know where the gold is." I looked over my shoulder. Thomson lay slumped on the back seat, his silvery hair spread wildly across the head rest. He still wore the astonished pop-eyed expression he'd assumed when he died. One side of his face was covered in mud from the garden and rivulets of dried blood covered his chin and neck.

"You're a murderous little bastard, aren't you Wheatley?" Haslitt said, still staring fixedly ahead.

"It's called self-protection."

"Frank Thomson was a good friend. He had style. He had brains... and you wasted him."

"Yes. I'm good at waste disposal. Fasten your seat belt... we don't want you injured do we?"

I'd never been behind the wheel of a superb machine like this one before. The bonnet stretched out in front of me like the prow of a ship and I was glad that it had automatic transmission. So all I had to do was press the accelerator. We moved slowly forward, turned round at the end of the cul-de-sac then headed east. It was well past one o'clock in the morning and the traffic was sparse. A light drizzle had started to fall and a film of condensation formed quickly on the inside of the car windows. Haslitt, who obviously knew the vehicle, turned the heater on, produced a sponge from the glove compartment and wiped the moisture from the windscreen. We drove along in silence for a while then he said, "It really is a game to you, isn't it, Wheatley? Cops and robbers. The good guys against the bad guys, honour amongst thieves, trust. Good God, how have you survived this long?"

"Well, I might regret it but I'm going to trust you, Haslitt. You get all the gold if you promise to take it, do what you like with it, but leave me and Sally alone."

There was a long pause. I was aware that he was staring at me, wondering if I was serious about handing over so much treasure, then he said gruffly, "Okay, you have my word," then after an even longer pause, he snarled, "I still think you're a pathetic little shit. You're not in the real world, Wheatley. Surviving is what it's all about. Grabbing what you can when you can cos if you don't grab it some other clever bugger will. You fucked up what was a sweet little job; you've killed four blokes who took their chances, used their brains to take what they did only to have you come along and mess things up."

I glanced over at him with contempt. "When you talk about your dead mates, Haslitt, I want you to know it was a case of kill or be killed. I didn't have any option. Did you have an option when you murdered Mike Paterson, a man old enough to be your granddad?"

"I didn't want him to die."

"Not at that moment maybe, but after he'd been tortured and given you the information you wanted you'd have snuffed him out without thinking about it. You don't have any humanity. Your only emotions are anger and greed. There's no place in your life for anything decent and clean. You're a rat, Haslitt, a sewer rat." I looked across at him. His hands were clenched together with anger. He was breathing hard and his face was contorted with fury.

I turned off the main road and drove the car down a narrow alley, the sides of the car almost touching the crumbling walls and scraggy bushes on each side. I had no idea where we were or what I intended to do at this stage but at least I'd got him away from Sally and I knew she was safe.

The smooth tarmac ended abruptly and had become a bumpy dirt-track, littered with deep water filled potholes and rocks. The car lurched from side to side, bouncing its occupants about and making the dead one pitch violently forward so that his face was almost resting on Haslitt's shoulder. He jerked himself away and elbowed Thomson's head so that the corpse fell on its side half on and half off the back seat.

"So much for good friends," I said.

On our left a huge, dilapidated building loomed suddenly against the night sky. Most of the roof was missing and the joists that once supported it stuck out like ribs of a dead animal from the cracked brickwork. We moved slowly forward. Another grey shape appeared, long and black with a row of broken windows. It was an old railway carriage, disused and empty, piles of discarded wood propped against its sides and a tangle of old cable cascading onto the roof from somewhere high overhead. A few more buildings then another line of carriages, newer ones this time. Possibly still in use. Then a continuous high brick wall rising slowly upwards to form the first of a series of dark archways.

Up ahead the lights of a motorway curved smoothly across a vast concrete bridge, illuminating the railway track beneath and transforming the shiny rails into brightly coloured neon tubes snaking out from the black depths under the archways beneath.

I brought the car to a halt but kept the engine running.

We sat in the semi-darkness staring forward at the lights of the bridge, neither of us speaking. Occasionally a car passed over the huge arc of motorway high above us, two yellow dots moving below the orange glow of the streetlamps, until the image became blurred and distorted as the drizzle outside increased and dribbled down the windscreen. Haslitt broke the silence at last.

He turned his head to me and said, "Romantic isn't it? Okay, what're we waiting for?"

"I just want a moment to think."

"Well, now you've thought, what did you come up with?"

I said, "I meant what I said, Haslitt… about giving you all the gold. I just don't know if I can trust you."

"I told you, you have my word. Hand over the gold and you won't see me again. That's a promise."

I wanted desperately to believe him but I looked at his hard granite face and knew that I could never be one hundred percent certain. I decided my only option was to risk it, but first I had to test out his promise.

I pointed my finger, "Do you see that archway straight ahead? The fifth one from the left?"

He nodded. "I see it."

"About ten yards into that archway there's an old metal door set back into the wall. It leads into a small room. God knows what it was used for. Piles of cables in there now and old electrical boxes. Hasn't been used for years. In one corner there's a long, galvanised water tank covered in rotten planks and a blue tarpaulin. The gold is in there."

Haslitt stared at me in astonishment.

"Christ! You took a chance. Any old tramp looking for a place to doss down could've found it."

"Nobody did though."

"Can we go and have a look?" He climbed eagerly out of the car and walked round to my side staring at the dark archway ahead.

"All in good time," I said. "I told you the gold is yours now. I don't want any more part of it. I'm sick of all the killing."

"Okay, okay. Now let's go and get it!"

"No. This is where it ends for me, Haslitt," I said. "You surely didn't expect me to load the gold into the car for you? Remember your promise. Remember I trusted you." I pointed the gun at the ground through the open window and pulled the trigger several times. On the first two pulls the gun bucked in my hand and the phut, phut of bullets hitting the gravel echoes around the dark yard then there was a series of clicks. I offered the empty gun to Haslitt.

"I won't need this any more, Haslitt," I said. "Take it." He took the gun. His face had taken on an expression of stunned disbelief. He looked at the gun, then at me, then back to the gun. At last he gave a short laugh before suddenly lunging forward and thrusting a long arm through the open window and grabbing me by the hair in his huge paw. "You stupid prat!" he screamed. "You stupid fucking prat!" He drew his other arm back and hit me on the side of my head with the butt of the gun. I yelped in pain. "Christ. You're so naïve it's ridiculous." He hit me again, this time on the mouth and I felt blood gush from a split lip. "You are going to die you pathetic piece of shit!"

"You gave me your word," I spluttered feebly.

"I don't believe you're fucking real," Haslitt screamed, yanking my hair painfully round so he could hit me again. I grabbed his wrist and hit the window control button. The toughened glass rose upwards and trapped Haslitt's thick arm just above the elbow. I held on tightly to his wrist and trod hard on the accelerator. The car shot forward about ten yards. I heard him scream then braked. Haslitt's massive bulk flew forward and I heard an audible crack as his arm snapped at the shoulder. I reversed, dragging him the other way then opened the window and let the useless limb go. Haslitt fell to the ground whimpering loudly and clutching his shoulder. I got out of the car and crouched down beside the stricken hulk.

"I trusted you, Haslitt. Big mistake."

There was no answer. He lay like a stranded whale, breathing heavily and groaning, his face contorted in agony. I waited, then when the words came they came in short gasps, almost a whisper.

"You bastard. You fucking bastard!"

"Yeah, I am, aren't I?" I said. "A bastard who offered to give you all that you wanted. A bastard who thought it might be possible to trust you." I took hold of his jacket by the collar and hauled him round so that his back was resting against the wheel of the car. The whimpering became a scream of pain.

"Who's the stupid prat now?" I asked. "You could've gone off and lived the life of Riley with all that loot as long as you left me and my girl alone. You failed the test, Haslitt."

"Test?"

"Yes, test." I crouched down directly in front of him. "That's why I brought you here. That's why I emptied the gun. It was a test. But you blew it. You could have had it all and now you've got nothing."

There was a long silence. The stricken Haslitt seemed totally deflated. He sank lower against the wheel, his eyes closed and his teeth clenched in pain.

For a full minute he lay unmoving then he looked up at my face.

"Got nothing? I think I've still got something," he said then drew his leg back and kicked me violently in the chest with his size twelve boot. I hadn't expected this and I sprawled back onto the muddy ground, gasping with pain and trying desperately to get my breath back. I struggled back onto my hands and knees. Haslitt had a gun in his good hand and was pointing it at my head.

"Trust?" he panted painfully. "See where it's got you. You're a fucking arsehole. While you were consoling your tart, I just walked back into the kitchen and picked up my gun. Easy eh, you little shit?" I couldn't speak, I was still struggling to get some air into my lungs.

He kicked out with his foot again, narrowly missing my face.

"I've wanted to kill you since I first laid eyes on you, Wheatley. Don't worry though, nice people like you go to heaven, don't they? You'll be seeing that little tart up there soon." He managed a grin. "After I've fucked her senseless! Goodbye little man!" He squeezed the trigger. There was a dull click. He looked startled and pulled the trigger again… another click.

I shook my head. "Sorry Haslitt. Another failed test."

I took the gun that Frank Thomson had been pointing at me before I shot him in my front garden from the waistband of my trousers and levelled it at Haslitt's face. "You see I'm not quite as trusting as you thought. I had an idea you'd follow me into the house for your gun, so I took the precaution of removing the bullets." I tapped the barrel of the gun with my finger. "This belonged to the late Mr Thomson. My, my, haven't we got a lot of guns between us?"

Haslitt groaned. His face in the dim light seemed suddenly to have sagged, grown older.

"What're you going to do with me?" he wheezed.

"As a human being, Haslitt, you're a bit of a failure. You enjoyed beating up my girlfriend who's about a quarter of your size and you probably would have enjoyed killing her after you'd disposed of me. You disgust me!"

I levelled the gun at his face. The big man, now totally beaten, cringed back.

"No wait! I'm sorry. Honestly, I didn't mean all that stuff just now," he pleaded. "How about if we share the gold? I… I could get rid of it for you. Turn it into cash…"

"What about the girl?" I snarled.

"For Christ's sake. Who needs her? We'll be rich. Fabulously rich. There'll be hundreds of girls. Young girls. She'll be trouble for you, Wheatley. She'll hold us back. We get rid of her, then…"

A huge wave of revulsion crept through me as I listened to this pathetic, cringing human ape.

I shot him. This time the phut sound from the silencer was magnified by the surrounding buildings, echoing off the walls for what seemed a very long time before all was silent again.

Haslitt's body had crumpled back against the wheel, a gush of blood spurting from the hole in his forehead; his astonished blue eyes stayed fixed on my face, still and unblinking, even when the blood poured into them turning them from blue to crimson.

I staggered to my feet and leaned on the bonnet of the car, my head in my hands. Five killings. It seemed endless. I hadn't wanted to kill again, had genuinely wanted Haslitt to take the bullion and get out of my life. I'd deliberately set up this test to find out if he could be trusted to leave us in peace, to leave me and Sally unharmed. I'd had to do it, had to kill again so that she might live. There had been no option. Suddenly my whole body started to tremble. I knelt down and clasped my arms around my knees and tried to stop the muscular spasms by pulling my body into a tight ball. I couldn't stop the tears welling up in my eyes. I fell back onto the wet ground.

"Oh God. What's happened to me?" I sobbed. "I didn't want to harm anybody. I didn't want to kill. Oh God... oh God!"

Over by the embankment a train clattered past sending strobe-like flashes of light fluttering across the interior of the car, picking up in sharp relief Thomson's head and the dead bloodied eyes of the man who had been Haslitt. I turned my face away and pressed my fists against my eyes, squeezing tight shut to cut out the horror of my surroundings. If only it was possible to turn the clock back. To return to the days before all this mayhem and violence had entered my life. Why had I been so nosey? Why had I returned to that house in the night so long ago? Why had I let greed take over and ruin my life? I looked down at Thomson's gun.

One more bullet. That's all it would take. Sweet oblivion. They'd find me in the car tomorrow perhaps, along with Haslitt and Thomson. They'd see the two gold bars on the floor. Connect me with the robbery. With the killings. The security guard and the policeman at the Fletton Stewart building.

The three men at the house. The two dead bodies I was with now. How would Sally take it? Dear trusting Sally. Until she died she would believe she had been betrayed by a criminal, a murderer. I winced. I couldn't let that happen. Everything would have to be explained to her.

I glanced at my watch. Over two hours had passed since I had promised to be back in an hour. I was late and there was so much to be done. I got up from the ground, shivering. I was wet through. The rain had stopped and a chill wind was blowing across the concrete strip that the car was parked in. I pulled up my collar and walked away from the car until I reached a grassy bank which sloped upwards towards a railway track on which stood the bulky, black silhouettes of a line of good trucks. I moved slowly along the bottom of this embankment staring hard at the ground until at last I found what I was looking for, a really big puddle. Then glanced back towards the car. Ten yards, maybe fifteen. I thought it was about right so went back and opened the car door.

Thomson's body was surprisingly light. I lifted it from the passenger seat and carried it carefully across the rubble and potholes then, after checking which side of the body was covered in mud from my garden laid him muddy side down in the puddle. I stood back and studied the effect. Fairly convincing. It did look as though he had fallen at that spot. Carefully I wiped Thomson's gun with my handkerchief then placed it in his, curling the stiff fingers as well as I could around the grip, the forefinger around the trigger guard. Then it was back to the car.

The interior light was not as bright as I would have liked it to be but it was enough for me to be fairly sure that the back seat was clear of Thomson's blood. Only a small trace showed on the spot where his head had rested and was easy to wipe away.

Next I took Haslitt's gun from his hand, wiped it clean and then put it in the glove compartment of the car. I replaced it in his giant mitt with the gun I'd shot Thomson with in my garden earlier. So now each man had a bullet in him from the appropriate weapon.

I left the passenger door wide open and walked a few yards away to survey my handiwork. Had I forgotten anything? I racked my brains to think of any clues I might leave behind but it seemed there was nothing more I could do. I turned and ran towards the lights of the distant motorway.

*****

At that time in the morning there was very little traffic on the road. I didn't have my phone with me so couldn't call for a taxi. So I ran frantically in the direction of home, constantly looking over my shoulder hoping to see the yellow light of a vacant cab going my way. Three taxis slowed up then accelerated fast when they saw my muddy and bedraggled figure but the fourth either didn't notice or didn't care. He stopped and I begged him to get me back as fast as he could. He obliged by putting his foot down but even so, by the time we got to my house, I had been away for three hours and ten minutes. I'd promised to be back in an hour.

Sally was standing at the gate when the taxi drew up. A pale, distraught figure against the dark backdrop of the garden. She stared anxiously at the taxi before I emerged, something in her stance betraying the fact that she was terrified and ready to run for her life, but when I stepped out from the taxi, she gave a sharp cry, tore open the gate and flung herself into my arms, weeping.

"Eddie!" she cried. "Eddie, oh thank God, thank God!" Her dress felt wet against my hands and I guessed that she had been standing at the gate for a long time.

"It's all right now, Sally. It's all right. I'm back."

"You were such a long time, I thought…" Her voice trailed away and she buried her face against my shoulder, her body trembling and cold. I turned and pushed a twenty-pound note into the taxi driver's hand.

"Is that enough?"

The man grinned.

"That's fine, mate. Thanks. Now get her indoors, she looks bloody frozen."

He swung the taxi round and took off in the direction we'd just come from and I put my arm around Sally's shoulders and guided her back into the house.

"I'm sorry I was late. It took longer than I thought." I kissed her gently on the forehead and closed the door.

"I've been so worried," she said. "I thought that man had killed you. I was about to call the police. Oh, Eddie... what's happening? I'm so confused."

I pushed her away and held her at arms' length.

"How are you feeling now?"

"Cold!"

I smiled. "I can see that. I meant how are you after being punched by that thug?"

She shook her head. "I'm fine. I just need you to explain everything to me. I don't understand all this."

I pulled her close again and said quietly into her ear. "Look, you've been patient this long. Do me a favour and go upstairs, get into a hot bath and warm yourself up then when you come down again I'll have a nice cup of tea waiting for you and I'll tell you everything."

"But I—"

"Please Sal," I said. "For me. Or you'll end up with pneumonia."

She stared up at me for a long moment unable to stop the trembling of her body and the chattering of her teeth, then nodded, turned slowly and walked up the stairs.

I waited until the bathroom door had closed then walked into the kitchen and stripped off my filthy, wet clothes. I filled the basin in the sink with hot soapy water and sponged the muck off my head, then I dried myself and ran up the stairs for some clean clothes. I was still chilled to the marrow so I put on a thick woollen sweater over a check shirt and corduroy jeans before coming back downstairs and lighting a fire in the sitting room.

Ten minutes later, Sally appeared. She was wearing my dressing gown and slippers and her wet hair had been brushed back behind her ears. She had a large strip of sticking plaster on her forehead and a smaller one on her chin.

I felt that familiar lurch as my heart somersaulted at the sight of her, but this time it was tinged with sadness. Sadness that she had been brought into this whole sorry mess and that I would soon lose her. I thought I had never seen her look more beautiful.

A sudden spasm of anguish knotted inside my stomach. This was probably going to be our last time together. The last time that she would want to be this close. The last time I would see her beautiful face, feel the invisible threads that bound us together and made is into a couple. After tonight, when she knew what I had done, it would be all over. She would be gone and my life would become a meaningless void.

I put the tray with the teapot and cups down on the low table and prodded the newly lit fire with my toe.

"Do you feel a bit warmer now?"

"Mmm, a lot better thanks."

"Would you like a scotch with your tea?"

She nodded and I brought the bottle to the table and poured out two generous measures. She sat down on one of the armchairs. Her face was still pale and she wore a haunted, sad expression around her eyes and mouth. She pointed at the other armchair and when I was seated, said, "Okay Eddie. Tell me." Then after a pause, "Tell me everything."

CHAPTER 14

Surrender

The shadow took a long time to emerge. For ages, the wall and everything around it was black, jet black. No colours, no shapes, total blackness, then very slowly patches of grey appeared and the shadow emerged like a photograph on sensitive paper in a bath of chemicals. My shadow, head bowed, shoulders slumped, sitting dejectedly in an armchair.

The pale glow of morning silhouetted the empty building site across the street and filtered into the room through the uncurtained window. The window at which I had stood hours ago watching the tail lights of the car go off down the street. The window at which I had continued to stand, gazing into the darkness long after the lights had disappeared.

Sally riding off into the night, her face white and confused, the look of shocked disbelief lingering in her eyes. Sally moving out of my life, refusing to stay the night, refusing to let me drive her home, accepting my car keys, walking off down the path along the pavement to the car. One glance back at the house. Pale-faced, bewildered, hurt. I wanted, with every fibre in my body, to rush out and take her in my arms. To implore her not to leave, to beg her forgiveness, but instead standing, as she had asked me to do, helplessly watching her go.

She'd listened in complete silence to the whole sorry affair. There had been no questions, no interruptions, no changes of expression even. I'd tried hard to fill in every detail of the story. My dull life before the robbery, my feelings about Miriam and my need to escape, walking the streets in the early hours of the morning. The fear I'd felt when I thought I was about to be shot. My remorse over the killing of the three robbers and my love for her and how my life had changed since our first meeting.

Afterwards, Sally had sat for an eternity staring into the fire, then she had turned to face me, looking tired and exhausted and said, "I want to go home now Eddie."

"Won't you stay here?"

A shake of the head. "No, I need time to think. This has been a shock." She stood up. "I want to go home."

I tried to hold her hand and said, "Of course. I'll run you back."

She pulled away and walked to the door, speaking in barely a whisper. "Please let me go Eddie—on my own."

I took the car keys from a hook beside the door and put them I her hand.

"I won't need the car," I said. "Keep it as long as you like."

She turned and looked at me, forcing a weak smile. "Give me a little time."

I nodded, unable to speak, despair making my body rigid, watching her walk out of the door, get into the car and drive off into the night.

That was then and now the shadow had slipped down the wall until it was just a small rectangle on the carpet.

I was glad the night was over. I rubbed my tired eyes, pulled myself to my feet and walked stiffly into the kitchen, put the kettle on and searched through the cupboards for something to eat. A hard piece of bread was all that could be found. I covered it with apricot jam and took it with a cup of tea over to the kitchen table and sat down.

In front of me were the remnants of the previous evening's supper with Sally. Two crumb-covered plates and mugs still containing the dregs of their tea. One of the mugs had a faint smear of lipstick on the rim.

I stared at the mug for a long time, a feeling of overwhelming sadness suddenly enveloping me. Eventually I reached out, picked up the mug and pressed my lips to the tiny red smudge.

I felt a warm trickle of tears run down my cheeks and a sudden constriction block my throat. For a brief moment I tried to fight it but then gave up the struggle. It was something I couldn't control. I started to blub. Huge choking, self-pitying sobs racked my body. I banged my fists against my head and cried as I had not since I was a child.

By seven thirty I was out of the house, meandering aimlessly through the London streets. Walking had always been my greatest therapy and anxious that I might miss a call from Sally, I took my mobile phone. But I had to get out. Anything was better than staying in the house.

The beginning of the early morning rush was just starting and the traffic was fairly humming along the streets, making the most of that period before the arteries into the city would be almost completely clogged. I plodded through it all, totally unaware of my surroundings, lost in my own thoughts. A plan was forming in my head. A plan to escape. I was sure that Sally would not return to me now and that I was on my own. I would sell the house and move away to try to start a new life somewhere else. To hell with the gold, it could stay where it was. After all, nearly three hundred thousand pounds in cash was hidden up the chimneys of the house. My God! The world would be my oyster. I could travel to wherever I wanted. Break free. Get away from the horrors I had endured over the past few weeks and see the world. Immerse myself in the sights and sounds of foreign parts. Forget about the gold bullion and violent men, forget about Miriam and Rufus and old man Hislop, forget about the house, forget about Sally... I stopped, rooted suddenly to the spot, staring down at the pavement. It was impossible to forget about Sally, easier to forget I had a right arm, easier to forget how to walk, easier to forget how to breathe. I sat down on a flight of steps leading to somebody's office and tried to keep the sluice gates shut. No chance. The tears welled up again and burst as though from a broken dam. My shoulders shook and soon I was blubbing like a little boy who had had his favourite toy taken away. I cursed as I cried. Embarrassed and annoyed at my own weakness, aware of the curious stares of passers-by, but at the same time strangely relieved that the floodgates were open and that I could let out all the emotions that had been bottled up so tightly over the past few weeks. Nobody stopped, nobody offered to help. I was glad of that, wanting to be left alone, quite happy to be cocooned in my own little shell of grief and self-pity.

When it was over, the tears stopped and the shaking shoulders still, I became aware of another organ causing turbulence apart from my heart. This time it was my stomach and it was telling me that I was hungry.

Another half mile down the road, a café with a glass-topped counter, dark, swarthy men serving readymade sandwiches and polystyrene beakers of tea to a queue of office workers. Lunchtime already? I glanced disbelievingly down at my watch.

Twenty past one. I'd been walking the streets for hours. I tried to remember what I had been doing all that time. Couldn't think so I joined the queue and bought myself a large beaker of steaming hot, sweet tea, a plate of sausage, chips and beans and a huge hunk of brown bread.

Two burly, brown-faced workmen, one of them puffing away at one of those cigarette substitutes called a vape, made room for me at one of the tables in the side room and watched silently as I wolfed the food down. I ignored them, the smoke wafting across my plate and the loud music blasting from a speaker overhead. My mind was in a turmoil as I tried to work out what to do.

By the time my plate was empty and the tea drained from my mug, I had made a decision. The fantasy of selling the house and skipping off abroad had been discarded. It was hard enough living with the deaths of six men on my conscience, but that plus not having Sally in my life would make it intolerable, no matter where in the world I chose to live.

I stood up and walked out of the café into the street, turning in the direction of home. I would give Sally one week. If she had not contacted me by then I would give myself up to the police.

*****

The killings of Haslitt and Thomson made the headlines in all the national papers. It seemed that Frank Thomson had been suspected for a long time by the police of being on the fringes of crime but they had never been able to prove anything against him. Now, however, the big black print screamed from the front page. EVIL CRIME MASTERMIND IN SHOOTOUT! MR BIG DIES IN GUNFIGHT! and BULLION MASTERMIND DIES WITH HIS SECRET.

There were photographs of the two dead men. Photos of their houses, of Haslitt's club, The Parrot Perch and another of Thomson in a laughing group of rather wealthy looking individuals at a golf club in East Anglia.

There were interviews with associates of the two men and the lead writers had raised the possibility that Thomson was the mastermind behind two other big robberies which had taken place a few years earlier.

Frank Thomson's wife had taken refuge at the home of Sir Arthur Freeman who, whilst throwing the press off his land, had publicly declared that any connection made between Thomson and the criminal fraternity was scandal-mongering, libellous and a downright scurrilous lie. He'd known Frank Thomson for years and there was not a stain on his character. There would be some good reason why he had been in that car with a known criminal. He wasn't sure what, but time would tell. In the meantime, he would not allow Thomson's widow to be interviewed. She was far too distressed and any statement from her would be to the police who were waiting until she was in a fit state to be questioned.

The police had been less reticent with the gentlemen from the press and had been eager to let the public know that the killings at the railway goods yard was their biggest break so far and that the small matter of finding the rest of the stolen gold bullion would be cleared up, they were sure, in a matter of days. Meanwhile, between the short period they gave Janet Thomson to recover from the shock of her husband's death and the non-stop grilling she would then face when able, her elegant home in Southwold was torn apart in the search for clues and left looking like the wreckage from an earthquake.

I followed the story of the great bullion robbery as it unfolded in the press and on television in a daze. There was no connection. It was not part of my world. It was as though the whole thing had happened to someone else and that I had spent most of my life sitting in this small sitting room watching television, reading the news and feeding myself from tins bought with the papers on my only outings each day to Patel's corner shop.

I watched the glaring headlines dwindle to one or two lines as the story was replaced by the riveting news that one of the Royals had produced a baby. A feat so wonderful and unusual that it warranted several pages of photographs and comment in the tabloids and would surely make the nation swell with pride to know that, unlike ordinary women, Her Royal Highness was capable of producing an extraordinarily handsome prodigy of a son who was twelfth in line to the throne and would within a few years be able to tell the same adoring reporters, with two fingers raised, "Why don't you all piss orf and leave one alone!"

Meanwhile the nightmares returned the same as before. The corridor with only one door, the dead hands clawing at my throat, only now there were five men. Five human beings who had died because of me, clutching and tearing at my clothes in a frenzied effort to drag me into their dead world.

The images stayed with me during the day too. Five faces constantly welling up in my consciousness, bringing me out in a cold sweat and making my body tremble. It was as though they were there physically lurking somewhere just out of the periphery of my vision, playing a game with me, taunting, teasing and jumping out when I was least expecting it.

I might be making a cup of tea and suddenly a picture of one of them, Winston or Thomson or Haslitt, would flash into my mind, their faces just as I had last seen them: eyes popping with astonishment, blood flowing from their wounds… dead!

I had never been a particularly religious man, but now, totally alone, Mike Paterson gone and no one to confide in or to share the burden, the enormous weight of guilt and remorse drove me often to my knees, and I would ask for help and beg for guidance and forgiveness.

Often I would see Mike Paterson again. Not the warm, genial friend, but a twisted, stiffened corpse. Unrecognisable and alien. This was the hardest to bear. The knowledge that I was directly responsible, that if it had not been for me, Paterson would still be alive, still popping out for an occasional pint, still taking his driving lessons. But then of course, if it hadn't been for me the others too would still be alive, spending their ill-gotten gains, still living a life of crime. Inflicting pain and suffering on others, but they would still be alive. They in their troubled world and me in my untroubled one.

On the third day I took one of the plastic bags full of money out of the chimney, extracted twenty thousand pounds and replaced the bag. I put the money into a large envelope and with it a letter to the Chief Constable. The letter said, 'A gift to the unfortunate families of the security guard and the policeman killed during the Fletton Stewart bullion robbery'. The letter also expressed the wish for the donor of the money to retain anonymity. Then, as an afterthought, just in case the Chief

Constable pocketed the money, I wrote another letter to the Home Secretary telling him what I'd done.

With Paterson dead there was no way that I could find the home addresses of the three bullion robbers, so that portion of my conscience had to remain unsalved but I trudged home after posting the envelopes feeling marginally better.

By the fifth day after the railway goods yards killing, the story had disappeared altogether from both the national press and the television news. Five days had made a marked difference to the appearance of my home. In that short time it had started to resemble a tramp's doss house. Newspapers lay scattered everywhere. Dirty plates and half empty mugs of tea were piled on the mantelpiece and window ledges, and empty cans of beer, beans and peaches were strewn across the floor. I had not fared much better. My eyes were dark-rimmed and my skin pallid and grey. A thin growth of hair sprouted patchily from my chin and my hair lay lank and uncombed. I was uncomfortably aware that I needed a bath but was unable to summon up the energy to do anything about it.

Using an old lipstick of Miriam's, which I found in a drawer, I had marked the days off in large circles on a calendar, which was propped up beside the television set. Five red circles. Two more and I would give himself up to the police.

As the days had dragged slowly past without a call from Sally, I had convinced myself that I was destined to a life sentence in jail. The concept terrified and appalled me, yet it seemed to me that life without Sally was an even bleaker prospect. I found I was constantly checking my phone to see if she had texted me a message and many times I'd made the decision to call her but each time I'd changed my mind and cancelled the idea. I wanted desperately to hear her voice yet I was afraid of what that voice might say. I was becoming a wreck. On the few occasions when I managed to sleep, those nightmares, vivid and horrific, had returned, tormenting and prodding me awake, leaving me gasping for breath, body bathed in sweat, still seeing the bodies of Winston and Smalley, Baseball Cap, Haslitt and Frank Thomson advancing towards me from each side, their dead faces staring at me, arms outstretched to claw at me with their cold, clammy hands.

On the seventh day, I stared dismally at myself in the mirror. I wondered whether I should clean myself up for the police. Have a bath, put on a clean shirt and a suit. Look respectable. What did one wear when confessing to five murders and grand larceny? After long consideration I decided to stay as I was – haggard and dirty – a much more believable image for a wanted criminal.

Across the room on the calendar, the seventh red circle had been scrawled around that day's date. The circle I had desperately not wanted to draw, knowing as I did so that all hope was gone and that my future now lay between the cold, grey walls of a prison.

I turned and walked into the hall. Halfway towards the front door I stopped for a moment and stared down at the landline telephone, then I shook my head and walked abruptly away, opened the door and walked out of the house.

Outside, in the bright sunlight, my new brick wall stacked full with the precious yellow metal that had caused the deaths of seven men and brought misery and grief to their families and all who had conspired to benefit from it, sat mockingly amongst the weeds of the front garden.

I paused at the gate and looked down at my handiwork for a second or two. Then, taking a pace forward, I spat angrily against the brickwork of the wall and watched the spit dribble slowly down until it reached the earth before I turned and walked away along the pavement towards the city.

The police station was a large Victorian building surrounded by high wrought iron railings and approached by a curving set of stone steps, which started at the end of a new shopping precinct. It was the only old building in about seven acres of new development and it stood defiantly on a mound overlooking the new shops and houses, like an aged dog surrounded by her pups.

On the left of the building was a long, sloping driveway which led to a new complex of garages and offices at the rear. I wandered through the shopping precinct and up the stone steps towards the main entrance. Now that the moment of surrender had come, I felt strangely calm. From now on my worries and cares would be taken care of. There would be no more anxiety, no more terror, no more problems. Henceforth my waking, sleeping and the hours in between would be governed by a higher authority. I would have no responsibilities and should I wish, not even be required to think. I was not frightened by the prospect but felt at ease and resigned and, in a perverse way, almost looking forward to seeing the effect that my bombshell would have on the desk sergeant.

Inside the building I found himself in a large room divided into sections by a frosted glass partition. A long, low desk ran across the width of the room and behind it sat a middle-aged policeman who was speaking into a telephone and writing notes in a large ledger as he spoke. Behind him, in yet another glass partition, I could see two or three other upholders of the law sipping tea and chatting. There was no one else in the room as I entered. The policeman gestured towards a row of chairs, which stood under the window facing his desk. I preferred to remain standing.

"What colour was the dog?" the policeman asked. He had a bored look on his face and was stifling a yawn as he spoke.

"And what name is it, madam?" Another yawn. "No, not your name. We've already got that. The name of the dog."

The conversation droned on. I glanced up at the posters on the walls and found myself staring at the faces of Haslitt and Frank Thomson on a large white card under big black letters proclaiming MURDER & ROBBERY and underneath the photographs an appeal for help or information from anyone who had seen either of the men on that night. I thought I might be able to help them.

The telephone conversation ended and the receiver was put down. The bored policeman scribbled something in the book then glanced over at me, looking me up and down and obviously deciding that I was a tramp.

"Yes?" he said without interest. "What can we do for you?"

I shuffled nearer to the desk, unsure now what to say, feeling my throat go dry and my knees feel suddenly weak.

I opened his mouth to speak but stopped when I saw the policeman's attention diverted. His eyes were looking past me at someone else who'd just entered the room. I plunged on, "I want to make a statement," I said. Then from the doorway beyond me I heard a cough and someone called my name.

"Eddie!"

I turned. Sally was standing at the door. Sally, her hair bedraggled, face anxious and tired was right there, only a few yards away. I was confused, unable to take it in, barely unable to speak.

"Can I speak to you for a moment?" she said.

I stood there helplessly, still unable to comprehend.

"Sally?"

She walked towards me and stood a yard away staring at me. I saw that her eyes were brimming with tears.

"Come home," she whispered. "Come home." She held out her arms and I stumbled blindly to her, encircling her body with my arms and burying my face against her neck.

"Sally," was all I could say. "Sally, Sally, Sally!"

Tears were coursing down my cheeks and I heard her whisper "I love you," felt her body tremble and the wetness of her tears mingling with my own.

The policeman who had been drinking tea in his glass cubicle came out and stood grinning on the other side of the desk and another member of the public who had just entered the building clutching a large ginger cat, stood awkwardly to one side of us with an astonished look on her face.

Eventually Sally stepped back. Her cheeks were streaked with tears but there was a small smile on her face.

"C'mon," she said. "Let's go."

I nodded and put an arm around her shoulders, a feeling of vast relief surging through my whole body. We walked towards the door.

"What about that statement you want to make?" the desk sergeant said.

I turned. "It's all right," I said. "I'd lost something... but now I think I've found it again." Then we walked out of the police station into the sunlight.

*****

Sally's flat was only marginally less tidy than my house. Again newspapers littered the floor and an assortment of plates and cups lay scattered everywhere, but as I entered the room and stood amidst the debris and clutter I felt as though I'd just walked through the gates of heaven. I smiled at her.

"Am I allowed to speak now?"

Once outside the police station I had wanted to talk, to ask questions but she put a finger to his lips and taking me by the arm had walked me through the streets of East London without a word being spoken.

She nodded. "Go ahead."

I sat down on the settee and patted the seat beside me.

"I'm so confused Sally. I can't believe this is happening," I said.

She sat down beside me and put her hand on mine.

"Does that feel real?" she asked.

I nodded and tried to put my arms around her but she pulled away.

"Eddie, we have to talk. I need to get things sorted out in my mind."

I sighed and sat back.

"Of course," I said. "I'm sorry."

For a while she was silent, nervously twisting a strand of her hair around her finger, then she said falteringly, "So many times over the past week I've wanted to call you... just to speak to you... only a word or two. I kept hoping that the phone would ring and it would be you. That you'd somehow explain everything away. That none of this had happened. I've tried to understand Eddie... I still can't believe all the things that you told me." Again she was silent, staring down at her hands, shaking her head slowly from side to side. "I had to have time to think... I've gone over it all in my mind, time and time again. It's all so unreal. I haven't been involved with anything like this before... last week, that night... I've never been so frightened in my life."

I sat, not knowing what to say. I hated myself for causing her so much distress. She looked so vulnerable and small. She did look tired. Her face was pale and drawn and her hair lank and untidy.

"I haven't slept much," she said, catching my glance and touching her hair self-consciously.

"I'm sorry," I mumbled lamely.

She shook her head. "I still don't understand what you were going to do. I mean about us. What would have happened? Would you have told me or was I to assume you were a very rich man?"

I shrugged hopelessly. "I don't know, I honestly don't know. Over the past few weeks things have just happened. I don't seem to have had any control over anything. I can't believe all this has happened to me."

"What would you have done?" she persisted.

I put my head in my hands. "A few days ago I couldn't have contemplated telling you that I was responsible for the deaths of five people. I couldn't have put that burden on your shoulders... couldn't risk you walking out on me..."

"What then?" she interrupted. "Would you have just lived a lie?"

I shook my head helplessly.

"I don't know. I hadn't worked anything out. I hadn't thought that far ahead. I didn't want to lie to you Sally. I just didn't want to lose you."

She sat looking at my face for a while, then said, "Knowing you I think you would have told me in the end. You're not a good liar. I believe you about the killings. I know that those men, those robbers would have killed you and you had to do what you did to save your own life... it was self-defence, I see that... but..." She faltered, then blurted out, "But the other two men ... what happened? Did they have to die? They weren't self-defence were they?"

She was looking at me so pleadingly, so anxiously that I wanted badly to take her in my arms but instead I reached across and squeezed her hand before explaining in detail my encounter with Frank Thomson and how he had died. I told her how Mike Paterson had been murdered and of the threats that Thomson and Haslitt had made about killing her. I told her about the chance I had given to Haslitt to take the gold and leave us in peace and then of the moment I had had to pull the trigger again.

The reliving of it all had brought out that old familiar cold sweat and by the time my story was done my hands were shaking uncontrollably.

Sally said in a quiet voice, "What would you have done about the gold?"

"I hate the gold!" I said savagely. "I would have left it where it is inside the wall. It's caused enough trouble!" I shrugged. "I would've tried to talk you into coming away with me. Anywhere. I wouldn't mind. Perhaps even leave the country. Just get away and start a new life. Leave this nightmare behind."

For the first time the anxious look disappeared from her face and she smiled.

"That's what I hoped you'd say."

"I was going to give myself up," I said.

"I know."

"But how did you suddenly appear? Where did you spring from? It was like being rescued by the Cavalry."

She leaned back against the settee.

"Just luck," she said. "I'd been cooped up here in the flat for most of the week, wondering what to do. I managed to get someone to fill in for me at the driving school and I just sat here fretting. I was running out of food so this morning I ventured out to go to the shops." She turned her head and looked at me. "I didn't recognise you at first." She put her hand on my cheek. "You've not been looking after yourself. I saw you walking through the shopping precinct. I was so shocked at seeing you I couldn't speak, couldn't call out your name. I watched you go right past and climb the steps up to the police station. Then I realised what you intended to do. I panicked. I couldn't bear the thought of you going to jail so I rushed after you… just in time it seems."

I grinned.

"It couldn't have been closer."

"No, not much."

"Thanks," I said. "Thanks a lot." She moved across the settee towards me and I put my arms around her shoulders and pressed my face into her hair.

"I've missed you, Eddie," she said.

"Me too."

She turned her head and looked up at me.

"I'll tell you what I'd like you to do."

"What?"

She smiled.

"Well, whilst we've been apart I haven't slept well and I haven't eaten properly but at least I have had the occasional bath."

"Oh God! Is it that obvious?"

"Let's say I think I love you just a tiny bit more pink coloured."

I stood up and walked across to look at myself in a mirror and groaned.

"Good grief! What a sight. You must be mad rescuing that. Should have left me to go to prison."

"You're right, but what's done is done. It's the first door on the right past the kitchen."

Half an hour later, I emerged from the bathroom wrapped in a large blue towel, smelling and looking decidedly cleaner. I saw that miraculously in such a short period of time she had tidied the flat, changed into a clean white blouse and red skirt, brushed her hair and put on some make-up. We sat at her little kitchen table over cups of coffee.

"Okay. What do you think we should do?" I asked.

"Well, that first suggestion of yours seemed a good idea," she said. "The one about us making a clean break, getting away from it all."

"Wow," I said. "You'd do that with me? Even after all that's happened?"

She nodded.

"Go abroad?"

She nodded again.

"What about the driving school?"

"I'd sell it. I think it might get a fair price from the big boys keen to buy me out."

"And this flat?"

"It's only rented."

I sat back, astonished.

"Oh, Sally, what a waste life was before I met you."

I raised my cup and clinked it against hers. "To our new start," I said. "I'll ring the estate agents today and put my house on the market."

"Yes," she laughed. "Let's do it!"

I fished in my pocket and took out my phone. There were quite a few local estate agents listed when I linked up to Google.

I looked up and saw that the troubled expression had returned to her face.

"What's the matter?" I asked anxiously.

"Promise you'll never forget," she said.

"Forget?"

"All that's happened." She shook her head sadly. "Here we are planning a new life and… those men… they…" she faltered to a stop.

I took her hands and squatted down in front of her.

"Sally. I never stop thinking about them and I never will. I'll have them on my conscience for the rest of my life. If I could turn the clock back and make it so none of this happened I would… as long as I could still have met you."

"Will we always be looking over our shoulders Eddie?"

"For the police?"

She nodded.

"No, I'm sure about that," I said emphatically. "There are no clues that point to me."

"What about the gold?" she asked.

"It'll stay where it is. It's caused enough trouble."

"But the new owners will find it as soon as they try to plant shrubs or flowers in the wall."

"I'll take the earth out, put a layer of concrete over the gold and then replace the earth."

She nodded, looking relieved.

"Don't worry. Everything will be all right… and if we pool our resources we should have enough to keep us going for a good while."

She was silent for a moment, then she whispered conspiratorially, "Longer than a good while. Haven't you got a little nest egg or two hidden up your chimneys?"

My mouth must have dropped open.

"Well," she said. "You're leaving the gold but surely you deserve something for all the trouble you've been through?"

I felt my expression of astonishment slowly change into a broad grin. I took her in my arms again and held her close.

"You know what you are, don't you, Sally Russell? You're a bloody crook!"

CHAPTER 15

New Owners

Sean Blakeney sat back in his armchair and took a long, happy swig at his can of lager. All things considered, he felt extremely contented and not a little smug. After all, it's not every day you become a house owner. His dad never owned his own house and as far as he knew neither had his grandfather. Maybe he was the first Blakeney to have been born with brains. Well, maybe not brains but courage. His father and grandfather had both been content to rent a place, to cough up money weekly for years and years to some rich bastard in the City and have nothing to show for it at the end. Well, he'd had the guts to get himself a mortgage. A hell of a big mortgage. It would stretch him a bit, but it meant he'd got his own place and if prices continued to go up like they had been, well, you just can't lose can you? Especially when you're a bit of a dab hand at bartering. Blimey, it was still hard to believe he'd got himself such a bargain.

It had done him a bit of good with Carol. Carol was dead proud of him. None of her mates had their own place. None of them had husbands with brains. Take Colin for instance. He glanced across at his friend Colin leaning over an old Trivial Pursuit board, wracking his brain for the answer to some simple question. Skinny little Colin with his spiky hair and tattoos and Neanderthal skull. No flesh on his bones and nothing in his head. He looked like a reject roll from Sanderson's wallpaper factory. Colin would never have the nous to buy his own place. Colin would be paying rent for the rest of his life. Probably wouldn't even move out of that grotty flat they had in Lewisham.

Sitting next to him, warm and soft against his thigh, was Colin's wife, Sharon. Lovely girl, Sharon. Smashing figure. Completely wasted on Colin. They wouldn't last long. She'd been flirting all night with him. He'd caught her eye a couple of times. Knew she was attracted. Well, a woman needs someone who's got a bit of go about him, not someone content to flog himself to death in a paint factory, paying rent and never owning anything.

He let his eye wander around the room. It was in smashing nick. Nothing to do to the place for years. Carpets had been thrown in and he'd managed to get most of the furniture from the previous owner dead cheap. Stupid sod had almost given it away. Either stupid or got more money than sense.

Funny bloke he'd been. Dead keen to sell. A bit too keen Sean had thought at first. Got him worried. Something wrong somewhere. Nobody gives anything away, not nowadays, not unless they're barmy. So he'd told him he'd go away and think about it. Gone home and told the old man and the old man had come with him and Carol on their second look. Searched around but couldn't find anything wrong, no matter how hard he'd tried. Whispered to Sean in the garden to try a ridiculous offer. Suspicions had been proven correct, the man was barmy. He'd accepted the offer.

Sharon's elbow nudged him in the ribs, jolting him out of his reverie. She was waving a card in front of his face like a fan.

"Wakey, wakey, Sean," she said. "It's not bedtime yet."

"Come on Sean, answer the bloody question," Carol said, banging him on the arm and scattering cigarette ash on the carpet. She was getting drunk. He'd better ease up on the Bacardi. Carol always swore a lot when she'd had too much to drink.

"Are you goin' to play or are you goin' to sit all night with that smug look on your face, staring at your palace?" Colin said.

"Sorry." Sean sat forward and tried to concentrate on the game. "What was the question again?"

Sharon read slowly from the card. "What is the only manmade structure visible from the moon?"

There was a long pause, then Sean said, "Tesco's down the High Street!"

They all giggled.

"You don't bloody know," Carol said. "Tell him Sharon."

"The Great Wall of China."

Colin said, "I'm fed up with this. We're going to be all night. Christ, we've been at it for ages and Sharon's the only one who's got a question right."

"Yeah, let's pack it in," the two women chorused.

"I would've got a few but me mind's been busy on property matters," Sean said.

"Well get it off property matters," Colin snorted. "… and bung us another drink."

Sean went off into the kitchen and brought back two more cans of beer. He topped up Sharon's glass from a bottle of Bacardi on the table and tossed one of the cans to Colin, ignoring his wife's glass completely.

"You be careful you're not picked up by the Old Bill. You've had a skinful," he said.

"No problem. I drive better this way."
Sharon picked up her glass and for the fourth time that night said, "Well, here's to Carol and Sean and their new house."

Carol and Sean responded enthusiastically. Colin pretended to be opening his can. His wife turned to him.

"When are you going to buy us a house?"

"One day. One day. We 'aven't been married as long as these two."

"There's only six months between us."

Colin stood up. "You'll have to be patient, won't you. In six months' time we might have one."

"Some hopes!"

Her husband ignored her and walked over to the
fireplace where he leaned on the mantelpiece and surveyed the
room. He spoke to Sean.

"How did you manage to get the bloke to sell it to you
so cheap?"

His host joined him at the mantelpiece and they stood
there as though they were propping up a bar. Both men felt more
comfortable in that position.

"Well, you have to know a bit about bartering, don't you.
Know the right time to put in an offer. Suss out how keen the
seller is to sell and all that. I wore this bloke down until he
dropped his price and hey presto!"

In actual fact, Eddie had taken the very first offer that
came for the house in his hurry to get away.

Sharon said, "Oh Sean, you aren't half clever."

Colin glared at her. "Are you sure there's nothin' wrong
with the place? Dry rot? Woodworm? It might be just about to
fall over," he said scathingly.

The proud owner laughed. "No problem. I got me dad
to look at it for me. He's a builder. He ought to know. S'matter
of fact he thinks I've got the best bargain ever."

"It's lovely," Carol slurred.

Colin emptied his can of beer. "I reckon we'd better go.
It's a long way to Lewisham."

His wife nodded. "Yeah, back to our rented hovel."

"Don't feel too envious Sharon," Carol said, struggling
out of the settee. We're mortgaged up to the eyeballs."

Sean nodded. "It's true. We won't be able to eat from
now on but I reckon if I sold the place again tomorrow I'd have
made twenty grand."

"What was the bloke like what sold it?"

"Funny bloke, wasn't he Carol? Don't think he was
married. Had a bird living near the shops; he was goin' to run
away with her. Going abroad I think. Seemed in a hurry to sell.

I think we came along just at the right time. Hard bloke to knock down though. Hang on, I'll get your coats."

They followed Sean into the hallway where he threw Colin's coat to him and helped Sharon on with her anorak, then opening the front door and putting on a passable imitation of a posh accent said, "Well, it's been awfully nice of you to visit our humble abode. Do call again, won't you? Just give the butler a ring and he'll fix up a date in the diary."

"Smug bugger," Carol said.

They walked out into the street. Sharon looked wistfully at the 'For Sale' notice standing in the garden of the property next door but decided against saying anything when she caught the warning look in her husband's eye.

"Thanks for a terrific evening," she said.

"Where's your car?" Sean asked.

"About a mile down the road," Colin said, pleased that at last he had found something to criticise. He pointed to the line of parked cars hugging the pavement. "Where do you park your van, for Christ's sake?"

"There's always a space somewhere," Sean said huffily.

His friend turned. "C'mon Sharon. We might be lucky and thumb a lift to our car." They walked off down the street.

"See you Sean, Carol, thanks a lot."

The proud new house owners watched their first guests disappear into the darkness. Carol sat down unsteadily on the brick wall that divided their garden from the pavement.

"He's as jealous as hell, isn't he?"

"Yeah, poor devil. I reckon Sharon will be bendin' his ear all the way home."

They were silent for a while. She squinting down at her feet, trying to bring them into focus. He staring admiringly at the light shining through the windows and door of his new house.

"Carol said, "Colin is right though."

"Eh?"

"He's right about the parking. It's nearly impossible to find a space. Murder when I've got a load of shopping to carry."

Her husband shrugged.

"Can't have everything I suppose."

Carol said, "Up near my mum's there's a bloke what's knocked down his fence and put concrete on his front garden so he can park his car."

Sean looked at the garden wall.

"Strewth Carol, we've only just moved in. I've got a lot of bills to pay. I can't afford a load of concrete now."

"Not now maybe, but it's worth thinkin' about."

He put his arm around her and helped her to her feet. A branch from a miniature rose bush growing in the wall had become entangled in her cardigan. Sean carefully pulled it free and patted the disturbed earth on the top of the wall back into place. They walked up the path to their front door.

"One day, maybe," he said. "When I get hold of some spare cash."

Stanley McMurtry, MBE

More usually known by his pen name "Mac", Stanley McMurtry was born in Edinburgh. The Family moved to Birmingham when he was eight years old and at 17 he enrolled at the Birmingham School of Art and soon afterwards landed his first job as a trainee shop-fitting designer but as this proved to be too restricting he left and worked as an Ironmonger's assistant until undergoing compulsory military service.

On leaving the forces, he became a trainee cartoon film animator, and it was here that he found true happiness and fulfilment doing a job that was to become his life. During breaks in filming, he began to contribute "Gag" cartoons to magazines and newspapers. He did rather well at this and was soon snapped-up by the Daily Sketch in 1968 to be the Political and Social Cartoonist. In 1971 the Daily Mail took-over the Sketch and Mac became its main cartoonist, during which time he was voted **Cartoonist of the Year** six times and **Political Cartoonist of the Year** twice.

Additionally, with a colleague, he wrote scripts for the comedians Dave Allen and Tommy Cooper, which is testament to his extraordinary good sense of humour and fun.

Mac was awarded the **MBE** in 2004 for services to the Newspaper industry, was a "Castaway" on **Desert Island Discs** in 2008, has been invited to **Number 10** by the then prime minister **Margaret Thatcher** and was voted one of the **Men of the Year** in 1983.

In the meantime, he has been a successful children's author with his acclaimed book "**The Bungee Venture**" being made into an animated cartoon by the fabled **Hannah & Barbera** team in Hollywood.

Mac is a widower with two children and five grandchildren who retired from the Daily Mail at the end of 2018 but was brought back to create a weekly cartoon for the **Mail on Sunday.**

He now spends his time writing novels and children's books.

Pressman
House

BV - #0011 - 010223 - C0 - 229/152/16 - PB - 9781915657121 - Gloss Lamination